Just some o̶f̶ ̶t̶h̶e̶ reviews for J. Kenner̶ erotic no̶v̶e̶l̶s̶

'Kenner may very well have cornered the ̶m̶a̶r̶k̶e̶t̶ dominant antiheroes and the women wh̶o̶ second installment of her Most Wanted s̶e̶r̶i̶e̶s̶ solidifying that claim. Her characters' scorching, scandalous affair explores the very nature of attraction and desire, redeeming and changing them beyond measure . . . Fans will no doubt love the games of power, overwhelming passion and self-defining relationship that Kenner has crafted, and come away eager for more' *Romantic Times*

'Fans of erotic romance will enjoy *Heated*. The plot is complex, the characters engaging, and J. Kenner's passionate writing brings it all perfectly together' *Harlequin Junkie*

'In Julie Kenner's typical masterful storytelling, nothing is as it seems. We are taken deeply into the plot twist and the danger of this erotic journey. The chemistry first felt by both Tyler and Sloane during their first encounter roars into an all-consuming fire neither one can put out . . . Take the same journey I did and you will not be disappointed!' *As You Wish Reviews*

'*Wanted* is another J. Kenner masterpiece . . . This was an intriguing look at self-discovery and forbidden love all wrapped into a neat little action suspense package. There was plenty of sexual tension and eventually action. Evan was hot, hot, hot! Together, they were combustible. But can we expect anything less from J. Kenner?' *Reading Haven*

'*Wanted* by J. Kenner is the whole package! A toe-curling smokin' hot read, full of incredible characters and a brilliant storyline that you won't be able to get enough of. I can't wait for the next book in this series . . . I'm hooked!' *Flirty & Dirty Book Blog*

'I loved this story! It had substance, lovable characters, and unexpected discoveries. And the love between Evan and Angelina was passionate, explosive, and utterly wonderful' *Part of That World*

'J. Kenner's evocative writing thrillingly captures the power of physical attraction, the pull of longing, the universe-altering effect one person can have on another. She masterfully draws out the eroticism between Nikki and Damien . . . *Claim Me* has the emotional depth to back up the sex . . . Every scene is infused with both erotic tension, and the te̶n̶s̶i̶o̶n̶ ̶o̶f̶ ̶w̶o̶n̶d̶e̶r̶i̶n̶g̶ ̶w̶h̶a̶t̶ ̶l̶i̶e̶s̶ ̶b̶e̶n̶e̶a̶t̶h̶ ̶D̶a̶m̶i̶e̶n̶'s̶ veneer – and how a̶ akers*

'*Claim Me* by J. Kenner is an erotic, sexy and exciting ride. The story between Damien and Nikki is amazing and written beautifully. The intimate and detailed sex scenes will leave you fanning yourself to cool down. With the writing style of Ms Kenner you almost feel like you are there in the story riding along the emotional roller coaster with Damien and Nikki' *Fresh Fiction*

'PERFECT for fans of *Fifty Shades of Grey* and *Bared to You*. *Release Me* is a powerful and erotic romance novel that is sure to make adult romance readers sweat, sigh and swoon' *Reading, Eating & Dreaming Blog*

'*Release Me* . . . just made the top of my list with Damien and Nikki . . . the way in which J. Kenner tells the story, how vulnerable and real Damien and Nikki feel, makes this story so good, and re-readable many times over' *In Love With Romance Blog*

'This is deeply sensual and the story packs an emotional punch that I really hadn't expected . . . If you enjoyed *Fifty Shades* [and] the Crossfire books, you're definitely going to enjoy this one. It's compelling, engaging and I was thoroughly engrossed' *Sinfully Sexy Blog*

'I will admit, I am in the "I loved *Fifty Shades*" camp, but after reading *Release Me*, Mr Grey only scratches the surface compared to Damien Stark' *Cocktails and Books Blog*

'It is not often when a book is so amazingly well-written that I find it hard to even begin to accurately describe it . . . I recommend this book to everyone who is interested in a passionate love story' *Romancebookworm's Reviews*

'The story is one that will rank up with the *Fifty Shades* and Crossfire trilogies. I am impatiently awaiting book two! A definite read for those who enjoyed *Fifty Shades* and *Bared to You*' *Incubus Publishing Blog*

'*Release Me* gives readers tantalizing pages of sensual delight, leaving us reeling as we journey with this couple and their passions are released. *Release Me* is a must read!' *Readaholics Anonymous*

J. Kenner loves wine, dark chocolate, and books. She lives in Texas with her husband and daughters. Visit her online at www.jkenner.com to learn more about her and her other pen names, and to get a peek at what she's working on. Or connect with her via Twitter @juliekenner or through www.facebook.com/JKennerBooks.

By J. Kenner

Most Wanted Series
Wanted
Heated
Ignited

The Stark Series
Release Me
Claim Me
Complete Me
Take Me (e-novella)

Ignited
J. KENNER

HEADLINE PUBLISHING GROUP
An Hachette UK Company
338 Euston Road
London NW1 3BH

www.headlineeternal.com
www.headline.co.uk
www.hachette.co.uk

headline
ETERNAL

Published by arrangement with Bantam Books,
an imprint of Random House,
a division of Random House LLC.

First published in Great Britain in 2014
by HEADLINE ETERNAL
An imprint of HEADLINE PUBLISHING GROUP

2

Cataloguing in Publication Data is available from the British Library

ISBN 978 1 4722 1515 4

Offset in Sabon by Avon DataSet Ltd, Bidford-on-Avon, Warwickshire

Printed and bound by CPI Group (UK) Ltd, Croydon, CR0 4YY

Headline's policy is to use papers that are natural, renewable and
recyclable products and made from wood grown in sustainable forests.
The logging and manufacturing processes are expected to conform to the
environmental regulations of the country of origin.

Acknowledgments

For all the wonderful Stark and Most Wanted fans I've met in person and through social media. Y'll are the best!

Ignited

one

Cons and games, lies and deceit.

Those aren't just words to me, but a way of life.

For years, I've tried to escape—to be other than my father's daughter—but time and again I have failed.

Maybe I haven't tried hard enough. Maybe I didn't want to. I like the rush, after all. The challenge.

I have more than twenty years of the grift behind me, and I thought I knew it all. Thought I understood risk. Thought I knew the definition of danger.

Then I saw him.

Raw and carnal, dark and dangerous.

I didn't know risk until I met him. Didn't understand danger until I looked into his eyes. Didn't comprehend passion until I felt his touch.

I should have stayed away, but how could I when he was everything I craved? When I knew that he could fulfill my darkest fantasies?

I wanted him, plain and simple.

And so I set out to play the most dangerous game of all. . . .

I stood in the middle of the newly opened Edge Gallery, my heels planted on the polished wood floor and the brilliant white walls of the main exhibit space coming close to blinding me.

Around me, politicians mingled with hipsters as they buzzed from one painting to the next like bees around a flower. Male waiters in sharply creased tuxes carried wine-topped trays with purpose, while their similarly attired female counterparts offered tasty morsels that were such works of art themselves it seemed a shame to eat them.

Tonight's sparkling gala celebrated the opening of this newest addition to Chicago's well-known River North gallery district, and everyone who was anyone was here. And not just because of the art. No, the crowd tonight had come as much to mingle with the owners as to celebrate the opening.

And why not? Tyler Sharp and Cole August were among Chicago's elite. They, along with their friend and frequent business partner Evan Black, made up the knights—a triangle of power within the Chicago stratosphere. The fact that their power stemmed from both legitimate and illegitimate means only added to their dark, edgy coolness.

Not that the illegitimate side of the equation was public knowledge, but it did add a sort of mysterious sheen to these deliciously sexy men who made the press drool. I knew the truth because I was best friends with Evan's fiancée, Angelina Raine, and that friendship had spread to include all the knights. At least, that's what Angie and the knights believe. In reality, I'd realized the guys weren't squeaky-clean entrepreneurs within a day of meeting them.

Like knows like, after all.

For that matter, like attracts like. At least, that's what I hoped. Because although I truly did want to celebrate the opening, I'd really come here for one purpose, and one purpose only: to finally and completely get Cole August's attention—and then get him in my bed.

Not that I was progressing like lightning toward that goal. I'd come without a solid plan—something I never do—and after ninety minutes of mingling, I'd spoken only fourteen words to Cole, and that was at the door as I'd entered. I knew there were fourteen words, because I'd played the encounter—I wouldn't go so far as to call it a conversation—over and over in my head. A form of mental torture, I guess, as I wallowed in my own insipidness.

"I'm so thrilled for you both."

"Thanks, Kat. We're glad you could make it."

"Me, too. Well, I'll let you mingle. Later."

I shook my head at myself. Honestly, if my father had been around to overhear that exchange, he would have disowned me on the spot. Hadn't he taught me the art of making small talk? Of pulling people in? Of getting close so that you can get what you want?

Planning and focus have always been second nature to me. I'd grown up in the grift, and I'd known the ins and outs of designing a long con even before I knew my multiplication tables.

Tonight wasn't about a con, though. Tonight was about me.

And apparently that one little fact was enough to throw me entirely off my game.

Well, damn.

I shifted slightly so that I could look at the object of my mission. I found him easily enough—Cole August is not the kind of man who blends. Right then he was working the room, discussing art with both serious buyers and casual friends.

Art was his passion, and it was easy to see how much tonight meant to him. The two featured artists—a South Side tagger whom Cole had found and pulled out of the ghetto and a world-renowned painter who specialized in hyperrealism—worked the crowd alongside him.

Cole moved with a raw power and casual arrogance that both suggested his own South Side upbringing and also defied it. I knew that he'd once been entrenched in a gang, but he'd pulled himself out of the muck to become one of the most powerful men in Chicago. As I watched him, it was easy to see the confidence and grace that got him there.

I stared, a little mesmerized, a little giddy, as Cole continued through the room. He was dressed simply in black jeans that showed off his perfect ass, and a white T-shirt that both accented the dark caramel skin of his mixed-race background, and subtly reminded the guests that Cole hadn't been born to money and privilege. He wore his hair short, in an almost military-style buzz cut, and the style drew attention to the slightly tilted eyes that missed nothing, not to mention the hard planes of his cheekbones and that wide, firm mouth that seemed molded to drive a woman crazy.

He was sex on a stick—and all I wanted was to taste him.

I've never played the relationship game, and I've rarely craved men. That bit of self-denial stemmed more from pragmatism than any lack of libido on my part. Why torment them and myself by revealing my sexual quirks, and then suffer the inevitable angst and hurt feelings when they're unable to achieve what a sixty-dollar cylinder of vibrating rubber could manage so easily?

And to be honest, most of the men who crossed my path were less stimulating—both intellectually and physically—than anything tucked away in my toy drawer.

Cole, however, was different.

Somehow, he'd snuck into my thoughts. He'd filled my

senses. I'd felt that tug the first time I'd laid eyes on him, and that was years ago. But over the past few months, he'd become an obsession, and I knew that if I wanted to get clear of him, I had to push through.

I had to have him.

I'd come here tonight determined to get what I wanted—and now I was more than a little perturbed at myself for not having immediately leaped fully and confidently into the dark waters of seduction.

I knew why I hadn't, of course. It was because I wasn't certain that my advances would be welcome, and I wasn't a big fan of disappointment.

Yes, I thought that he was attracted to me—I'd felt that zing when our hands brushed and the trill of electricity in the air when we stood close together.

At least once or twice when I'd caught his eyes the illusion of friendship had turned to ash—burned away by the heat I'd seen in him. But those moments lasted only a few brief and fluttering seconds. Just enough to whet my appetite, and to make me fervently hope that the heat I saw was real—and not simply the desperate reflection of my own raging desire.

Because what assurance did I have that it wasn't all me? Maybe I was projecting attraction where none existed and, like a moth, I was going to get singed when I fluttered too close to the flame.

Still, I'd never know if I didn't go all in and find out. Maybe I'd fumbled the ball with my crappy conversation, but the night was young, and I gave myself a mental pep talk as I wandered the gallery, gliding through the flotsam and jetsam of gossip and business talk. Everything from catty comments about other women's clothing, to speculation as to the best place for a post-gala meal, to praise for the undeniable skill of the various artists represented at the opening.

A few people I knew casually made eye contact, politely shifting their stance as if to welcome me into their conversation. I pretended not to notice. Right then, I was lost in my own head, trying to wrap my mind around what I wanted and how I intended to get it.

The gallery was shaped like a T, with the main exhibit hall—which displayed the work of tonight's two featured artists—being the stem, and the crossbar being the more permanent exhibits. I'd been to the gallery before, so I knew the general layout, and I wandered the length of the room to where the two wings intersected.

There was a velvet rope blocking guests from entering the permanent area, but I've never paid much attention to rules. I slipped between the wall and the brass post that held the rope secure, then moved to the right so that I would be out of sight of the rest of the guests. After all, I wasn't in the mood for either a lecture on proper party etiquette or company.

The last time I'd been in this area, the section had still been under construction. The walls had been unpainted and the glass ceiling had been covered with a dark, protective film. The long, narrow room had been gloomy and a little claustrophobic. Now it extended in front of me like a walkway to paradise.

Tonight, the glass ceiling was transparent. Outside, lights mounted on the roof shone down to provide the illusion of daylight, and all around me the area glowed with artificial sunlight and the bright colors of the various pieces on display.

Beautifully polished teak benches ran down the center of the room, each separated by bonsai trees, so that both the seating and the decoration were as artistic as the architecture and the contents. And yet there was nothing overpowering about the room. Even tonight, with the hum of voices flowing in from the main gallery, I felt the blissful freedom of solitude.

With a sigh, I sat on one of the benches, realizing only as I did that I'd chosen this spot for a specific purpose. The image in front of me had caught my eye. No, more than that. It had compelled me. Drawn me in. And now I sat and studied it.

I knew a little bit about art, though not as much as my father. And certainly not as much as Cole. But it's fair to say that I've paid my dues in the kind of art gallery that caters to clients who embody that perfect trifecta of too much money, too much time, and too much property.

I couldn't count the number of days I'd spent in high heels and a pencil skirt, extolling the virtues of a particular piece. I'd rave about the astounding deal the buyer could get because our client—"no, no, I can't share his identity, but if you read the European papers, you've surely heard of him"—was desperate to unload an original master that had been in the family for generations. "Hard times," I'd say with a resigned shake of my head. "You understand."

And the buyer would frown and nod sympathetically, all the while thinking about this amazing bargain, and how they could one-up the Smiths at the next garden party.

I'd never sold an actual work by an actual master in my life, but the pieces I had passed held an equal appeal, at least to the eye if not to the investment portfolio.

But this painting before me put all the others I'd dealt with to shame. It was the view of a woman from behind. She was seated on the edge of a fountain, so that from the artist's perspective she was seen through shimmering beads of water that seemed to form a living curtain. A kind of barrier between her and the world. It gave the illusion that she was a creature of pure innocence, and yet that was not an asset. Instead, her innocence rendered her untouchable, even though it was clear that all anyone had to do was slip through the water to reach her.

The angle of view was such that her hips were not visible. Instead we saw only the curve of her waist, the unblemished skin of her back, and her blond hair that fell in damp curls that ended near her shoulder blades.

There was something familiar about her. Something magnetic. And for the life of me, I had no clue what it was.

"It's one of my favorites."

The familiar deep voice pulled me from my trance. Flustered, I turned to face Cole, then immediately wished I hadn't. I should have taken a moment to prepare myself first, because I heard my own gasp as I sank deep into those chocolate eyes.

"I—" I closed my mouth. Clearly I had lost all ability to think or speak or function in society. I fervently hoped the floor would just open up and swallow me, but I'd be okay with an alien abduction, too.

Neither of those things happened, though, and I found myself just sitting there staring at him while the corner of his mouth—that gorgeous, rugged, kissable mouth—twitched with what I could only assume was amusement.

"I'm sorry I slipped back here. It was getting too crowded in there for me, and I needed some air."

Concern flickered across his face. "Is something wrong, Catalina? You looked preoccupied."

"I'm fine," I said, though I trembled a bit, unnerved as always when he called me by my given name. Not that he actually knew my real name. As far as Cole and all my friends in Chicago were concerned, I was Katrina Laron. Catalina Rhodes didn't exist to them. For that matter, she didn't exist for me, either. She hadn't for a long, long time.

Sometimes, I missed her.

About eight months ago, a group of us had been having dinner together. Cole started talking about an upcoming trip to Los Angeles, and how he intended to visit Catalina Island. I don't even remember the details of the conversation, but by the end of it, my new nickname had stuck.

I'd rolled my eyes and pretended to be irritated, but the truth of it was that I liked the intimacy of hearing my birth name on his lips. It meant that we shared a secret, he and I, even if I was the only one of us who knew it.

Not that Catalina was an exclusive nickname. Cole also called me "blondie" and "baby girl," though he tended to reserve the latter for Angie, who had been a teenager when he'd met her.

Catalina was my favorite of the endearments, of course. But I wasn't picky. However Cole wanted to mark me was fine by me.

Right then, he stood to my right and frowned down at me. "I'm fine," I repeated, with a little more force this time. "Really. I was lost in thought, and you startled me. But I'm back now."

"I'm glad." His voice was smooth, almost prep-school cultured. He'd worked at it, I knew. He rarely talked about the time he'd spent in gangs, the things he'd had to overcome. Hell, he barely even talked about the two years he'd spent in Italy, studying art on scholarship. But it had all come together to make the man. And right then, in that moment, I was glad he never talked about it to the press or his clients. But I fervently wished that he would talk about it to me.

Yeah, I was a mess all right.

I stood up, then wiped my hands down the red material that clung provocatively to my thighs. I hoped it looked like I was smoothing my skirt. Instead, I was drying my sweaty palms.

"I'm going to go track down one of the girls with sushi," I said. "I didn't eat dinner and I think I'm feeling a little light-headed." I didn't mention that he was the reason my head was spinning.

"Stay." He reached out and closed his fingers around my wrist. His hand was huge, but his grip was surprisingly tender. His skin was rough, though, and I remembered how much of the work in the gallery he'd done himself, assembling frames, hanging canvases, moving furniture. Not to mention painting his own canvases. He must spend hours holding a wooden brush, moving carefully and meticulously in order to get exactly what he wanted—color, texture, total sensuality.

Slowly, as if he was intentionally trying to drive me crazy, he let his eyes drift over me. I fought the urge to shiver—to close my eyes and soak in the fantasy of this deliberate caress.

Instead, I watched his face. Watched his expression grow hot, almost feral, as if he wanted nothing more in that moment than to touch me—to take me.

Do it, I thought. *Right here, right now, just do it and let me have thought and reason back. Take me, dammit, and free me.*

But he didn't pull me close. Didn't press his hands to my ass and grind his cock against my thighs. Didn't slam me against the wall and press his mouth to mine while one hand closed tight around my breast and the other yanked up my skirt.

He did nothing but look at me—and in looking made me feel as though he'd done all those things.

He also made me feel better about the abuse I'd put my credit card through to buy this outfit. The dress was fire engine red, had a plunging neckline, and hugged every one of my curves. And while I might sometimes think that my curves were more appropriate for a 1940s film noir wardrobe, I can't deny that I filled out the dress in a way that Cole seemed to appreciate.

I'd worn my mass of blond curls clipped up, letting a few tendrils dangle loose to frame my face. My red stilettos perfectly matched the dress and added four inches to my already ample height, putting me just about eye level with this man. If you looked up "fuck me heels" in the dictionary, a picture of these shoes would be on the page.

I wanted to stay right there, lost in the way he was looking at me.

At the same time, I wanted to run. To get away and regroup.

To figure out how in hell I could manage to control a seduction when I couldn't even control myself.

Escape won out, and I tugged gently at my arm to free it.

To my surprise, his grip tightened. I frowned at him, a little confused, a whole lot hopeful.

"I'd like to hear your thoughts."

"My thoughts?"

"The painting," he said. "What do you think of it?"

"Oh." Cold disappointment washed over me. "The painting."

I gave my arm another tug and this time, to my regret, he released me.

"You like it?"

"I love it," I said, both automatically and truthfully. "But there's something—I don't know—sad about it."

His brows lifted slightly, and for a moment I thought he looked mildly amused. As if he'd understood the punch line of a joke a few moments before I did. Except I never got there at all.

"It's not sad?" I asked, turning back to look at the image.

"I don't know," he said. "Art is what you make of it. If you think it's sad, then I suppose it is."

"What is it to you?"

"Longing," he said.

I turned from the painting to him, sure that my face showed my question.

"Not sadness so much as desire," he said, as if that explained his response. "Her desires are like gemstones, and she holds them close, and each one presses sharp edges into the palm of her hand."

I thought about that as I looked back at the painting. "Do you think that way because you are an artist? Or are you an artist because you think that way?"

He chuckled, the sound both mild and engaging. "Shit, Catalina. I don't know. I don't think I could separate one from the other."

"Well, the most eloquent thing I can say is that I like it. I realize it's not one of the featured pieces, but I hope you're going to show more of the artist's work. It's compelling." I leaned closer, looking for a signature on the canvas or an information card on the wall. I found neither. "Who's the artist?"

"Don't worry, blondie," Cole said, his eyes flicking quickly to the painting. "We'll keep him around." Now I was certain I heard amusement in his voice, and since I wasn't sure what the joke was, it ticked me off.

I cocked my head, feeling more in control now that he was irritating me. "Okay, tell me. What am I missing?"

He moved to step in front of me, blocking the painting. Hell, blocking everything. He filled all of my senses, making me a little drunk merely from his proximity. From the sight of him before me and the scent of his cologne, all spice and wood and male. Even the echo of his voice played in my head, those radio-quality tones making me want to shiver.

I didn't have his touch, but the sensation of his hand upon my skin still lingered, and I clung tight to the memory. And as for taste—well, a girl could only hope.

Eternity passed in the space of seconds, and when he spoke, there was a musing note to his voice, as if he were speaking more to himself than to me. "How do you do it?"

"Do what?" I asked, but by the time the words escaped my lips, the spell was broken, and it was as if he hadn't spoken at all.

"It's an important night for Tyler and me," he said, his voice now tight with formality. "I'm glad you came, but I should get back to the rest of the guests."

The abrupt change in his tone disappointed me, but I clung greedily to the words themselves, and tried to ignore the rest. He'd said *I'm glad*. Not *we're glad*.

And I, apparently, had reached a new level of pathetic if I'd sunk so low as to be analyzing pronouns.

"I wouldn't have missed it for the world," I said, hoping my own voice didn't reveal the loose grip I had on my sanity.

He flashed me that killer smile, then turned toward the main gallery. But after only two steps, he stopped, then looked back at me. "By the way, you owe me," he said, and this time there was no denying the humor on his face.

"Oh, really? And why is that?"

"How is it you started working here three months ago and I didn't notice? That's not like me at all. And, frankly, Kat, if you'd spent that much time at my side, I assure you it would have caught my attention."

That spark of heat was back in his voice, but I barely noticed it. Instead, I'd turned a little cold. A string of curses whipped through my mind, and I had to force myself not to spit out a choice one or two.

Instead, I did what I'd been trained my whole life to do—I got my shit together and ran with it. "Oh my god, Cole, I'm so sorry. I meant to mention weeks ago that the mortgage company might be calling, but I got caught up in helping Angie with wedding prep stuff, and now I'm closing next week and I've been packing, and then—"

"It's okay," he said. "I get it."

"It's just that my hours at the coffee shop haven't ever been steady, and I didn't want the underwriting people to think I don't have the means to make my payments."

"It's okay," he repeated. "Buying a house is a very big deal. It's cool. It's been well over a week since they called, and I verified everything. If they haven't requested any more information from you by now, then I'd say you're good to go."

He met my eyes once more, trapping me in his gaze just a little too long for comfort. Whatever humor had been in his face before had vanished. Instead, I saw only a vibrant, sensual intensity. "But like I said, you owe me."

I swallowed, and despite the dryness in my mouth, I managed to form words. "Whatever you want," I said, and I could only hope that he understood the full meaning of my words.

His gaze lingered a moment longer. Then he inclined his head as if in dismissal. "I'll see you back in the main gallery."

Once again he turned and walked away from me.

This time, he didn't look back.

two

It took me a few minutes to gather myself before I returned to the party, and the moment I slipped around the rope barrier and felt the press of gaiety and chatter all around me, I knew that I should have taken a few minutes more.

You owe me, he'd said.

Whatever you want, I'd promised.

Did he understand how completely I meant those words? Had it really been desire I'd seen when he'd looked at me? And, if so, what was he going to do about it?

For that matter, what was *I* going to do about it?

Apparently I'd just come full circle. I'd started the evening with the intention of seducing Cole August. And despite the electricity that had crackled between us, I don't think I'd come even the slightest bit closer to that goal.

How's that for a complete failure to meet a mission objective?

Once again, I was not doing my father proud. Maybe if I thought of Cole as a mark rather than as a man . . .

I started to run my fingers through my hair, then caught myself before I accidentally pulled it out of the clip. Since I desperately wanted something to do with my hands, I waved down a svelte, dark-haired waitress. I spent a moment debating between a spring roll and sushi. I ended up taking one of each, then cursed myself. Food, Cole, my whole damn life. Apparently I was doomed to shoulder the curse of indecisiveness.

Great.

I moved toward a wall to get some breathing space away from the throng and tried to find Cole. It wasn't hard. He'd moved away from the crush of bodies and now stood in an alcove beside a portly man with a ruddy, unattractive baby face. The man was talking animatedly, his skin becoming more splotchy by the moment and his hands fluttering as if in punctuation of his words.

Cole showed no reaction at all—which told me right there that he was pissed as hell and doing a damn fine job of holding it in. Cole's temper was famous, and whoever this man was, he wasn't scoring points by threatening to incite an explosion during the gala.

I considered going over and interrupting—if nothing else I figured that should distract Cole's current nemesis. But fortunately, the gallery's business manager, Liz, slipped up, offered the man a drink, and artfully led him away.

Cole watched them go, and I saw his fist clench at his side. I started to count, and when I got to ten, Cole pushed away from the wall. Anger management tricks, I knew, and he was putting them all to use.

I wondered what he was angry about. I didn't, however,

wonder enough to go ask him. No, I was much more selfish than that. I was still focused on my own problem with Cole—and it wasn't his temper that I wanted to see explode.

I considered calling Flynn, my friend and roommate of the last few months. At best, he'd have a useful guy perspective on the whole mess. At worst, he'd offer a few soothing words. But I knew he was working tonight—if he wasn't, he'd be at the gala. Flynn wasn't one to miss a party. Especially not one that serves free alcohol.

Even a girl perspective would be good, but Angie and Evan had been double-booked tonight, and had already left to meet her parents for a wedding-planning dinner, and Tyler's girlfriend, Sloane, hadn't yet arrived.

I knew she was working late because last night over martinis she'd told me about the surveillance job she was on, but I'd thought she would be here by now. Selfish, maybe, but we'd become tight, and I wanted her around for moral support.

I glanced at my watch, then frowned. Then I told myself that it wasn't fair to be annoyed when Sloane was off doing her job and had no clue that I was contemplating seduction and needed hand-holding.

Then—thankfully—the gal pal fairies took pity on me, because when I glanced toward the front of the gallery, I saw her pulling open the glass door and gliding over the threshold.

Despite the late hour, the air was stifling from an unseasonably hot May. Even so, Sloane looked bright and fresh and pretty—like the girl next door who just happened to have the hard edge and cynicism of a former cop. I started to head in that direction, then stopped when I saw Tyler approach her, his eyes bright with appreciation.

He pulled her close, and despite the room full of people, his welcoming kiss was long and lingering, and I swear I could see her glow from all the way across the room.

My stomach tightened in sudden, unexpected longing. I wanted to be that girl—precious in a man's eyes. And with the power to bring him to his knees.

No. Not just any man. Cole.

I watched as Sloane brushed her hand possessively over Tyler's arm, then whispered something to him. He laughed, then kissed her cheek. She moved away from him to enter the party, and he stood for a moment, his gaze lingering on her as he watched her go.

Since I was watching Tyler, I didn't realize that Sloane had been coming my way until she eased up beside me. "Any news on the house?"

"We close next week," I said. "I'm suffering from mild terror that it's all going to get ripped out from under me. Like we'll find out that something is horribly wrong with the foundation. Or the sellers will back out. Or the loan will fall through."

The house had started as a whim. My natural state is to be in constant motion, everything from my habit of fidgeting to my general tendency to uproot myself every few years and move to a new city.

Over the last six years, though, I'd eased off that last trait. Instead of bouncing out of Chicago, I'd just bounced between apartments.

A few months ago, I decided that living in a house could be fun. I'd started out looking solely at rentals, but once I saw the tiny two-bedroom frame house, I knew it was like Charlie Brown's Christmas tree. All it needed was a little love. More important, I knew it had to be mine.

I hadn't even realized I'd been contemplating ownership until I'd picked up the real estate agent's flyer, but I was tired of feeling uprooted. I wanted to settle. I wanted . . . *more.*

And now I was on the verge of having it.

Honestly, I liked the way that felt.

Sloane's brow was furrowed as she pondered my words.

"You've had the inspections, the tenants have already moved out, and the sellers live—where? New Mexico, right? And I think you would have heard by now if there was something wrong with the loan." She narrowed her eyes. "The employment stuff checked out okay, right?"

"Yeah, but talk about a snafu. The call must have come when Liz wasn't here." I'd hit Liz up before I told my little fib on the loan application, and she'd promised to back me if the underwriters called.

"Shit. What happened? Tyler didn't say a thing to me."

"Apparently Cole got the call."

Her eyes widened. "Oh, really? When?"

"It's been over a week."

"And he didn't say anything?"

"Not until just a few minutes ago," I said.

She held her hands out, gesturing for me to continue. "Hello? What did he say?"

"That I owed him," I admitted.

Her laugh was filled with pure delight. "Well, that's convenient, isn't it?"

"Excuse me?"

"If he said you owed him, you just need to ask him how he wants to get paid."

I crossed my arms over my chest. "And what exactly are we talking about?"

"Oh, please, Kat. Don't play coy. I'm a cop, remember? I know how to read people. And that goes for you, too, Katrina Laron, even though you think you're impenetrable."

I did think that, and it was a little disconcerting to know that I was wrong. This was why I'd spent most of my life avoiding making close friends. They got into the cracks of your life, knew you too well, and made you vulnerable. But Sloane was right—as a former cop, she was used to watching people and noting the details. More than that, it wasn't that long ago that she'd been in a similar position, plotting out a way to seduce Tyler Sharp. Considering she and Tyler were now desperately in love and deliriously happy, I had to figure she understood the game.

She looked me up and down, the movement very deliberate. "Nice dress." Her mouth curved in a wicked grin. "Seems like the kind of thing Cole would appreciate."

"Bitch," I said, but I was laughing.

"So other than the dress, what have you got in your repertoire?"

"Isn't that the question of the day? You're right about the intentions," I admitted. "But I'm doing a piss-poor job on the execution." I ran my fingers through my hair, remembered the clip too late, and cursed.

I gave her the rundown of what had happened in the gallery while I freed my hair and fluffed it with my fingers. "But I'm not sure if he was really interested, or if it's just me being hopeful."

"Please tell me you aren't really that naive," she said. "The guy's completely gone on you."

"You are such a liar," I said. Frankly, I couldn't imagine Cole being gone on anyone. He was too damn good at keeping everything in check. As far as I'd seen over the years, that temper was the only thing that managed to escape his walls—and even that burst out like a rocket and was quickly snuffed.

"I've seen his face when he looks at you," she said. "Or, more accurately, I've seen his face when he looks at you and you're not looking back." Her mouth quirked up. "You know as well as I do that Cole doesn't give anything away that he doesn't have to."

"There's one of the century's biggest understatements."

"I'm serious," she said. "When Tyler looks at me the way I've seen Cole look at you, I know to expect a very long night, with very little sleep."

"Oh." I drew in a breath, then licked suddenly dry lips.

"That's something," I added, unable to keep the smile out of my voice. "Thanks."

"Sure," she said. "But, listen. Are you—" She cut herself off with a shrug. "Never mind."

"Oh, no," I said. "No way are you pulling that with me. You've got something to say, and it's about me or it's about Cole. And I want to know."

"It's just—are you sure about this? And why now?"

"Yes," I said, because despite my nervous moments and hesitations, I'd never been more sure about anything. I took her arm and steered her to a far corner, where there were no paintings displayed on the walls and therefore no guests to overhear us. "And as for now, I don't think I have a choice anymore. I can't get him out of my head," I admitted. "He's getting into my dreams. I've never had a guy get this far under my skin, and it's driving me a little bit crazy."

"So this is an exorcism?"

"Maybe. Hell, I don't know. Why?"

"Because we're friends, Kat. All of us. Me and Tyler, Angie and Evan. And even you and Cole. I don't want it to get weird, and I don't want—" She shook her head. "Sorry, that's none of my business. Shouldn't go there."

No way was I letting her get away with that. "Go where?"

"I just don't want you to get hurt," she said.

"What are you talking about?"

She dragged her fingers through her hair. "I just happen to know that Cole doesn't date. I don't want you disappointed. And—to be perfectly selfish—I don't want to lose the dynamic between the six of us."

"I don't, either," I said truthfully. "But I need to do this." I didn't try to explain that if I didn't, the dynamic between us would change anyway. I'd crossed a mental line, and no matter what, I couldn't go back to being Friendly Kat, the girl with the secret crush on Cole. Because this wasn't a crush. This was a need. This was a hunger. I'd opened Pandora's box, and even if I'd wanted to, I couldn't shove everything back inside.

"What do you mean he doesn't date?" I pressed.

"That's what Tyler told me. He fucks," she said with a quirk of her brow. "But he doesn't date."

"That's part of what makes him perfect," I admitted, because although I had no way of knowing for sure, I'd watched him long enough and intently enough to guess that Cole was at least as fucked up as I was. "I just want to scratch this itch. And if you're right, then Cole has the same itch, and this should work out just fine."

"So you're just looking for a fuck buddy?" She narrowed her eyes, obviously dubious.

"Yeah," I said, though I hadn't really put it in those terms before. "Yeah, I guess I am."

"Kat . . ." She trailed off, and there was no way to miss the censure in her voice.

"What?"

"That's a load of total bullshit."

"No," I said firmly, "it's not." And it wasn't. I'd admit—at least to myself—that the attraction I felt for Cole pulsed hard and drove deep. But that didn't mean I wanted to date the man—or, more specifically, it didn't mean that I *would* date him, no matter how much I might want it.

Not that I could explain all of that to Sloane. We might have become friends since she'd rolled into town late last summer, but no way was I opening my closet so she could see all of my skeletons.

I didn't need a degree in psychology to know I was fucked up, and I didn't need a degree in human sexuality to know that I wanted Cole's hands on me. The second one I could do something about. The first one I just had to live with.

"Trust me, Sloane," I said, hoping that I wasn't about to screw up royally. "I know what I'm doing."

For a second she didn't answer, then she nodded. "It's your life. Go get him."

I laughed, then signaled to a passing waiter. He paused in front of me, and I grabbed a glass of chardonnay.

I held up my finger as I downed it, silently signaling the waiter to stay. Then I exchanged my empty glass for a full one. "Liquid courage," I said, more to Sloane than the waiter, though his lips twitched as well.

He tilted his head in both acknowledgment and farewell, then slid off into the crowd. I watched him go, knowing that my turn was next. Because Cole was somewhere in that throng, too.

I caught Sloane's eye, and took strength from her encouraging grin. "Here goes nothing," I said, then moved away from her and back toward the throng, determined to see this through.

It took a moment, but I finally found Cole surrounded by a group of well-heeled guests, all of whom were gazing with rapturous expressions at a canvas that seemed to be in motion, it was so full of color and life. I couldn't hear Cole, but I saw the animation in his face, the way he got when he spoke of art.

He used his hands, his body, and with every word and motion he captured the crowd. Hell, he captured me, too, and I moved closer and closer, until finally I could hear his words and I just stood there, letting his smooth voice roll over me and give me courage.

After a moment, he wrapped up his spiel and left the guests to contemplate the painting on their own. When he did, he turned and saw me, and I felt the impact of that connection all the way to my toes.

There'd been heat between us earlier tonight—of that I no longer had any doubt. But Cole had been in control then. This time, I'd caught him unaware, and I could plainly see the pulsing hunger that raged through him as he took in the sight of me.

Go. Now.

I drew in a breath for courage. Yeah, it was time to do this thing.

And so I took one step, and then another and another. Each taking me toward Cole August. Each fueling that fire inside me that raged for him—a fire that had the power to either raise me up or reduce me to ashes.

I could only hope that tonight I would capture the man, and not destroy myself in the trying.

three

It's not sex that messes you up. It's desire.

Once sex enters the equation, everyone has something to bargain with. It's like a contract, and there's consideration on each side. Maybe the sex isn't great, or maybe it's mind-blowing, or maybe the participants are so wrapped up in their own neuroses that it overshadows all the rest. But even then, the basic parameters are there and everyone knows what's expected of them.

That's not the case with desire.

With desire it's all one-sided. You have nothing to go on except perception. A smile. A nod. A handshake that lingers too long. The stroke of a finger over hair.

But all those things can be hidden, and all those things can be faked.

When you grow up in the grift, you know how to fake a lot of things, and you know how to read people.

You think you do, anyway.

I thought I knew how to read Cole. I thought I'd seen the subtle signals that validated my own desire. The little hints and movements, the casual glances and offhand touches.

I thought I'd seen them—but I couldn't be certain. And if I wanted an answer I had to put myself on the line.

That is why desire is a bitch.

That bitch currently had her iron hand on my shoulder and was steering me through the crowd toward the object of my desire. He'd been pulled aside by an elegant seventy-something woman who appeared to be interrogating him and the artist about the subtle distinctions between two of the pieces on display.

I had three things going for me, and I clung tight to them like a child to a security blanket. First, my upbringing made me a chameleon, both changeable and adaptable. It also gave me a thick skin and the ability to fake confidence. Some kids thank their parents for forcing them to endure Little League in order to build character. I thanked my dad for teaching me how to pull off long and short cons.

Second, I'd seen desire in Cole's eyes at least twice during the gala. Maybe I was projecting, but I didn't think so. And if he wanted me, too, then that made my goal that much more attainable.

Finally, I'd slammed back two glasses of wine within the space of five minutes, and I am a lightweight where alcohol is concerned. That meant that I was floating on a cloud of liquid courage, just like I'd told the waiter. And as far as I was concerned, that was a damn fine thing.

"You can analyze," Cole was saying as I approached, "or you can feel." The two paintings he was discussing were huge, the canvases each eight feet tall and four feet wide. They stood side by side, the vibrant colors seeming to jump from the canvases. The artist, a South Sider who looked to be on the shy side of twenty and went by the name of Tiki, nodded vigorously from his post beside Cole.

"That's what I been sayin'." He thumped his chest with the heel of his hand. "You gotta go with what you feel here. You can pick it apart and hold up color swaths and call in your high-price decorators, but that ain't gonna tell you what's gonna feel right when you walk into the room and see that canvas on your wall."

The woman sniffed. "That may be so, young man, but my husband just paid six figures to our designer to redo the den, and I assure you that if what I purchase clashes with the decor, it won't be your art I'm feeling."

Tiki laughed. "You got me there, Amelia."

I expected her to chastise him for his impertinence, but she only joined his laughter.

"What do you think, Kat?" Cole asked.

I looked up at him, surprised that he was pulling me into the discussion. More than that, I had the distinct feeling that he'd been watching me while I'd been watching Tiki and Amelia.

"I think that your six-figure decorating job isn't worth a nickel if you don't make the room yours." I stepped closer to the canvases, sliding into operator mode. *This* I knew how to do. "If you had a completely empty room to work with, which would you choose?"

I looked from one to the other as Amelia considered. "It's a hard choice, I know," I said. "They're similar, and yet at the same time each stands alone. They're evocative," I added. "The bursts of color. The subtlety of the muted areas." I glanced at her, saw that she was nodding slightly, and started to reel her in.

"I don't know about you," I said—because we were just talking girl to girl now—"but I look at these, and they lift me up." I did a quick inspection of her appearance. The classic lines of her dress. Her carefully styled hair. She was considering buying modern art, yes, but this was an elegant woman with roots that probably sank for generations.

That analysis told me where to go next. "It makes me feel like . . ." I drifted off, as if considering. "It's like being at the symphony," I finally said. "When the music seems to lift you up and carry you away."

"Yes," she murmured, nodding. "Why, yes."

"What I find particularly compelling is the way these two pieces blend together. You see? The colors complement each other. The red here draws out the purple on this one." I indicated each painting in turn. "They work in tandem—honestly, I'd be afraid that separating them would be like removing all the violins from a performance of Beethoven's Fifth."

I glanced at Cole and saw that his eyes were narrowed just slightly. But whether he was impressed with my efforts or concerned that I was about to screw up a sale, I didn't know.

Tiki was easier to read. His wide grin suggested that he knew exactly where I was heading.

I pushed them both out of my mind. Right then, I didn't need performance anxiety adding to my already existing soup of emotional turmoil.

"How would you choose?" Amelia asked.

"Honestly?" I leaned toward her conspiratorially. "I'd cheat."

Her eyes widened, as if I'd just said the most scandalous thing imaginable.

"If I had an empty room to fill, I wouldn't leave with just one. I'd insist on acquiring both."

She turned her attention from me back to the paintings. I could see the spark of interest, and then I saw the way her brow furrowed to form a deep V above her nose. "But all this is hypothetical. I don't have carte blanche."

"Actually," I said, grinning broadly, "you do. What's the color scheme of your room?"

"Earth tones highlighted with peach."

"These colors," I said, indicating a portion of the canvas on the left. I looked to Tiki for confirmation and help. He gave the confirmation, but he didn't jump in as I'd hoped.

Cole, however, picked up the thread. "She's right, you know," he said to Amelia. "Alone, the other painting might not work with that scheme. But see here?" He gestured between the two paintings, his movements highlighting the colors and patterns. "These browns and greens are a perfect complement to the peach and pinks over here."

"Yeah, man, they're right," Tiki said. "These canvases, they're like a team. Like bread and butter, you know what I'm sayin'?"

I watched Amelia, and saw the slow spread of a smile. It was a smile I recognized from my days and nights in Florida, pushing paintings with my dad. It was a smile that said a woman with too much money had just figured out a way to justify her spending.

In other words, my work there was done.

I pressed my palm gently against her arm. "I'm sorry. I didn't mean to run on like that. At any rate, I'll let you and Tiki talk. I really should go mingle."

"Well, I don't think we need any further debate," I heard her say as I melted into the crowd. "We just need that nice young girl with the credit card machine."

"That was quite the performance," Cole said a few moments later. He took my arm and steered me to one side. I went willingly, my entire body tingling simply from the firm grip of his fingers against my bare elbow.

He walked slightly behind me, so I couldn't see his face. "Good performance?" I asked. "Or bad performance?"

"As far as I'm concerned, you get a standing ovation."

"Really?" I asked, ridiculously pleased that I'd impressed him.

He let go, then moved to face me. I missed his touch, but the trade-off was worth it. I'm not the kind of girl who swoons over hunky firemen calendars and I've only seen *Magic Mike* once. But as far as eye candy went, Cole was a walking, talking Milky Way bar, and at least as tempting.

"Really," he confirmed. An easy smile bloomed on his face, and he shook his head slowly, with obvious pleasure. "I didn't realize that working as a barista required such honed salesmanship."

"I'm a woman of many talents," I said, then fluttered my lashes.

"Damn right you are." He drew in a breath as he looked at me, and try as I might, I had no clue what he was thinking.

"That was quite the commission you just brought in," he finally said. "I have a feeling you'll be getting Christmas cards from Tiki for the rest of your life."

"I look forward to it. What about you?" I asked boldly, and blamed it on the wine. I met his eyes, and fervently hoped that mine really were a window to the soul, because right then I wanted him to see straight inside me. "What will I get from you?"

"That depends on what you want."

"Want," I repeated. Where Cole was concerned, what didn't I want?

"I told you earlier that you owed me," he said. "Do you want to call us even?"

"Do you?"

He was silent for a moment, and then one moment longer. "No," he finally said.

I lifted my chin. "Good."

His expression remained perfectly stoic, but he lifted his hand toward my face, then dropped it, as if he were a child who'd caught himself about to do something naughty.

"It's okay," I said, my voice almost a whisper. "I won't break."

"Don't be so sure, blondie. I've been known to destroy even the most resilient things."

"I'm not a thing. And you won't destroy me." I hesitated only a second, then took one step closer. The difference was only inches, but the air seemed suddenly thicker, as if my lungs had to work harder to draw in oxygen. "It's okay," I said again.

All around us, the party continued, but I'm not sure either one of us was aware. Instead, it felt as if we'd stepped into a vortex, and at least in our little corner of space and time nothing else mattered or even existed.

I held my breath, wanting his touch so badly I could taste it. And when he finally brushed the side of his thumb over my cheekbone, it was all I could do not to moan aloud.

All too quickly he took his hand away, leaving me bereft.

All too quickly he stepped back, forcing the world around us to come back to life.

"I just had to see if I was right," he said.

"About?"

"Your skin. It's like touching a promise."

"Is it?" I murmured.

"Tender," he said. "And a bit mysterious. With layer upon layer just waiting to be discovered."

My breath stuttered in my chest. "I didn't know you thought that," I said. "I didn't know you thought about me at all."

He was silent for so long I began to fear he wasn't going to answer. When he spoke, his words cut through me, sharp and sweet. "I think about you more than I should."

It was suddenly very warm in the gallery. Little beads of sweat gathered at the hairline on the back of my neck. I needed air, because it seemed as if all the oxygen had been sucked out of the room.

Somehow, miraculously, I formed words. "What are you thinking now?"

I saw the answer I craved in the lines of his face and the stiff control of his body. I felt it in the way the air between us crackled and sparked. I even smelled it, that warm and musky scent of desire.

The reality of his answer surrounded and enticed me, and yet when he spoke, his words denied me. Denied us both.

"I'm thinking no," he said, destroying me with nothing more than those three simple words. "And I'm thinking that I need to get back to my guests."

four

I watched him go, numb from the knowledge that despite being so close I had failed so spectacularly.

I couldn't even take any solace from the fact that when he denied me, he was denying himself, too. I wanted his touch, not just the knowledge that he wanted me.

Then take it.

The thought was so simple, so accurate and so compelling, that I actually took a step toward him. I'd seen the heat. Hell, I'd practically smelled the sulfur. If I pushed the issue, I knew damn well that I could force an explosion.

Determined, I aimed myself toward him. One step, then another. And then—with the crowd swirling around me and the voices meshing together like a discordant soundtrack—I simply stopped.

Did I want this?

I did, yes. Oh, god, I did. I wanted to feel Cole's hands on my bare skin, his naked body hot against mine.

And yet . . .

And yet I couldn't quite make myself go further. I could force an explosion, yes, but what then? If we burned together hot and hard, what would happen next?

Would we rise from the ashes like a phoenix?

Or would that fire simply destroy everything that already existed between us?

I'd told Sloane that I'd passed the point of no return—that I had to move forward even if that meant risking our friendship—and I'd meant the words when I'd said them. But now doubt and fear had crept into the equation.

I cared about this man, and in so many ways. Did I really crave him so much that I was willing to risk destroying everything else?

"Are you okay?"

I blinked, drawn from my thoughts by the woman's voice. "Yeah," I said. She was a tall brunette, and somewhat familiar. "Just distracted—and a little light-headed. Too much wine."

"Cole and Tyler know how to throw a party. I'm Michelle. I think I've seen you once or twice at Destiny."

"Oh, right." I took the hand she offered and shook it. Destiny was the well-heeled gentleman's club the knights owned. I didn't go there often, but I'd been a couple of times with Angie for drinks while we'd waited for Evan, and Sloane had actually worked there for a while. She'd even confessed to me that she still performed occasionally. "Tyler likes it," she'd said with the kind of smile that suggested that she liked it, too. And liked even more what happened after the dancing.

I tried to place Michelle, but couldn't manage it. With her body, she could have easily been a dancer, but I didn't think so. I had a vague memory of her at the bar. And, as the memory grew stronger, I started to see Cole there beside her.

"You're Cole's friend, right?"

Her eyes crinkled slightly at the corners. "Yeah," she said, with an amused lilt to her voice. "We're very good friends."

"Well," I said tightly, as green strands of jealousy started twisting in my gut, "it's really great to see you here."

She said a few more hollow words about the gala and I responded with equally hollow chitchat. Then she continued on her way. I waited a moment, then decided that those knots of jealousy confirmed that I needed to just get the hell out of there. I needed to think and to regroup.

And I needed to put distance between me and Cole.

I planned to make the circle, say my goodbyes, then go home and drown my lust and indecision in a bottle of Shiraz and a really sappy movie. With any luck, Flynn would still be at work, and I could have the entire bottle to myself.

I started to meander toward the door, but didn't make it very far. Instead, I ended up pausing just a few steps from my starting point, jerked to a stop by the sight of Michelle and Cole, her hand on his shoulder and her mouth near his ear.

True, she could have been telling him something mundane—*I thought you should know your car has a flat*—but my imagination was drifting more in the direction of *why don't we slip in the back and I'll suck your cock*.

Shit.

Yes, I was an absolute, indisputable wreck—and it was entirely Cole August's fault.

I steeled myself to continue toward the exit, and kept the thought of a glass of wine and a movie dangling in front of me like a carrot. But then I saw Cole's hand on the small of Michelle's back, and his face as hard as stone. And then, when the two of them stopped in front of the bloated, baby-faced man Cole had been talking with earlier, my curiosity got the better of me.

I couldn't hear the conversation, but I could tell that Cole was royally pissed off—and Baby Face looked pale and frightened.

Michelle said something to Cole, and from the way he took three long, measured breaths, I had to assume he was trying to control his temper. Then he and Michelle led a very unhappy-looking Baby Face through the gallery and into the closed-off section.

I debated for only a minute, then followed.

When I reached the velvet rope, I peered into the closed section, but didn't see them. The painting that had caught my attention earlier was to the right, and I knew that the offices were toward the left. Both were beyond the velvet rope, and I knew that if I slipped past it a second time, I'd be kicking good manners to the curb even while embracing my inner snoop.

I shrugged. Seemed like a reasonable trade-off to me.

I slipped into the gallery, took off my shoes so as to walk more softly, and made my way to the end of the hall and the large door that led to yet another corridor. This one ran parallel to the main gallery and housed the staff offices, studio space for Cole and the featured artists, restrooms, and supply closets.

The door was cracked open slightly, and since that was practically an invitation, I didn't even hesitate. I was almost to Cole's office when the door opened and Michelle slipped out.

I flattened myself against the wall, certain that the red dress was shining like a beacon and she would see me. But she walked in the opposite direction, continuing down the corridor until she reached the end and the door that led into the small front office that served as Liz's primary domain.

The moment she disappeared through the door, I sagged with relief. Then immediately jumped when the sharp explosion of shattering glass echoed through the area, followed by Cole's deep, angry, and tightly controlled voice. "Goddammit, Conrad. Do you have any idea how easy—how goddamn fucking easy—it would be for me to kill you right now? What a goddamn pleasure it would be to snap your neck and put you out of my misery? Do you? *Do you?*"

I couldn't hear Conrad's reply, but I had the feeling it involved whimpering.

"If I ever hear that you've come sniffing around my people again, I swear to god I will rip your heart out. Now get the fuck out of here before I lose my goddamn temper."

Conrad must have taken Cole at his word, because he stumbled out of the door, as white as a sheet and moving so fast he jiggled. He turned toward me, then jumped even more when he saw me standing there.

He said, "Oh!" then jogged past me toward the door. I sagged back against the wall, relieved. And determined to follow Conrad out as soon as my heart rate slowed a tiny bit.

Determined or not, tonight no longer seemed like the best night for a seduction.

I drew in a breath, pushed away from the wall, and started to walk quietly toward the exit.

I'd gone only two steps when I froze, suddenly certain that Cole was behind me. I'd heard nothing. Seen nothing. But the air around me seemed to crackle, as if the remnants of Cole's anger were making him hum like a live wire.

"I'm sorry," I said, as I began to turn around. "I didn't mean to—"

But the words died on my lips. He was right there, his huge frame filling the hallway, his muscles tight, his expression ferocious.

His hands were clenched in fists by his sides. I could see the effort that was required to hold himself together, and I knew that all it would take was one wrong word to completely rip him apart.

I spoke anyway.

Maybe I was trying to soothe. Maybe I wanted the explosion.

All I knew was that I wanted to hear his name on my lips and see that fierce intensity in his eyes directed at me.

I was playing with fire, and so help me, I didn't care.

"Cole," I said, then stopped when my voice seemed to set him in motion. His long strides brought him right in front of me. Instinctively, I took a single step back, then felt his hand close around my upper arm.

I felt the brush of his breath against my face as he issued one single command. *"No."*

Heat seemed to radiate through me, spreading out from that spot where his hand remained pressed to my bare skin. I could practically smell his anger—that violent, wild fury. He was heated and unpredictable and if I had any instinct for self-preservation, I knew that I should be terrified.

I wasn't.

Instead, my whole body tingled in reaction to the undiluted sensuality of this man, and I wanted to close my eyes and soak it in. I wanted to feel it hotter, wilder.

I wanted everything he had to give—and it pissed me off that he wasn't giving it.

Deliberately, I turned to look at my arm. At that singular spot where he was touching me. Then I tilted my head back so that I was looking straight into his eyes once again.

"Yes," I said, and despite the deep, fathomless brown, I could see the way his pupils dilated in response to my words.

I held my breath, wanting the touch that I was certain would come, then almost screamed in frustration when he released me.

"Go back to the party, Kat," he said, then turned away from me and very deliberately walked back to his office.

What the fuck?

"Goddamn you, Cole August," I shouted, ignoring the irony that it was me—not him—who'd actually popped. I hurried after him, then reached out and grabbed a handful of his T-shirt just as he reached his doorway. "Do you think I'm scared of you? Of this? I'm not."

"You should be." His voice was as low and as ominous as his expression.

He was on edge. I knew it. I could see it. And I really didn't care. I was on edge, too. For that matter, I'd jumped headlong into the chasm, and now I was tumbling through space.

I didn't know where I would land. All I knew was that I wanted Cole to be the one to catch me.

"Maybe I should," I admitted. "But I really don't give a damn." And then, before I could talk myself out of it, I used my grip on his T-shirt as leverage, drew myself up on my tiptoes, and closed my mouth over his.

The kiss was like falling through hell to land in heaven. His mouth was hard at first, unyielding. Then his fingers twined in my hair and his other hand cupped the small of my back, pressing me forward until I was right against him.

I felt his erection like hard steel trapped inside his jeans, the swell of it pressing provocatively against my abdomen.

Had I really been thinking about dropping this quest? Of walking away from this man who could make me feel so incredible?

What kind of idiocy was that? And thank god I hadn't listened to my own foolish notions.

He shifted against me, and I released a groan of pure, self-satisfied lust. The sound seemed to break something inside him, and the kiss turned wilder, our mouths joined as I wanted our bodies to be. His tongue exploring, tasting, driving me crazy and making me spin just a little bit out of myself, because otherwise how could I survive this onslaught of sensation?

He broke the kiss, then leaned back, breathing hard.

I grabbed his collar and drew him back. "Don't you dare," I said, not the least bit surprised that my voice sounded more like a growl than spoken words.

"Christ, Kat."

Because I feared his words were a protest or a dismissal, I tightened my grip on his shirt and yanked him forward, unbalancing him. He barked out a curse, and I saw the mixture of irritation and heat and lust flash across his face.

There was power there, too, but the control I'd seen earlier was gone now, replaced by a wild, determined need.

For the flash of an instant I feared that I had pushed too far. Then he was on me, and there was no room for fear anymore. Just need and heat and lust and passion.

His hands closed over my shoulders, and I vaguely acknowledged the sound of the door banging shut. Then the room was spinning as he whirled me around and slammed me hard against the wall.

The gallery space had once been a warehouse, and he had me pressed against the original exposed brick. I felt its rough texture grating against my shoulders and bare arms, and each sting of that contact seemed to heighten the thrill of Cole's hands upon my body.

His fingers closed around the collar of my dress, and he yanked it down, ripping the material. I gasped, thrilled and delighted as he closed his hand tight over my breast, his fingers teasing my already tight, overly sensitive nipple.

With his other hand, he tugged my skirt up, and as his mouth closed over my breast, he shoved my panties aside, then moaned when he realized I was waxed.

"Christ, you feel good," he said, as he thrust his fingers roughly inside me.

I was wet and open and ready—and my body clenched around him, wanting to draw him in, to be as close to him as humanly possible.

"Kat," he murmured as he moved from my breast to my neck to my mouth. "Christ, the taste of you."

"Don't stop," I begged, as his fingers thrust harder and harder inside me.

"You make me—"

"What?"

"Feel," he said.

"Yes," I said, surprised that one word could convey so much. "Oh, yes."

His mouth closed over my breast again, and I writhed against the rough wall, each scrape of the rough brick against my skin like an underscore to our passion.

I wanted him inside me, and I silently begged for him to just take me, to fuck me, and not to ask or tell, but to just *do*. I wanted to be his—I wanted to simply belong.

There was a couch about three feet to my right, and he took my hand and drew me roughly toward it. His mouth covered mine, and as his tongue teased me, his fingers yanked my skirt up the rest of the way up to around my waist. Then he whipped me around, his palms on my ass as he bent me over to spread me, to take me, and I moaned aloud in sweet anticipation, because wasn't this what I'd been wanting this entire night? Hell, this entire year?

I felt his fingers graze over the raw and sensitive skin on my shoulder. And I sucked in air, realizing for the first time how thoroughly the brick had abraded my skin.

"I hurt you."

"No," I said, as something cracked inside me. It hurt, yes. But I liked it.

I didn't know what that meant, but I knew that it was true. I liked the pain—not pain by itself, but pain that came from him. From our shared passion.

I wanted him to have that—the power to hurt me. I wanted him to keep it close like a gift. Because somehow that made me his.

I wanted to explain that, to make him understand, but I couldn't find the words.

"I hurt you," he repeated, and this time I heard the low, agonized tone of self-loathing in his voice.

"You haven't," I whispered, rushing to reassure him and cursing myself for not finding the words sooner. "Please, Cole, no."

But he wasn't listening, and I felt suddenly cold and exposed. I started to turn, to shift, to put my dress right. I couldn't, though. He had one hand on my waist and the other on my shoulder.

The one on my waist kept steady pressure, keeping me bent forward and helpless.

The hand on my shoulder grazed lightly over my newly raw skin. Skin that only moments before had burned with a pain that punctuated pleasure, but that now just stung, almost shamefully.

"Christ," he said, and this time his voice was so low that I almost couldn't make out the word.

"Cole," I said gently. "It's okay."

"Okay?" His voice was taut, a precursor to an explosion. He released me, and I stood up, carefully smoothing my skirt down even as I felt my cheeks burn. What had been one of the most erotic and exciting moments of my life had shifted totally off-kilter.

He held out his hand, and I saw that his fingertips were streaked with my blood. "I did that to you."

"You didn't," I said. I turned around, then tried to adjust my dress. "Cole," I said softly. "Please. I want this."

"What?" The word was harsh. "What do you want, Kat? What could you possibly want from me?" He held out his hand again. "Pain? Blood?"

"Maybe." I lifted my chin and met his eyes. "You said I owed you. Well, I'm willing to give whatever payment you want."

"You have no idea want what I want or what you're saying."

"The hell I don't," I countered. "Don't you get it, Cole? I want you. Whatever or however that means, I want you."

Something flickered in his eyes, something that looked a bit like hope. But it was gone before I could be certain.

He took a step backward, and I had never seen him look more sad. "I may not have a lot of self-restraint. But I have enough. And I'm not taking you down with me."

"Cole, please."

He turned to leave, then paused at the door to look back at me. "I tore your dress."

I fingered the rip in the neckline that exposed the lace of my bra and the swell of my breast. Despite my confusion and embarrassment and total frustration, my impulse was to rip it further. To rip the whole goddamn dress off. To stand naked in front of him. Tempting him. Testing him.

Instead, all I said was "Yes."

"I'll have Red drive you home," he said, referring to the driver he shared with Evan and Tyler.

"Fuck that. I can find my own way home."

Our eyes met, and for a moment I thought I saw regret. Then it cleared, and he simply nodded. "Take a jacket if you want," he said, indicating a coat tree on the far side of the room.

Then he left, leaving me standing alone in his office, my dress ripped and my emotions equally in tatters.

five

"Avocado, salmon, and cream cheese," Flynn said as he slid a plate loaded with the world's biggest omelette in front of me. "Orange juice," he added, following the plate with a champagne glass. "Of the mimosa variety. And—because what is breakfast without bacon?—a nice, crunchy side of pig fat."

I lifted a brow as he put a plate of bacon on the small wooden table that took up most of the apartment's minuscule breakfast area. "And I'm supposed to eat all of this how?"

"One forkful at a time." He filled his own plate, then plunked himself down in the chair opposite me. "Consider it guilt food. I was out getting laid last night while you were home doing the morose girl routine."

"When you put it that way," I said, then dug in.

There are many benefits to rooming with Flynn. He's the

best cook I've ever met. He's diligent about paying the rent on time. He works as a flight attendant, so he's often gone for long stretches, thus fulfilling my need for alone time. And when he's in town, he often picks up a shift at John Barleycorn, a local pub, which also fulfills that solitude thing, but has the added bonus of providing a place to go for drinks with good service guaranteed.

He's been friends with Angie for years and gets along great with Sloane, so there's none of the awkwardness that sometimes comes when circles of friends overlap. More than that, he's easy on the eyes. And he's straight.

It was that last characteristic that had intrigued me the most when I woke up that morning. Not because I wanted to sleep with him, but because he could provide insight into Cole. At least, I'd hoped he could.

I'd shared the basic overview of what had transpired at the gala while he cracked eggs and fried bacon. Once I had the lightly edited sordid tale out there, I asked him to play shrink and get into Cole's head for me.

"Like anyone could get inside Cole August," he said. "Or any of them, for that matter. But Cole . . ." He trailed off with a shrug and a shake of his head.

"What?"

"I've known him for as long as Angie has, although I didn't hang out with him or the others as much, especially once Jahn started spending most of his time in the condo instead of the house," he added, referring to Angie's uncle and the downtown condo that she'd inherited when he'd passed away a little over a year ago.

"But?" I pressed.

"But I know him well enough to know that I don't know him at all." He shrugged. "He's not one for oversharing."

"Neither am I. For that matter, neither are you."

He lifted his hands in a gesture of peace. "I'm not criticizing. I'm just stating a fact. And as for me, you know all my dark secrets."

I tapped the omelette with my fork and grinned. "Which is why I get such good treatment."

"True that." He sucked down some of his mimosa. "I'm just worried about you. It's like he's become an obsession. And you're not the kind of girl who obsesses."

Because he had a point, I said nothing.

"You ought to just walk away. I mean, for one, he pretty much told you to. And for another, there's nobody in the world worth all the mental energy you've tossed toward this guy."

I frowned, turning his words over in my head. "Do you really believe that?"

"Believe what?"

"That no one is worth it." The thought made me sad. And made me think that Flynn felt more alone in the world than I'd realized.

He lifted a shoulder. "I don't know. Maybe. Maybe not. I guess the real question is whether Cole is worth it." He flashed a wicked grin. "I mean, if you're just looking to get laid, I'd be happy to oblige."

I rolled my eyes. "Not in a million years. Your professional expertise would make me self-conscious."

He smirked. "I'm retired, remember?"

"And I'm glad." For a few months, Flynn had supplemented his income by sleeping with bored, older society women. I think Angie suspected the truth, but I was the only one who knew for certain, primarily because I'd become suspicious and called him on it.

But while I might know his secrets, he still didn't know mine. And I didn't see any reason to alter that status quo.

"Even so," I continued, "it would be weird. I know how tempting it must be to see me day in and day out, and not have a piece of me," I added airily. "But I know you'll survive the blue balls."

He grinned. "That's why I love you, Kat. You don't take my shit."

"I don't take anybody's shit."

"Except Cole's."

I frowned, because I had to silently admit he had a point.

Because this was Pity Katrina Day, Flynn gave me a pass on our usual deal where he cooks and I clean. So while he gathered the plates, rinsed, and loaded the dishwasher, I looked idly on, my mind wandering over the conversation.

The truth was, even if there wasn't the whole awkward friend thing hanging between us, I still wouldn't sleep with Flynn. I rarely slept with anyone, actually, because I knew damn well what would happen. How I would react. How I would shut down.

That's the main reason I knew that this craving for Cole was legitimate—and why I had to either pursue it or shut it down hard and fast and forever. Because even though I knew what would happen—even though I knew what I would remember, and even though I was certain that the shadows would creep up and consume me—I still wanted him more desperately and more tangibly than I'd ever wanted any man.

I caught myself shivering, and I hugged myself to ward off the memories.

Flynn caught the movement and frowned. "You okay?"

"Just a chill. I slept crappy last night."

"Big surprise there." He finished off his drink and looked at me hard. "You need to talk to him, plain and simple. You know that, right? If you're not going to just drop it, then you need to suck it up and have the conversation. The guy wants you. You want him. You've come damn close, and yet he hasn't laid you out and tossed up your skirt. You need to ask why."

"I've tried."

"Try harder."

I shrugged. I was getting tired of this being all about me. "You're still cool with renting a room in the house, right?"

He didn't answer for a second, and I was afraid he was going to comment on my very obvious tactic to change the subject. To my relief, when he answered it was to say, "Hell, yes. But you really should let me split the mortgage."

"No way. It's my house. Or it will be next week. You're renting a room. We already made this deal." I knew that money was tight for him. The airline kept cutting his shifts, and the tips for tending bar only went so far. I really didn't want him to go back to the gigolo thing, but if money got tight, I was afraid that he'd do just that.

I pushed back from the table. "Thanks for the breakfast and the conversation. I should get out of here. I have errands and then wedding planning and then I'm going to crash early, because tomorrow I'm spending the predawn hours slinging coffee. My life is so freaking glamorous."

"I know I've said it before, but it's pretty damn cool the way you managed to pull together buying a house on a barista's salary."

"I'm the kind of girl who gets what she wants," I said, not mentioning that my plan had required faking a job at the gallery and pulling the down payment from the safe deposit box where I stored the cash I'd saved over the years from my various cons.

"Is that what this is about?" he asked.

I looked at him, baffled. "What are you talking about?"

"Cole," he said. "Are you pushing so hard because he's something you want but didn't get?"

"No," I said automatically. "Of course not." But as I walked to my room to finish getting dressed, I had to wonder. Was everything I thought I felt for Cole just tweaked pride? Or was it truly something deeper?

And when you got right down to it, how the hell was I supposed to know the difference?

Since I thought that Flynn might be right, I decided to blow off a few house-related errands in favor of going by the gallery to see Cole.

"He hasn't come in yet," Liz said. She was a pretty blonde who used to be one of the dancers at Destiny.

One of the cooler things that the knights did was help the girls who worked at the club find the kind of jobs where they didn't have to take off their clothes if they didn't want to. They even paid for school or vocational training, and Tyler owned a placement agency that a lot of the girls used when they were ready to move on.

The *really* cool thing was that a number of the girls had been snared in a white trafficking ring, and the guys had managed to get them cut loose and gainfully employed. It was a low-profile operation, but both Angie and Sloane were so proud of what their men had done that I had heard about it as well.

Now all three of the knights worked on and off with a federal task force that had taken down the ringleaders of the trafficking scheme. The case was still being investigated, but I imagined there would be a huge, media-circus-worthy trial one of these days.

"The gala went over great," I told Liz. "You did an awesome job putting it together."

"Thanks," she said, looking pleased. "Do you want to leave him a note or something?"

I wasn't sure that I did, but it seemed odd to show up and not say a thing. Besides, leaving a note was what civilized people did. "Can I just go back and put it on his desk?"

"Sure," she said, giving me a winning smile.

This time, when I walked down the corridor of offices and

workspaces, I saw that the door to Cole's studio was open. I caught a glimpse of something familiar and paused, then found myself drawn in by the image of a woman's naked back—an image I'd seen before.

The canvas was propped on an easel, and though I'd originally thought that this was the same portrait that had intrigued me last night at the gala, I soon realized that the angle of this one was slightly different. It was another study of the same woman.

There was, however, one very obvious difference. This one was signed in a familiar scrawl.

Cole.

I remembered our conversation and bit back a smile. No wonder Cole had said the gallery would continue to feature the artist's work.

Without realizing it, I'd walked all the way into the studio. Now I was only inches from the canvas. The perspective on the woman was almost the same as that of the portrait displayed in the gallery, with some subtle yet important differences.

Like the original portrait, the woman in this painting suggested beauty and purity. She seemed vibrant, yet in control. Alive and aware and exceptional. A goddess, only here on earth.

It was a testament to Cole's skill that he could evoke such a range of emotions and such vivid interpretations simply from his paintbrush. I'd known he was talented, but standing here now I was struck by the fact that his talent edged up against genius.

I took a step back, wanting to simply soak in the image. Right then, it was as close as I was going to get to Cole, and I didn't want to waste the moment or the opportunity.

Unlike the portrait hanging in the gallery, this image wasn't shielded by the fountain, and so there was no barrier between the woman and the audience. The details of her back were more clear, including a tan line that gave her a more human quality.

On top of that, the image dipped lower, showing a few more inches of her hips and the two small dimples just above the swell of her ass.

I had dimples like that. When I was a kid, I'd hated them. Now, I considered them an asset. A little sexy, a little flirty. I had to assume Cole thought so, too, otherwise why choose—

I froze, my eyes drawn to an area just below the model's left dimple. Was that . . . ?

I bent closer, then sucked in air. *It was a tattoo.*

More than that, it was the tattoo of a Latin expression. *Ad astra.* To the stars.

Automatically, my hand snaked around to my own back, just below my own dimple. To my own tattoo of those exact words. Words that I'd grown up with because they were my father's favorite saying.

I stepped back so that I could take in the entire portrait. It was me. I had no doubt anymore. That was my waistline. My hair. Even the way that the model's head was tilted slightly to the side, the way I often did when I was thinking.

I'd been staring at myself, interpreting my own portrait, and I hadn't even known it.

More than that, I'd had no idea that Cole was using me as a subject.

What the hell?

I thought about all the times I'd sunbathed on the roof of the condo with Angie. The times that Evan had taken all of us out on his boat.

Cole had been watching me?

And not just watching me, but studying me.

Restless, I moved around the room, realizing as I did that the canvas on the easel wasn't the only image of me. Rough sketches littered a worktable, and as I looked down, I found myself staring back into my own eyes, taking in the curve of my own cheek, the swell of my own breasts.

Empirically, the work was exceptional. But that wasn't what intrigued me.

Cole wanted me.

At the very least he was attracted to me, intrigued by me. Obsessed with me.

That, apparently, was something we had in common.

So why the hell was he fighting so hard to stay away from me?

I drew in another breath and looked around this bright, airy room, seeing it this time as Cole might see it. It was filled with me. Or, at least, a version of me.

But the girl on the canvas and in those sketches was filled with light. She suggested purity and sweetness. There was nothing harsh or secretive about her.

She was me—and yet she wasn't. And the pleasure I'd been feeling began to shift into something cold and unpleasant.

I don't know who Cole saw when he looked at me, but he wasn't seeing Katrina Laron, or any of the other names I'd used throughout the years.

He wasn't even seeing Catalina Rhodes, the girl I'd started life as, but who had been erased long ago.

Had he not really been looking at me at all?

Or did he see something in me that I'd been hiding from everyone? Including myself?

six

I'd planned to go straight from the gallery to The Drake hotel, where I was meeting Sloane and Angie for a liquid lunch before Sloane and I branched off to discuss Angie's bachelorette party. That would have been the smart thing to do, considering I could have walked between the two locations in under fifteen minutes, and the drive would take less than five.

But I was restless and out of sorts, and so I detoured from River North all the way to my soon-to-be new neighborhood of Roscoe Village, adding an hour to my travel time when you factored in the return trip and traffic. Not to mention the minutes that would tick by as I sat in the car and gazed at the second thing in my life I was obsessing about.

Like Cole, my house was going to need a lot of TLC. Unlike Cole, its curb appeal in its present state left a lot to be desired.

Then again, that was why I'd been able to get it cheap. Or

relatively cheap. Considering the house consisted of less than one thousand square feet, had only one bathroom, and needed all new appliances, I wasn't really sure that the six figures I was shelling out for the property could be considered "cheap" in anyone's book.

But the place was about to be mine, and that made it worth any price to me.

Maybe that's why I'd felt compelled to come here after seeing those drawings. They'd left me feeling edgy and unsure of who I was and what I wanted. And the fact that they had been so meticulously and lovingly created by Cole left me just as confused about what he wanted.

Considering all the canvases devoted to my image, you'd think he would've seized the opportunity to take me. But he'd walked away, and now my head was all but spinning.

The house soothed me. It was tangible. It was wood and brick and stone and nails.

With the house, what you saw was what you got.

With Cole, not so much.

I sighed, because that was the bottom line, wasn't it? Why I'd driven miles out of my way and was going to end up late to meet my friends? Because every second of every day my mind was trying to unravel the mystery that was Cole. And not doing a very good job of it, either.

Frustrated, I got out of the car and walked to the front porch. I pressed my face against the window and looked inside, noting the battered hardwood floors that I would soon be sanding and refinishing. The dingy walls that seemed to cry out for a coat of paint.

This was more than a house, I realized. It was an anchor. Nine-hundred and twenty-four square feet tying me to Chicago and this life and my friends.

Katrina Laron.

Somewhere along the way, that's the girl I'd settled on.

I pressed my forehead against the glass and sighed. Had I really just been griping about not being able to figure out Cole? Had I actually been frustrated because he saw me as pure and innocent? Pretty unfair considering I changed who I was every five minutes.

Hypocrite, thy name is Katrina. Or Catalina. Occasionally even Kathy.

God, I really was a train wreck.

Because the house didn't yet belong to me, I technically wasn't allowed inside. Technicalities rarely bothered me, though, because they only became a problem if you were caught breaking the rules. And even then, I could usually talk my way out of it.

The key was stored in the real estate lockbox, to which I also didn't have access. I'd been here before, though, usually with my agent, Cyndee, and I'd been around the block enough times to know that one never misses an opportunity.

So when she punched in the combination, I'd paid attention to the code. I recalled it now easily enough—my father didn't give a flip about my grades in school, but fail to remember something he told me to memorize, and I'd end up grounded for a week.

I entered the code, grabbed the key, and let myself in.

The air was stale and thick, and already stifling even though it wasn't yet noon. But I breathed in deep anyway, because this stale air and everything surrounding it was going to be mine soon.

There was no furniture, so I didn't sit. And I hadn't come with any particular purpose, so I just started to wander, taking in the rooms, imagining how I would fix them up. Knowing that I *could* fix them up.

I sighed, understanding now why I'd been so determined to come here. Maybe I couldn't get what I wanted from Cole. But I could damn sure get this house to fall into line.

It didn't take long to circle through the living room, kitchen, bedrooms, and bath. I took a peek at the backyard, then turned back toward the front door, my car, and my friends.

I was about to step out onto the porch when my cell phone rang. I dug it out of the back pocket of my jeans, then sucked in a breath when I saw the caller ID. *Cole.*

I hesitated a moment, but there was no way I was going to let this call roll to voicemail, even if I should. So I bit my lower lip, then pressed my thumb on the green button.

I didn't, however, say anything. Just my little nod to passive-aggressiveness.

"Liz told me you came by the gallery." His voice was steady. Smooth. And I couldn't read one damn thing into it.

"I did."

"If you were looking for an apology—"

"No!" I blurted out the word, then immediately winced. So much for cool and collected. "Dammit, Cole," I said, and though the words were harsh, my voice was gentle. "Don't you understand that there is nothing to apologize for?"

There was such a long pause before he spoke again that I started to fear the line had gone dead. When his words did come, they seemed to hang between us, heavy with emotion and regret.

"You tempt me, Kat."

"I guess that makes us even."

His low chuckle was like a balm, and I found myself smiling. "You're a goddamn fool, blondie."

"But I'm not," I said. "I'm smart, Cole. And I know what I want. You know what else?" I asked, but I didn't wait to give him time to answer. "I know what you want, too."

"Really? And what is it I want?"

"Me," I said, then hoped that I hadn't just taken another giant step away from him.

He said nothing—neither agreement nor protest—and so I pressed gamely on.

"I saw your studio space. I saw me."

"All right," he said slowly. "And what did you think?"

"The images are stunning, but I told you that last night when you found me looking at the one in the gallery."

"That was a poignant moment. The beautiful woman unaware she was looking at her own reflection."

"Beautiful," I continued, "technically perfect. Pure. But not me. Not really me at all."

"You're wrong," he said.

"The hell I am. I'm not pure. I'm not innocent. Christ, Cole, you had your fingers inside me less than twenty-four hours ago, and it wasn't me who walked away."

"Kat—"

"No, listen to me. Please, Cole. Don't you get it? I'm not the girl you painted. I'm not a goddamn angel. Do you have any idea how badly I wanted you last night? *All* of you. Your mouth, your cock."

"Jesus, Kat."

I heard the heat in his voice, and my pulse kicked up with the knowledge that maybe—just maybe—I was getting through to him. "And when you left me hanging, I swear to god I cursed you like a sailor. Would your innocent little model do that?"

He said nothing, and I pressed on, determined to win this battle. Hell, determined to win the war. "You wanted it, too," I said. "Tell me. Please. I need to hear that I'm not crazy. I need to know that last night you wanted me just as much as I wanted you."

"I've wanted you from the first moment I saw you."

I closed my eyes, my body sagging from the pure relief of hearing the acknowledgment of what I'd been so sure about. I leaned against the dingy wall of this house that would be mine, sighed, and slid down to the floor in bliss.

"You can have me," I said. "Any time. Any place. Any way you want," I added, saying the last in a whisper.

"No," he said. "I can't."

I cringed from the resolve in his voice.

"I can't," he repeated. "I can't choose when, or where, and certainly not how. But when I look at you—when I paint you—"

His voice had taken on a lyrical quality, and I held the words close, wanting to soak in this moment, because who knew how many more I would get? "Tell me."

"Put your phone on speaker," he said. "Set it beside you."

I pressed the button to turn on the speaker. "All right."

"Good. You need to understand that when I paint you, it's not just an image of you that is in front of me. It's flesh. It's blood."

"It's me."

"Yes. The spill of your hair. The curve of your neck. The swell of your breasts."

Gone was his earlier hesitancy. Instead, each word held masculine power. As if by painting me, he had claimed me, and I had no other choice but to submit.

"Go on," I whispered. My eyes were still closed, but in my imagination, I saw myself sitting on a blanket at the Oak Street Beach. I was looking out at the water, but Cole was there, too, off to one side, so that I could see him only in my peripheral vision.

But though I could barely see him, I could feel him. Every scrape of pencil over canvas was a tease, every stroke of paint from his brush was a caress.

"You're mine when I paint you, Kat. Mine to touch, mine to stroke, mine to see."

My pulse pounded in my ears and my skin felt hot. I pulled up my T-shirt to expose my abdomen, then sighed from the caress of cool air upon my overheated flesh.

"And I do see you, Kat," he said. "My brush doesn't lie, and when I trail it over the curve of your waist and the swell of your hips, it's not just lines and form that I'm bringing to life on the canvas, but you. Tell me, Kat. Tell me you understand that."

"Yes," I said, because right then I couldn't seem to think of any other word.

"When I paint you, I capture you. Light. Shadows. I see more than I put on the canvas, Kat. I see everything. The face you show the public, the most intimate parts of you that you keep hidden."

I made a small noise that might have been a protest, because that couldn't be true. He couldn't know me that well; he couldn't see my secrets.

"Don't you feel me, Kat? Don't you feel my eyes exploring, assessing, deciding what I am willing to show to the world and what I want to keep to myself?"

My body, I thought with relief. *He doesn't mean my secrets, but my body.*

"I feel you," I whispered, my voice like air.

"My brush moving softly over your lips," he said, as I drew my fingertip gently over my mouth. "Then down, lower and lower until I can tease your breasts. Until I'm exploring the shadows that fall between them and the way your skin glows, almost translucent when the sun teases your nipples. Are they hard now, Kat?"

"Very."

"Take your nipple between your fingers and pinch it. I want it harder, a deep, sensual red. I want to paint you aroused, Kat. The glow on your face and the flush of your skin. Do it, Kat. Do it and let me see."

"You're not here," I protested, though I willingly complied.

"I'm always there," he replied, and those words combined with the tight pinch of my own fingers against my sensitive nipples brought a moan to my lips.

I arched up, then whispered his name and was rewarded with a low, masculine groan.

"I want to paint you while you come," he said. "I want to capture ecstasy, Kat. Let me do that, angel. Let me do that now."

"Cole . . ." I heard the protest in my voice. An unwelcome, unexpected shyness.

"No," he said. "No argument, no denials. I want to see you. I want to watch your body tighten and then explode. I want to see it, Kat, even if only in my imagination."

I licked my lips, wanting it, too, but unsure if it was even possible. I'd never come with a man calling the shots in my bed. Not since—not in a very long time. But this . . .

Maybe this . . .

"Where are you?"

"My house."

"Alone?"

I thought about the words he'd been saying to me. "Well, duh."

He chuckled. "Some women like an audience."

"Oh." I considered what he'd said earlier about me being innocent. Maybe he wasn't so far off the mark. "I'm alone."

"What are you wearing?"

"Jeans. A T-shirt."

"Take off the jeans. Leave on your panties."

"I—"

"No," he said. "You don't argue. You simply do or hang up."

I felt my mouth curve up in pleasure as I kicked off my sandals, then shimmied out of my jeans. "All right," I said.

"In your house," he said, his tone musing, "there's a row of windows overlooking the front porch, and it's a gorgeous day. The sun should be streaming in."

My gaze flicked to the checkerboard pattern that the sunlight made on the battered wooden floor, blocks of light intersected by the dark shadows made by the frames that held each small pane of glass in place. "How did you know that? You've only been here once."

"I paid attention," he said.

"Because that's what you do? Or because this house was going to be mine?"

"Move to the light," he said, and though it wasn't an answer I heard the truth in his voice. Maybe he did pay attention out of habit, but he'd noticed this house because it was my house. Because he noticed me.

How could I have been unsure before? How could I have feared that whatever attraction I saw on his face was only a reflection, especially now that it was becoming so obvious that he had seen me—wanted me—long enough to make me mourn the lost opportunity of all the months that had passed in silent longing?

"Kat," he said, his voice firm. "Now."

"Oh." I shuffled into the stream of sun, then sighed as I felt the intensity of the warmth across my body. There was no air-conditioning in the house—not with the tenants having moved out—and so my body was already close to melting. But now, with the sun tickling my bare legs, I felt logy and sensual, soft and sleepy.

At the same time, I felt turned on.

It was an interesting mix, and I couldn't deny that I liked it.

"I want to paint the patterns of light as they hit your abdomen," he said. "Trace them for me. Drag your fingers over your skin. Are you doing it? Can you feel the way the warmth is seeping into you?"

"Yes."

"That's the sunlight, Kat. And it's my brush. My eyes. I'm studying you. The way your muscles quiver as I touch you. The way your belly tightens when you're aroused."

I swallowed. He was right. My body was doing exactly what he said, and between my thighs, my sex was clenching, too, wanting his touch even though he wasn't even in the room.

"Tell me about your panties."

"Cotton. Bikini. Boring."

"Not boring. I can picture you in them. You naked and aroused in your boring cotton panties—innocent, and yet not," he added before I could protest. "Tell me something, Kat. Are they damp?"

"Yes. Oh, yes."

"Are you sure?"

"I—"

"Slide your hand down and let me see. Let me paint that picture in my mind. You, arched back, your T-shirt pulled taut across your breasts, and your fingers inside your panties as you touch yourself. As *I* touch you."

"Cole . . ."

"She protests?" he asked, his voice light with amusement. "You're the one who offered this, Kat."

"The hell I did," I countered, but there was laughter in my voice, too.

"Anything I want," he said, and this time when he spoke there was no amusement. There was just heat and need and demand. "Touch yourself, baby. Touch yourself, and think of me."

"I—" But I didn't finish the thought. Primarily because I had no thoughts. My mind was in a haze, filled only with the promise of pleasure and the sweet temptation of Cole's hands upon me, even if only in fantasy.

Slowly, because I wanted to draw out the pleasure, I placed my palm over my lower belly. I eased my hand down, slipping my fingertips under the cotton waistband, then gasping a little as I did. Because that wasn't my hand I felt, but Cole's. Not my desire I was breathing in, but his.

"That's right," he murmured. "Don't stop. I want to feel how wet you are. I want to watch you open for me in the sunlight, all hot and wet and wild. Lower, Kat. Slide your hand lower, then tell me what you feel."

"I'm wet," I said, which was the understatement to end all

understatements. I was soaked. I was desperate. I was nothing but carnal desire and wild, wicked heat. "I'm so wet, and I want this to be your hand. Your fingers."

"But it is. Well, not yet. Do you feel that? The slight tickle up your inner thigh? Do you know what that is?"

I couldn't speak, so I just shook my head. He must have understood, though, because he continued. "That's my brush, the bristles stroking and teasing all the way to your cunt, then dancing over your clit, so soft, so sensual."

I gasped, realizing suddenly that I'd forgotten to breathe.

"Light touches, baby. Tease yourself like my brush. A light finger over your clit. Then slide a finger inside yourself. Imagine it's my finger, then the tip of my brush, because I will claim you that way, baby. I'm going to claim you every way possible."

I was whimpering now, wanting what he described, naughty and wild and so unexpected, and yet so personal to him—to us—that it turned me on more than I would have ever thought possible.

"It's time to come for me, baby. Is your clit hard? Sensitive?"

"God, yes."

"Then softly at first, harder if you need to. It's my mouth on you now. My tongue tasting you. My tongue flicking over that sweet nub. Do you know how good you taste? I could eat you all day, all night."

"Please," I murmured as my hand teased my clit, faster then slower, as the world seemed to spin and I seemed to float, carried away on the swell of Cole's deep, caramel voice. The sensation was wonderful—passion and pleasure that had such incredible potential.

I didn't expect to fulfill that potential, though. But that was okay. Just the journey with Cole was amazing. Just the knowledge that he was the one who made me feel this way, like my skin was sparking with electricity. Like I could fly if just given the chance.

"That's it, baby. You're so wet. You're so hot. Just a little more. Just a little bit higher and then I want you to come for me. Come on, baby. Explode with me right now."

I cried out, then arched up in surprise and amazement and pure, golden pleasure. The orgasm rocked through me, hard and fast and all the more violent because I wasn't expecting it and had no defense against it. I tried to breathe, tried to bring my body back down to earth, but all I could do was ride it out until, finally, I found myself curled into a ball on the wooden floor, my arms around my knees, and my body still trembling with the aftershocks of ultimate satisfaction.

"Katrina," he murmured.

"Cole." I rolled to my side so that I could see the phone and tried to imagine that it was Cole beside me, touching me, stroking me. That he'd brought me to orgasm—a feat that amazed me—then held me tight. And that he was holding on to me still.

"Hear me, baby," he said. His tone, more serious than the moment called for, brought me to full attention. "I don't see what isn't there, and I don't paint what I don't see."

I frowned, not understanding what we were talking about.

"You say that's not you on my canvases and sketches, but you're wrong. You've filled my days and occupied my nights. I know you, Katrina Laron, and you're more innocent than you think. I've claimed you, baby, and that makes you mine. But maybe not in the way you think."

"I don't understand."

"I know. But you will. Right now, I just want you to know that I will do whatever it takes to protect you. Even if that means protecting you from me."

seven

"To husbands and houses," Sloane said, lifting her Manhattan so that Angie and I could clink glasses with her. "Just a few more weeks, and you'll each have one."

Angie shot me a wry glance. "I'm claiming the husband," she said, making both Sloane and me laugh.

"Not a problem," I said. "I'm content with the house." At the moment, I was *very* content with the house. And with the man. But I didn't feel the need to share with my friends the fact that I'd just had phone sex in my soon-to-be living room. Especially not since I was still enjoying the glow.

"For now you're content with a house," Sloane said. "But soon you'll want a man for changing lightbulbs and mowing the front yard. That's just the way the world works."

"Is that why you're so keen on Tyler?" Angie teased. "His excellent lightbulb-changing skill?"

"That's one of the benefits of living in a suite at The Drake," Sloane said archly. "We don't have a front yard, and maintenance takes care of the bulbs. Which frees up our schedule nicely for sex."

And since neither Angie nor I could argue with an answer like that, we all clinked glasses and took yet another sip.

We'd been in Coq d'Or, the historic bar inside The Drake hotel, for over two hours now. I was on my third Manhattan, and was enjoying the kind of pleasant buzz that comes from a mixture of good alcohol and great friends.

Angie propped her elbow on the bar, then rested her chin on her fist as she looked past Sloane to me. "It occurs to me that your house is going to need more than a few fresh lightbulbs and a neatly trimmed yard. I imagine Cole's pretty handy with a toolkit." She caught Sloane's eye, and they both snorted with laughter.

I just shook my head in mock reproach.

"Aren't you going to tell us what happened?" Sloane asked. "You were both at the gala, and then you both disappeared."

"A woman doesn't kiss and tell," I said archly.

"At least there was kissing," Angie said.

I held up my hand. "Stop the madness." I wasn't inclined to discuss the strange development of my relationship with Cole, but I grinned and let some laughter into my voice, just so that my friends wouldn't pick up on my hesitancy. "We're running out of time and we need to talk about the wedding. Just a few more weeks," I said to Angie. "Are you nervous?"

"About what?" she asked, so sincerely that I knew she wasn't joking.

"Aren't brides supposed to be nervous?" I asked.

She lifted a shoulder. "If they are, I'm not sure why they get married. How could I be nervous about spending my life with Evan?"

"I think it's the wedding more than the husband that stresses out most brides," Sloane said.

"Fortunately, we both have my mother for that," Angie said, looking pointedly at me.

"And for which I am completely grateful." When Angie had asked me to be her maid of honor, I'd told her that I would be happy to take on the role, but if she wanted a sane and stress-free wedding, she probably didn't want someone as clueless as me handling all the traditional wedding-y things that the bride's right-hand gal usually took care of.

Since Angie's mother was a senator's wife with very particular ideas about what her little girl's wedding should look like—not to mention a huge and energetic staff to help pull it all together—my utter lack of resourcefulness was not a problem.

My role had been limited to drinking with the bride, calming wedding day jitters, and organizing the bachelorette party with Sloane.

Maybe not traditional, but it worked for us.

"Speaking of," I said, glancing at my watch. "Aren't you supposed to be doing something incredibly important and wedding planning-ish this afternoon? Your mom told me that Sloane and I could only have you for three hours, and since I was late getting here . . ."

I might not have the traditional maid of honor job, but I figured if I could keep the bride on schedule and her mother happy, then I was more than earning my keep.

She pulled out her phone to check the time herself, then cursed. "Okay, then," she said, before downing the last of her drink in one long swallow. "Don't have too much fun without me."

"Damn," Sloane said with a quick glance in my direction. "That kills our plans for the afternoon."

Angie rolled her eyes, then left. As soon as she was out the door, Sloane held up her hand to signal the bartender for another round.

"Are you crazy?" I asked.

"A little," she admitted. "And we'll be here at least another hour or two, so you have plenty of time to sober up. You're not working tonight, are you?"

"Tomorrow morning," I said, then made a face. When I'd first taken the job at Perk Up, it had been because the coffee shop was close to the Northwestern campus, and I'd been targeting a certain senator's daughter who I thought might be gullible enough and bored enough to get pulled into a scheme I'd been concocting around a fake multilevel marketing operation.

I'd tabled the plan once I'd actually gotten to know that senator's daughter, and to this day, Angie doesn't know that a plan for larceny was the instigating factor in what became a BFF kind of relationship.

The point being that I had never intended to remain at the coffee shop. But once the sheen of my cons had worn off, I needed a way to earn money. The hours were decent even if the pay was crappy, and I liked having the freedom to do my own thing when most people were pulling a nine-to-five. Besides, I was already on the payroll, and the idea of looking for another job made my head ache.

For years, I'd been telling my dad that he should get out of the grift. That he was getting too old and that there was no point in taking the risk when he should have more than enough cash stockpiled from his various successes over the years to allow him to live comfortably in Palm Beach or someplace equally retirement friendly.

So it was particularly ironic that I became the one to get out of the business first—more or less, anyway. But the "less" side of that equation was growing more every day, and once I closed on the house I was going to have to schedule a serious talk with myself about my life, my future, and everything.

Because once I had roots, I couldn't continue to run cons—even loose, easy ones that I set up primarily for my own amusement and to keep myself on my game.

Like my dad always said, only fish poop where they live. Maybe not the most classy of statements, but he was right. And that was the reason we never stayed in one place when I was a kid.

"Where did you go?" Sloane asked, and I turned my attention toward her, only to find her peering intently into my face. "I asked about the coffee shop and you took off for someplace a million miles away."

"Sorry. I've just been less than satisfied with my job lately."

"I could talk to Tyler. We might be able to use you."

The bartender brought our drinks, and I took a long sip of mine before answering. "I think what you do is exceptionally cool," I said. "But it's not me. And I'd end up resenting you because I'd be doing filing and correspondence and you'd be out taking surveillance photos while hanging upside down from lampposts."

As a former cop, Sloane was well qualified to work in the knights' high-end investigation and security company. Me, not so much. Not unless I wanted to be a consultant on the fine art of fraud. Which, of course, I didn't.

"I rarely hang upside down," Sloane said. "But I get what you're saying. Got anything in mind?"

"Maybe," I said. The truth was I'd been toying with a possible new career option, pulling the idea out from time to time and taking it on a mental spin around the block. So far, I was still intrigued. But not enough to talk about it. Not yet. I was still in that magical honeymoon phase. I'd talk about it once the sheen had worn off and I was ready to knuckle down and think about whether or not I could really make it work.

And speaking of honeymoons . . .

"It's not me we need to be discussing," I said. "We have a party to plan. And we ought to do it while we've still got a buzz," I added, with a nod to our glasses.

The trouble with having a bridegroom who owned a strip club was that it took the wow-factor out of taking the bride to a strip club, even one of the male variety. But with the Manhattans flowing through our veins, Sloane and I decided that a hot-guy version of Destiny could be just the ticket. And, because we were totally juiced, we also decided that bringing Angie to Destiny afterward and having her put on her own little show for Evan would be even more amusing.

Only time would tell if it was a good plan, or just one of those schemes that sounds fabulous when you're plastered.

"And speaking of the knights and sexy encounters," Sloane said, propping her chin on her fist and studying me through narrowed eyes. "Where did you disappear to last night?"

"Home," I said firmly.

"By way of . . . ?" she prompted. "Come on, Kat, give. There's no way that amazing dress failed to make an impact."

I thought of the dress, now crunched up in my trashcan, and smiled. "It made an impact, all right."

"Ha!" she said, her tone triumphant. "I knew it. Tell."

Sloane, apparently, was pretty damn perceptive.

"It didn't go exactly the way I planned," I admitted, which was about as close to a moment of deep, girly sharing as I intended to get.

"All right," she said slowly. "Bad end of the spectrum or good end of the spectrum?"

"Both."

Her brows lifted. "Oh, really? Care to elaborate?"

"Not in the slightest."

"But it was good?"

I had to laugh. "For a former cop, you don't listen very well. Yes, it was good. I had a moment of jealousy before it was good—some woman named Michelle who says she's seen me at Destiny wrapped herself around Cole. And then I realized that she and Cole and some guy were all caught up in the business side of things, so I pushed the jealousy down, for which I gave myself bonus points. Then Michelle left and I had some Cole time and it was . . . quite delicious," I decided. "At least until it got strange." I thought of the encounter earlier at the house. "And then it got delicious again."

"Delicious is good," Sloane said, then added, "I've met Michelle."

"Yeah? So she works for them, right?"

"Sure," she said, but she didn't quite meet my eyes when she said it. Instead, she took a sip of her drink, then reached down the bar to snag a menu another customer had left behind. "We should order. I'm starving."

"Uh-huh," I said. "I've met toddlers who are more subtle. What's up?"

"Nothing is up. My blood sugar, however, is down. Must eat. Want to split french fries?"

"I want you to tell me whatever it is you're not telling me."

"Two orders of fries," she said to the bartender. "And add in some of those stuffed mushrooms, too. Just for fun."

"Sloane."

"It's no big, really."

"People never say that when it's true," I pointed out. "It's about Michelle, so just spill it. Did she and Cole used to date? Christ, are they dating now?"

"They're definitely not dating." Her voice was oddly firm.

"What's that supposed to mean?"

"Oh, hell, Kat. I don't know. I already told you that Cole doesn't date. He fucks. And he's fucking Michelle."

"I see." And I did see. I just wasn't sure I liked what I saw.

"I don't think it's like that."

"Like what?" I asked.

"Like anything other than two people who are convenient to

each other. I just thought that I should tell you because despite your Fuck Buddy speech last night, I get the feeling you want more than that."

I focused on trying to stab the cherry in my drink with a toothpick. "I'll be honest," I said. "I don't know what I want. But, yeah, I think *more* probably comes close."

"I'm sorry," Sloane said.

"Don't be. I don't have a claim on him. And from what you just said, neither does Michelle."

"There's more. And it's really none of my business, but we're friends, and I feel like you should know what you're getting into, because it may not be your thing."

"All right," I said, a little worried, a little intrigued. "Tell me."

"Cole and Michelle—they both belong to a local club. The Firehouse. Have you heard of it?"

I nodded. "I've heard of it." I'd never been there, but Flynn had gone once or twice with clients. A local BDSM club. Very high end. Very exclusive.

And very much not within my realm of experience.

"Like I said, it's none of my business. But I do know that Cole goes there. And I know that he doesn't date. So if you're either looking for a relationship or if that's not your kind of scene, you may want to back off. I love you and I love Cole, and I don't want either one of you getting hurt."

I nodded, acknowledging her words even as I turned the possibilities over in my head. Was that what I wanted? What I needed?

I didn't know.

All I knew was that I was screwed up nine ways from Sunday where sex was concerned.

But this . . . this intrigued me. I didn't know if it would help, but I did know that I was curious.

And there was no way in hell I was backing off now.

*   *   *

Mornings come early when you work in a coffee shop.

Since I was opening, I got to Perk Up by five, then got the brews going before I unlocked the door. Two cars were already parked outside, and the moment I flipped the lock, the drivers killed their engines and made a beeline for the shop. Less than five minutes later the drive-through was four cars deep.

Just another day in the life of our fabulous commuting culture.

The morning went by in a blur of coffee, scones, lattes, espressos, and granola-topped fruit cups. By the time I was able to finally breathe, it was past ten and time to get ready for the lunch rush.

The only thing that worked out well was that I didn't have any time to think or angst or otherwise fret about Cole.

I told myself that was a good thing, but the moment I had the space to breathe, he filled my head again.

"Take your break," Glenn, the manager, said to me. "And if you take it outside, clear the tables on your way back in."

I nodded, then dumped a gallon of cream in my coffee to cool it off quickly, grabbed yesterday's paper from the break room, and headed outside to the patio. The heat was almost unbearable, but I liked it.

My life had been a series of financial peaks and valleys, and all too often we would hit the valleys in the winter. Since my father's favorite money-saving trick was to pile on the covers and ignore the radiators, I spent a lot of winters beneath old quilts and fleece blankets. And despite what I told my dad, my fingers and toes were always chilled, and the cold would spread right through my bones.

I flipped casually through the paper as I soaked in the sun. I wasn't interested in Chicago politics or the local society gossip. Mostly, I was looking at the ads. Old habits die hard, and you can tell a lot about what folks in a particular town want by what is advertised in their local paper. And with the right information, you can sell anybody anything—from oceanfront property in Arizona to a far-off planet named after their dearly departed grandma.

Today, I saw nothing interesting in the various advertisements, but the entire double-page spread of the Style section featured the gala. There were photographs of the guests, the artists, even the appetizers. But the only picture I was interested in showed Cole.

I'd never known the man not to look incredible, but in that photo he looked like a fallen angel, beautiful yet dangerous. The photographer's angle was wide, but he'd been standing close enough to Cole that the flash reflected off his skin, making him not only glow but seem to pop away from the background. The effect was exotic, and ensured that every eye perusing the paper was drawn to the man.

The man, however, was focused on something else entirely.

It wasn't obvious at first. And to be fair, I was probably the only person in the entire world other than the photographer who knew what Cole was looking at. But that didn't change the basic fact—Cole was looking past the crowd of people vying for his attention. His eyes were on someone near the bar. A female someone in a red dress and red shoes.

A someone who was me.

But it was the expression on his face that truly grabbed my attention. Lust. Longing. And the kind of intense desire that inspired love songs and sonatas.

Damn the man. Damn the man for denying himself. And, in doing so, denying me, too.

I'm not naive. Not by a long shot. But after yesterday's incredible morning of phone sex, Cole had said that he would protect me even from him. At the time, I had no idea what he'd meant. But Sloane's revelation about the Firehouse answered that question.

He wanted me. He'd said it, and this photo showed it. But he thought I couldn't handle what having him would mean.

I intended to prove otherwise.

I wasn't, however, entirely sure how to go about that yet. But that was okay. I didn't have any plans to see him until Friday night cocktails on Evan's boat. A small prewedding gathering for friends and family. That was almost a week away. I knew from experience that I could pull a con together in under a week. How much harder could this be?

I tried to focus on various scenarios as I went about the rest of my workday, but foaming cappuccinos and blending icy coffee drinks didn't mesh well with detail-oriented thinking. And by the time I was finally off-shift, I was just too damn tired.

I kept the top down on my Mustang when I drove home, wanting the feel of the wind through my hair. I've had the car for over a decade, and she's my pride and joy, never failing to put me in a good mood. I drove her too fast and cranked the radio too loud, and by the time I pulled into the lot behind my Rogers Park apartment I was feeling exceptionally awesome.

I climbed the stairs humming the latest from Taylor Swift, then called out for Flynn.

He didn't answer, but I could hear him clattering around in the kitchen. Even better, I could smell something baking.

Cookies?

I picked up my pace, calling out to him as I hurried to the kitchen. "If those cookies I'm smelling are for some party you're going to and I'm not allowed to taste, you and I are going to have words."

I took a minute to drop my purse in my bedroom and change into shorts and a tank top. Then I hurried to the kitchen, only to skid to a stop when I saw the man standing by the stove, an apron around his waist and an oven mitten on his hand.

"Catalina," he said, with the kind of smile that would always look like home to me. Then he spread his arms wide. "Hello, sweetheart."

"Daddy?" For a moment, I just stood there, a little dazed and a lot confused. Then the bits and pieces of reality that make up my world shifted back into place.

"Daddy!" I repeated. And that time, I ran toward him and threw myself into his waiting arms.

eight

"So you're really out?" I asked, as I moved cookies from the sheet to a plate with a small green spatula. "No more cons?"

"It's more complicated than that," Daddy said, as I slid the plate to the center of the table, then sat down across from him.

"You're bullshitting me."

"What a thing to say to the father who loves you."

"As opposed to the father who doesn't love me?"

He made a vague harrumphing noise, then busied himself with selecting two cookies.

I took one for myself, then leaned back in my chair. "You're the one who told me we had to sever ties, Daddy. Remember? You gave me a whole long speech about how if you got in trouble, you didn't want them tracking you back to your little girl."

"Damned eloquent speech it was, too."

"It was," I agreed. "Must have been, since you managed to

convince me. Do you realize I haven't seen you since that last con you were planning went south, and that was the one that was supposed to make us richer than Midas."

He grimaced, obviously remembering his stories to me about how I'd soon have a condo in Paris and an apartment in New York and a mattress made of hundred-dollar bills if I wanted it. And also remembering how he'd caught the eye of at least a dozen cops and Feds during that deal. It had been dicey for a while, and when he'd told me to lie low, I'd thought that it had been a wake-up call to get him out of the life.

"I haven't talked to you unless it was on a burner in more than a year. I haven't got a clue what's been going on in your life, and I was okay with that because I knew that you were protecting me. And that you'd get out of the grift soon, and when you did, you'd show up on my doorstep with your arms open wide and tell me everything's going to be okay."

He cleared his throat and took a bite of cookie, but he didn't say anything. And he didn't look me in the eye.

"And now here you are," I continued, "and your arms were wide, but what's wrong with the rest of the picture?" I didn't mention that I knew something was wrong just by looking at him. He was putting up a good front, being all smiley and jolly. But underneath the facade, he looked tired and worried and just a little off his game.

"This is the one, Kitty Cat. I swear to you, I've got it all set this time. Nothing's gonna knock your old man back now. Nothing at all. At least not once I get just one tiny detail sorted out."

I stood, feeling a little numb, and moved to the sink. I didn't want my dad to see my face, so I busied myself with rinsing out and refilling the coffee carafe. *One little detail* didn't sound good. *One little detail* sounded like code for *I'm a walking dead man*.

"What detail is that, Daddy?"

"Nothing you need to worry about."

I closed my eyes and counted to ten. Did the man not remember who trained me? Was he really trying to set me up like a mark? Plant all the pieces so that I'd offer my help just like he wanted, and all the while I'd think it was my idea? Just how gullible did my dad think I was?

More important, how scared was he that he'd put his own daughter at risk? Because no matter how far off true north my dad's moral compass might be, I knew one thing for certain: There was nothing in this world he valued more than me, with one simple exception—his own neck.

He had me in a pretty crappy position at the moment. I didn't know if whoever he'd screwed was days or hours behind him. I didn't know if we were dealing with an organization or a single pissed-off man. On the cheap or well funded? Was this the kind of deal my dad could fix, or did they want him to go down on principle?

And, for the love of all that is holy, I needed to know if there was even the slightest chance they knew about me.

Forget prancing around the mulberry bush. If someone was playing Pop! Goes the Weasel in my house, I was damn well going to be in on the game.

The carafe was full to overflowing now, so I poured water into the machine's reservoir, added the grounds, and started a pot brewing. Then I went back to my seat across from my dad, put another cookie in front of him, and said one simple word: *"Tell."*

"Kitty, sweetheart, I—"

"Stop it, Daddy. I have a life here. I have a roommate, who you may have put in danger. I have a house here, too. Or I will next week. I've got a real job and I'm getting settled. Putting down roots, you know?" *And there's a guy, and maybe it'll go somewhere.* I wanted to add that, but I hardly saw the point.

"Good for you," he said, and I could tell that he meant it. "My little girl. Who would have thought it?"

"Daddy," I said sternly, "did danger follow you here?"

He shook his head. "No. Swear to god," he added, drawing an X over his chest with his forefinger. "I won't deny I may have gotten in over my head, but I still know how to watch my step and my back."

I believed him. For now, anyway. "So tell me the rest," I said. "Why don't you start with exactly how you got in over your head."

He took another bite of cookie, and this time even the confection didn't make him look happy. "Have you heard of Ilya Muratti?"

"Sure," I said. "Some big mafia type, right? Owns casinos in Vegas and Atlantic City, and I'm sure he has his fingers in dozens of other pies, too." I exhaled. "Daddy, no. Tell me you're not involved with him."

He waved my words away as if they were gnats. "Just a little thing. One little thing in the grand scheme of his world, but it's gonna make your daddy a rich man."

My stomach twisted unpleasantly, and I regretted the cookies. "Just spit it out. Tell me."

And, god help me, he did.

He told me all about how he'd wheedled himself in tight with some of the men in Muratti's organization. He started out playing the role of a fine art broker, then dropped enough hints so that the guys could "discover" that he didn't worry about all those pesky laws any more than they did.

Eventually a job came up, and when they contacted him to see if he wanted a piece of the action, he jumped at the chance.

"Daddy, you didn't." I had my elbows on the table and my

fingers twined through my hair. "You did exactly what you taught me never to do. You got mixed up in organized crime."

"Just on the periphery, sweetie. Just around the edges."

Except that was bullshit, because the more he talked, the more I realized how deep he was.

"They just needed a document. One tiny little document."

"What kind?"

"A will. A holographic will, they call it. Handwritten, that means."

"I know what it means, Daddy," I snapped. "Keep going."

He did, and it kept getting worse and worse and worse. Apparently one Frederick Charles intended to leave three hundred acres of prime Atlantic City property to his niece, Marjorie Calloway. And that would do Muratti no good.

The living Frederick wouldn't negotiate with Muratti, believing him to be a no-good mafia prick. But a dead Frederick couldn't argue if his will showed that he'd changed his mind about dear Marjorie and decided to leave the property to a distant cousin who just so happened to be neck deep in gambling debts to Muratti. And who would, in settlement thereof, sign over the land.

Muratti, of course, would seed the land with casinos that would grow into thriving money trees.

"They're going to kill the old man," I said after he'd told me all of that. "As soon as the will is forged, they'll take him out." I met my father's eyes. "You got mixed up in a deal where someone is going to end up dead."

He'd gone completely pale. "I didn't know, Kitty Cat. I swear I didn't know."

I believed him. My dad had the stomach for a lot of things, but killing people wasn't one of them.

"You couldn't forge your way out of a paper bag," I told my father. "Who are you working with?"

"That's the thing," he said. "I lined up Wesley. You remember him?"

"Sure. How is he?" Wesley had mad skills—and what cemented him in my childhood memory was a seemingly endless supply of Tootsie Pops. I'd adored him.

"Passed away," Daddy said. "The big C."

"I'm so sorry to hear that."

"Yeah, it was a pisser."

"But if he's dead, he can't do the job. So what's the problem?" I asked, then turned right around and answered my own question. "Jesus, Dad. You were going to screw Wesley?"

"Not screw him," my dad said indignantly. "His share was going to be perfectly reasonable. But I'd found the deal and I'd brought him in. I was taking all the risk. Gotta be some compensation for doing the legwork."

"You're taking all the risk, all right. Now that Wesley's dead and you can't make the deal happen, Muratti's going to want his pound of flesh. Christ, Daddy," I said, as I stood and started to pace. "Do you know what the mafia does to men who can't deliver what they promised?"

"Why do you think I came here? They didn't follow me," he rushed to say. "I'm sure of it. And no one knows who you are. We buried that connection long ago. They won't find me. How the hell could they find me?"

I hugged myself, numb with fear. "They'll find you because they'll never stop looking."

"But Charles will eventually die, and the property will go to his niece, and then that will be that. Muratti will move on and I can come out of hiding."

"Hiding," I repeated. "That's what you're doing here?"

He didn't answer.

"No," I said sadly. "You're not hiding. You came here looking for me to find someone to take Wesley's place. You know as well as I do that a man like Muratti has a long memory."

"Just one document, Catalina. Surely you know someone who can do just one document."

"I'm out of the game, Daddy. Mostly, anyway," I amended. "And I haven't pulled an art con since Florida. I don't have the connections," I lied, because the truth was that I knew one person who could pull this off. But if I asked him, I'd have to tell him the truth about everything. And I wasn't sure I was ready to do that.

I ran my fingers through my hair again.

"Let me think about it. Maybe I'll come up with somebody."

"Yes. Yes, you think." He stood up and yawned. "I know it's barely past five, but I'm wiped out. You got a place for your old man to crash?"

"Nope," I said. "But come on. I'll get you settled in a motel."

His mouth curved down into what could have been a pout.

"Forget it, Daddy Dearest. It's too risky for you to stay here. You have a mafia boss sniffing around you. Do you really think I'm going to let Flynn get caught in the cross fire?"

He made a noise that sounded like agreement. Reluctant, maybe, but agreement nonetheless.

I shook my head, exasperated. "It's a motel, Dad. From the story you told me, you should be glad it isn't a prison cell."

"If it doesn't have room service," he said with a sigh, "it might as well be."

nine

Evan Black lived on a boat before he moved into the high-rise condo he now shared with Angie. Tyler Sharp rented a suite in The Drake hotel that had once served as the residence for royalty.

But as far as I was concerned, Cole's house put both Evan's and Tyler's addresses to shame.

He lived in Hyde Park near the University of Chicago and, yes, near the famous gang-riddled South Side that the old song about Bad, Bad Leroy Brown had made famous. I knew Cole had grown up in that part of the city, but he didn't live in the dicey area now. Instead, Hyde Park was funky and eclectic. A place where pretty much anything goes.

And Cole's house stood like the topping on a very delicious and exotic dessert.

It had been designed in the late 1800s by Frank Lloyd Wright, and with the straight lines, sharp angles, and overall geometric design, there was no mistaking the architect's work. The place had come on the market about five months ago, and Cole had immediately snatched it up. I had no idea what he'd had to pay in order to acquire it, but I had a feeling that no amount would have deterred him.

At the housewarming he'd told me that Frank Lloyd Wright was as much a master as Michelangelo or Da Vinci, and that there was no way he could have passed up the chance to live in something created by genius.

Now, standing just outside the huge wooden door surrounded by intricate stonework, I once again thought how much the house suited Cole. Not only was it artistic but it was impenetrable without being off-putting.

And wasn't that the same as the man? Because unless he let you past his walls, there was no getting inside Cole August.

I hadn't called first because I didn't want him to make an excuse not to see me. Liz had assured me that he planned to spend the evening at home catching up on some paperwork, but that didn't necessarily mean he'd told her his actual plans.

For all I knew, he was at the Firehouse. And as intrigued as I might now be by that place, I wasn't quite ready to go search for him there.

I hesitated another moment before knocking, feeling a bit like a fool. I wanted to see him—hell, I wanted to hear his voice. That smooth, sexy voice that had pushed me over the edge just the other day.

At the same time, though, I feared his reaction. He couldn't have been more clear about his intent to stay away from me if he'd taken out an ad in the *Chicago Tribune,* so finding me at his front door might not brighten his evening.

Then again, this wasn't about me and it wasn't about him and it damn sure wasn't about sex.

This was about my dad, and Cole was the only person in my life right now who might actually be able to help him.

And that meant that whatever issue Cole had with me at the moment was going to have to be shoved aside. I needed help. And Cole would just have to deal with it.

I rang the bell.

At first, there was no answer. Then I heard his voice crackle through the intercom. "Be right there."

I waited, and a moment later the door opened to reveal the man himself wearing nothing but a towel slung around his hips. "Kat," he said, and for a moment, I saw heat flare in his eyes. Then his expression turned carefully blank.

My mouth went completely dry, while my more southernly parts had the completely opposite reaction.

"Kat," he said again, in a voice that suggested neither pleasure nor irritation. Just confusion. "Sorry—I thought you were the messenger. I should have checked the monitor."

As if on cue, a skinny guy in a Speedy Messenger cap hopped off a bicycle at the curb. He trotted to the front door and passed a thin, manila envelope to Cole along with a clipboard. Cole signed the receipt, handed the clipboard back to the guy, then looked at me expectantly.

"What?" Why was he looking at me? I didn't know what was in the envelope.

"Why are you here?" he said, then added, "Kat? Is everything okay?"

I jerked my head up, realizing that I'd been staring in the general area of his crotch—and the definite bulge beneath the thin, white towel.

Oh my.

I drew in a breath to gather myself, and hoped he couldn't see the way my skin had flushed or the way tiny pinpricks of perspiration now dotted my hairline.

"I need to talk to you," I said. "Can I come in?" When he didn't immediately move to let me pass, I added, "It's important."

He stepped to one side, opening the door wider as he did so. "This way."

I followed him into a stunning sitting room, full of gleaming, polished wood features and modern-style furniture that accented the elegant simplicity of the architecture. The evening light swept in through high windows, and the whole room seemed to glow.

"Have a seat," he said, indicating a blue love seat. He turned to a small bar built into a corner, and as he walked away, I studied the intricate tattoo of a dragon that covered most of his back. I'd seen the entire tattoo only once before at a party on Evan's boat when Cole had stripped down to swim trunks. More frequently, I would catch a glimpse peeking above his shirt on the back of his neck.

The work was detailed and beautiful, and I had no idea why he'd gotten such a large, involved tattoo. I assumed it meant something to him, but when Sloane had asked him once, he'd brushed the question away, and I had never tried to press the point.

Despite the dragon's beauty, the image was edgy, and it gave the illusion that Cole was unpredictable and wild.

Then again, that wasn't really an illusion, was it?

"I'm glad you're here," he said as he brought me a shot of whiskey, straight up.

"Let me guess," I said dryly. "We have to talk."

The corner of his mouth quirked up. "It would be a good idea."

He sat in the chair opposite me, still wearing only the towel that was now stretched taut across his knees. I could see the shadow beneath the towel leading up to the juncture of his thighs. And though I could see nothing in those shadows, I could imagine. And I could want.

And I could get very, very distracted.

I lifted a brow and then nodded toward the towel. "Is this

why you're so successful in business? You know how to keep the other party on edge?"

"I do," he said. "Though in most business meetings I'm fully clothed."

"More's the pity," I said, and made him laugh.

"Give me a minute." He got up, then moved to the far side of the room where a pair of gray sweatpants hung over the back of a chair. He dropped the towel, and I drew a sharp breath in response to the unexpected—and quite exceptional—view of his bare ass.

All too soon, he pulled on the sweats and turned back to me, and though he was now modestly covered, the view was still pretty damn enticing.

"I made a mistake," he said without preamble. "The other morning on the phone. And I made a bigger one the night before that."

"You're wrong," I said calmly. "But it doesn't matter. Not right now. That's not why I'm here."

But it was, though. I'd come for me as much as for my father. And I was determined to walk out of this room with everything I wanted.

That was my plan—now I just had to make it fly.

He eyed me uncertainly for a moment, then sat across from me. "All right," he said. "Tell me."

I did, laying it all out for him. I left out the part about my childhood, about growing up in the grift. But I told him what my dad did. I told him about Muratti. I told him about needing someone to forge the will.

I told him more than enough to incriminate my dad, not to mention pull me into the web for conspiracy. In other words, I put my life and my dad's life in Cole August's hands. I did it because I trusted him. Because I'd seen the good that he'd done for the girls at Destiny, and I knew where his heart lay.

I thought I did, anyway.

I damn sure hoped I wasn't wrong.

"Where is your dad now?"

"I drove him around for about an hour making sure we didn't have a tail, then I checked him into the Windy City Motor Inn. You know. That ratty-looking place about a mile from Destiny."

"I know it," Cole said. "Fake name?"

"Of course. And we paid cash. He knows not to leave the room, not to charge phone calls to his credit card, not to call me on his cell phone, yada yada. I got him a burner in case he has an emergency." I lifted a shoulder in a shrug. "He knows the drill."

"Sounds like it. Sounds like you do, too."

I met his eyes. Felt that shock of connection. "I told you," I said. "I'm really not innocent."

I kept my voice low, my meaning clear. And I could see on his face that he knew what I meant—and what I wanted.

Dear god, how I wanted. I wasn't doing anything right then but sitting across from him, and yet I could feel him as tangibly as if he was touching me. The rough calluses on his hands. The smooth, taut muscles of his thighs. Those lips that I wanted pressed against me, exploring me.

How had I come to this? I felt as if my whole life I'd been walking around made of some sort of combustible material, and I'd only just realized it. I'd been safe, so long as I stayed away from a spark.

But then I'd edged too close to Cole and he'd ignited me. I was going to burn—that much was inevitable. But dammit, I wanted to pull him into the fire with me.

He sat watching me, silent, waiting for me to go on. But I didn't know what else to say. "So that's it," I finally said. "Will you help?"

"What makes you think I can?"

"I know about the Da Vinci," I said, referring to a forgery of a famous Da Vinci notebook that I knew he'd created years ago.

His brow lifted almost imperceptibly. "What Da Vinci?"

I cocked my head. "The one that's in Angie and Evan's condo. Do I really need to elaborate? Or maybe I should recite the litany of your various criminal activities over the years? I've been right here, remember? I've seen a lot. And I understand what I see."

There was a moment of silence, and then he leaned back in his seat, so cool and so casual that it was easy to see how he'd become so powerful. Nothing rattled the man. Or, at least, nothing rattled him until he exploded. And then the entire world shook.

"If I'm understanding you right, you're looking to retain the services of someone who could forge a holographic will."

"I am," I said after a brief moment's hesitation. "Honestly, I don't know what else to do." The truth was, I understood what giving that forged will to Muratti would do—it would put the old man at risk. But right then, right there, I had to think about my dad. And hope that somehow, some way, everything would work out.

"Even if I could find someone to retain, why should I?"

"Because I'm here and because I'm asking," I said. "And because I need your help." I thought of the girls at Destiny that the knights had been helping for years. I thought of the art students that Cole taught in his nonexistent free time, and the professional artists like Tiki who he mentored.

He wouldn't deny me—I was certain of that. And, yes, I was playing a game and using his good nature to roll the dice, but I had a feeling that in my position, Cole would do the same.

"All right," he said. "Done." He rose, then moved across the room to get another drink.

I watched him go, appreciating the view, but also feeling a

bit shell-shocked. "That's it? No negotiation? No back and forth?"

"Disappointed?"

I shook my head. "How long will it take to make up the forgery?"

He leaned against the bar and took a long sip of his whiskey. "I'm not going to make a forgery."

"But you said—"

"I said that I'd help. I didn't say how."

I opened my mouth to argue, but shut it again almost immediately. I wanted a solution that didn't require a forgery, after all. And considering the kinds of deals and schemes Cole manipulated and skirted every second of every day, I was confident that he could come up with a plan that both made sense and kept my father—and the property owner—alive.

"All right," I said. "I trust you."

The corner of his mouth twitched. "That's good to know."

I drew in a breath, then got up off the couch. I moved to him, hoping that he would put his arms around me and draw me close. He didn't, though, and I was left standing there, a little lost, a little aroused, as the air between us hummed hot and heavy.

"I really do trust you, you know," I said softly. "Whatever it is that you think we need to talk about, I promise you, we don't."

"Kat." He pressed his hands to my face, then held me gently as he peered into my eyes. I swallowed, unnerved by his intense inspection, but my gaze didn't waver, and what I saw in his face gave me hope.

He bent forward then and captured my mouth with his. I could taste the whiskey on his breath, and I felt suddenly light-headed. But I wasn't sure if it was the liquor or the man.

Unlike our kiss the night of the gala, this one was soft and sweet and a little sad, and I was already shaking my head in anticipation of his words as he pulled away.

"I can't be the man you need."

"You're wrong. You can't be anything else."

He reached into a pocket in the sweatpants, then pulled out a smooth green stone. It was oval-shaped and flat, with a thumb-sized indention on one side. He held it in his hand as I'd seen him do numerous times before, turning it over and over as he stroked and toyed with it.

"I know it confuses you," he said. "But I care about you, Katrina. And you can scream and rage and hate me all you want, but this isn't going any further. I can't stand the thought of hurting you, and you deserve someone a whole lot less fucked up than I am."

"Hurting me?" I repeated. "What the hell do you think you're doing? You say that you want me—that you care about me. And you know damn well that I care about you, too. But you're pushing me away? *That's* what hurts, Cole. Not this." I turned so that my back faced him, then tugged down the sleeve of my T-shirt to reveal the still-red scrapes on my shoulder.

"Jesus," he said, his voice like a low, pained curse.

"You didn't hurt me," I said, emphasizing each word. "How can I make you see that? It's just scrapes. It's just flesh. It's nothing compared to what there could be between us."

I wanted to throw up my hands and scream in frustration and bewilderment. Frustration that I couldn't get through his irritatingly thick skull. Bewilderment that I cared so much. I'd never cared so much. Not about anything, really, and certainly not about a man.

Things were changing, though. Or rather *I* was changing. I cared about my house. I cared about finding a better job. I cared about my friends and my father. About getting settled. About those roots I'd told Daddy I was planting.

And I cared about this man. I cared so desperately that I wasn't sure if I wanted to slap him or kiss him or cry on his shoulder.

Slowly, he reached for me, then gently stroked my shoulder, careful to avoid the worst of the scrapes. I felt my pulse increase in tempo, and I drew in a long, stuttering breath. His hands were like magic upon me, sending swirls of enchantment all through me. Awakening me. Warming me.

"You see?" I said, looking at him over my shoulder. "I'm way more resilient than you think."

He said nothing, and I took that as a good sign. I turned so that I was facing him more directly, wanting to read the expression that he was working so damn hard to keep closed off.

"You didn't hurt me, Cole. You didn't even scare me. I'll tell you what you did do, though. You made me wet. You turned me on." I edged closer so that I caught the clean, fresh scent of his soap. "Do you have any idea how much I wanted you in your office? How much I still want you?"

I looked into his eyes, hoping to see a desire that matched my own. Instead, I saw only steely determination.

Dear god, I wanted to break that control. It was like I was on a mission. As if I merely had to break this man for all the mismatched pieces of my own life to fall into place with Cole right there at the center.

I took another step toward him, so close now that I felt the flutter of his breath on my hair. So intimate I could see the pulse of his chest in time with his heartbeat, and each tiny pore on his bare skin.

Slowly, I pressed my palm against his abdomen, my fingers pointing down. His already tight muscles twitched under my hand, and I bit back a smile, knowing that, if nothing else, my touch had affected him.

I tilted my head up and found his eyes again. This time, I saw the heat that I craved, and that gave me courage to continue.

Slowly—so very slowly—I eased my hand down until my fingers slipped beneath the loose tie that kept those sweatpants from falling off his hips. I didn't stop, I didn't think, I just continued on, keeping my eyes on him, judging my impact on this man by the fire in his eyes and the tightness of his jaw.

A thin line of hair traced down his midline to his cock, and I followed the path eagerly. He was hard and thick, and I greedily closed my hand around his length to stroke him.

Cole groaned, then bit out my name like a curse. I only smiled, stifling my own sigh as I shifted from one foot to the other as the sweet, demanding pressure between my thighs increased.

"Do you want me on my knees?" I whispered, moving my hand in slow, sensual strokes. "Do you want your cock in my mouth? Or should I turn around, bend over the arm of your couch, and let you fuck me from behind? Whatever you want, Cole. And however you want it."

He reached down between our bodies, and for a moment I was certain he would tug my hand away. But all he did was hold it in place through the thick fleece of his pants, so that I ended up stroking his cock to a pressure and speed that he controlled.

"I told you," I said. "I'm not pure. I'm not innocent."

"Maybe not," he agreed. He let a moment pass, and I saw the regret on his face when he gently tugged my hand free. "But you also can't be mine."

The words, so unexpected, acted like a spark on kindling. My temper spiked, and without thinking about it, I reached out and slapped his face.

"Bastard."

"Goddammit, Kat, you're special." He reached up and massaged the red spot on his jaw. "Maybe you don't see it, but I do, and I'm not going to risk destroying that by having you get twisted up with me. Because there is nothing clean or pure or special about the shit I live with every goddamn day."

"That's a lie," I said. "It's fear and it's an excuse and never once in all the time that I've known you have I believed that you were a coward."

He exhaled, then ran his hands over his head in obvious frustration.

"I know about the Firehouse," I said. "I get that you're into BDSM. I understand, Cole. It doesn't bother me."

"You don't understand shit," he said.

"Then explain it to me."

"Fuck that," he said, then lashed out and kicked over an end table, making me jump. "*Shit*." There was anger in the word, but also frustration.

"You surprised me," I said sharply. "You didn't hurt me. And if you actually want to scare me you'll have to do better than tormenting a table."

As I hoped, he almost laughed. Almost. But he did calm down. He drew in a breath, then another. After a moment, he pinched the bridge of his nose and looked at me. "Do you think what I need makes me proud?" he asked softly. "It's not a road you want to walk with me, Kat."

"Dammit, Cole, don't you dare tell me what I want or don't want. You don't have a clue about what I need, and you sure as hell don't know my boundaries."

"Maybe not," he admitted. "But I know my own."

"What the hell is that supposed to mean?" I demanded.

With a sigh, he cupped my chin, his expression so sad I wanted to weep. "It means that you're a hard limit for me, blondie. And that's just the way it is."

ten

"Fine," I snapped. "But stay away from me, Cole. Stay away from me and my dad. And while you're at it, stay out of my life."

I turned and stormed toward his door. He caught my arm and yanked me back. "I'll help you with your dad. But not the rest."

"No. This isn't a negotiation. I told you what I want. You don't want to help on my terms, then don't help. But right now, I want you to get out of my way."

"Why?"

"Because I already owed you for the employment verification. I'm tired of owing you, Cole. I'm tired of owing you and not being able to pay the way I want to."

"I'm not tossing your dad to the wolves."

"Then fuck me," I said.

"Kat."

"Hard limit? That's bullshit. Do not tell me what I do and do not want and what I can and cannot have. I'm a grown woman, damn you. I know what I want, what I need. But you're so god-damned hardheaded."

I was stalking toward him now, and I was supremely pissed off. So was he. I could see the fire in his eyes. Cole wasn't defied frequently. I wasn't sure he quite knew what to do with me.

"How do I convince you that you don't scare me? This?" I grabbed my shirt by the hem and ripped it up over my head. I tossed it aside. "This?" The bra went next, and as soon as I'd dropped it on the floor I grabbed his hand and tugged so that I was standing right there—right in front of him.

Before he could think or protest, I cupped his hands on my breasts, and as he sucked in air through his teeth, I let go so I could reach down and unbutton my shorts. I tugged the zipper down, shimmied out of the damn things, and then hooked my thumbs in the band of my tiny lace thong.

"No," Cole said, closing one of his hands over mine.

I aimed a look of pure defiance right back at him, then kept right on going.

He grabbed my hand, then pulled me hard toward him so that I slammed against his chest. I gasped, then found myself breathing hard into the small indentation at the base of his throat.

"I'll do it." His mouth was at my ear, and he growled out the words in time with his action so that I heard the firm, no-nonsense tone of his voice playing melody to the brutal ripping of material as he tore the lace right off my body, rendering me completely naked, desperately hot, and utterly open for him.

"Cole!" I cried out, but he silenced me with his mouth firm over mine. But this was no sensual kiss. It was brutal, demanding. *Hot*.

As his tongue and teeth destroyed my mouth, his hands slid down my arms to find my wrists. He closed his hands around them, then forced them behind my back.

I winced from the awkward position.

"Did I hurt you?"

I shook my head. It did hurt—just a bit—but I damn well wasn't going to tell him that.

He tightened his grip, forcing the angle even more and making me cry out—because this did hurt—but I liked it. I liked being at his mercy. I liked knowing that I was under his control. And I especially liked what I realized he was doing with my now-destroyed panties—twining them around my hands and wrists to bind my arms behind my back.

He led me to the couch, then had me bend over the arm so that I was facing the seat cushion. He bent over me, his sweats brushing my bare bottom and his chest grazing my back. He nipped my ear with his teeth even as he thrust a finger deep inside me.

I wasn't expecting it, and I cried out in both surprise and pleasure. I was wet—god, had I ever been wetter?—and my body clenched greedily around him, wanting so much more. Wanting everything I could force him to give me.

"What if I told you I wanted to hurt you?" He pulled the finger out, then thrust in again—hard—this time with two fingers, then again with three. And each time I pulled the sensation tight around me, a welcome blanket, because this was what I wanted, to let go, to be free, to be *his*.

"What if I told you it got me hard? And that sometimes I just lose my grip? There are loads of shit I have to deal with, Kat, and you don't need any more crap in your life."

"But I need you," I murmured.

"What would you do," he continued, as if he hadn't heard me, "if I told you all that? If I said that I got off on the pain. That I like it. That I need it. Would you finally get it through your thick skull that you're in over your head with me? Would you finally run?"

"No," I whispered, breathing hard. "I'd beg. I'd beg you to

use me. To hurt me. To do whatever you want to me." I tilted my head so that I could see a little bit of him. "You make me *feel*, Cole. And oh, god, I want to feel more."

His weight pressing on my back lessened a little. "What the hell did you say?"

"I mean it, Cole. I've never—"

"Done this?"

"No. I mean, yes. I've never done this. But I've never—" I drew in a breath. Considering he had me naked over the side of a couch with my ass in the air, I was being ridiculously prudish and shy with my words. "I've never been this turned on. That's what I wanted to say."

Gentle hands closed around my waist as he helped me stand. Then he moved to the sofa, sat properly, and tugged me down as well so that I was straddling him, my knees on the cushions on either side of him, and my sex completely open to him.

He took full advantage of the position, and thrust three fingers inside of me. "Tell me," he said. "Tell me how you feel."

"Aroused," I said.

"No—ride me while you talk."

"I—what?"

The hand that wasn't twisting lazily inside me was on my waist, and in demonstration it eased me up and then back down again so that I was fucking his fingers. "I don't think I can do this with my hands tied."

"You'll do that and more," he promised. "Right now, I want you to tell me."

I lifted myself, my thigh muscles straining a bit as it had been a while since I'd had a decent workout. But it was worth it. I sank deep on him, hard, and he thrust upward each time I pistoned down, driving himself deeper and deeper inside me. He was filling me, and the sensation was magnificent.

And that, coupled with the brush of his hand against my clit, had my whole body tingling with promise. And, yes, with the hope that maybe—just maybe—I would actually explode in Cole's arms tonight.

He reached out and twisted my nipple hard, an interesting touch that had me gasping as a billion electrical sparks seemed to skitter all over my body to finally gather at my clit, taking me closer—so very much closer.

"You've stopped talking," Cole said. "I want to hear. Tell me. Make me feel what you feel."

"You've set me on fire. Like those stunt players who let the blue flames writhe all over their body. I think I'm the flame, Cole. I feel like my whole body is my center. Like you could brush the pad of your thumb over my nipples and I'd explode into a million pieces."

"They are wonderfully sensitive," he said, teasing my areola by drawing soft lazy circles, then flicking my sensitive nipple hard with his fingertip.

I cried out in surprise when he did that, and my sex clenched tight around his fingers, still deep inside me.

"I think the lady likes that. We'll have to try nipple clamps next time," he said, and I almost wept with joy knowing that there would be a next time.

I didn't know exactly what I'd found in Cole's arms. A new side of myself? A new type of pleasure? Was it just Cole I would react this way for? Or had I discovered an as-yet-unexplored side of my sexuality?

I didn't know. All I knew for certain was that I would do whatever he wanted me to.

"Considering how hard I am and that I've got my hand in your cunt, this may seem out of the blue. But you crossed the line into bitch mode today, Catalina."

"Bitch mode! I did not. I was just—"

"And that requires a punishment," he said, firmly enough to shut me up.

"Oh." I squirmed a bit, which had some rather delicious results from the way I rubbed against his hand.

"Have you ever been spanked?"

"No." I meant it literally. I'd never even been spanked as a child.

"Turn around," he said as he withdrew his fingers. "Over my knee."

My first reaction was to ask him if he'd lost his marbles. But I knew he hadn't. As far as sex went, my experience had been pretty vanilla, but I read books and magazines, and I knew spanking was reasonably common and, if the articles were any indication, highly arousing.

I also knew that it was very low on the serious BDSM totem pole, and I could only wonder what I'd graduate to once Cole decided it was time to remove the kid gloves.

The thought—and the possibilities—made me shiver.

"I like that," Cole said, running a finger over my skin. "I like seeing you anticipating. Nervous. Excited."

"I am," I said.

"Too much for you?"

"Not even close," I assured him, then almost melted in the long, slow burn of his smile.

I thought he would say something else, but all he did was tell me to bend over his knee. I felt a little silly, but that soon faded under the sting of his palm against my bare ass. I cried out, then sucked in air through my teeth as a warm tingly sensation spread through me, helped along by the soothing circles he stroked with his hand.

"I thought you would use a paddle or something."

"And deny myself the pleasure of striking such beautiful flesh?" he asked, even as he landed another blow. Then another and then another. By the time he had given me eight solid smacks on the ass, I was so close I was certain that one more paddle would push me over the edge and send me tumbling into a chasm that I hadn't entered in over a decade.

He stopped, though, leaving me turned on and bereft and confused.

He chuckled, obviously reading my expression. "You like it," he said. It was a statement, not a question, but I nodded agreement anyway.

"Here," he said, then drew me down to the floor and onto a soft, plush area rug. "I have to taste you."

I expected him to have me lay down, then spread my legs. Instead, he was the one with his back on the floor. I straddled his face, spreading my legs so wide that the stretch almost hurt. *Pain,* he'd said, and he was right. But there was something about this position. About the pain in my inner thighs. About the angle with which his tongue flicked at my clit. About the way his left hand caressed my ass, soothing the still-stinging skin, and occasionally pressing me forward so that he could suck hard on my clit or fuck me deeply with his tongue.

And there was the way he reached up, found my breast, and twisted my nipple in time with the way his tongue teased my sex.

All in all he was a one-man symphony, giving pleasure with the licks and strokes. Giving pain with the twists to my nipples, the small spanks, and even the sharp nips of teeth against my overly sensitive clit.

Like a symphony, the pain and the pleasure rose, dark and light, swirling and spinning. Building to a sensational climax.

Unlike a symphony, I didn't know if we would ever reach those ultimate heights. After all, I never had before with a guy, and despite everything that had happened tonight—all the new sensations, and all these glorious new experiences—at the end of the day, an orgasm was still an orgasm, and I couldn't escape the memories and shame that were tied up with letting that sorry bastard take me there.

But Cole wasn't him. And he never could be. Cole wasn't a sneak or a worm. Cole demanded what he wanted; he didn't steal it like a thief in the night.

When Cole touched me, it didn't make me want to hide. Instead, it lifted me up.

I thought of Cole. Of his mouth on my clit. Of his fingers on my nipple. Of the pleasure he was shooting through me.

I thought of him and I flew a little bit higher and wondered if, really, this could be possible.

And when I heard his voice—that demand-filled, no-nonsense voice—telling me to "come, come now, Catalina," I reached out with all my might, thrust my hand into the nearest star, and knew that it was a day for miracles.

Because even as my mind tried to fathom this inconceivable truth—even as Cole cried out my name and urged me to go over *now, now, now*—my body shattered into a billion points of light that shimmered and burst and sparkled and shimmied. And then, finally, were still and satisfied.

And, most of all, content.

eleven

Cole's arms were tight around me, my back pressed to his front, my ass nestled tight against him. I felt warm and safe and satisfied, but something wasn't quite right.

It took me a moment to realize that I was hearing Cole's voice. Low and worried, telling me that it was okay, that I was fine.

The concern in his voice confused me—until I realized that slow tears were rolling down my cheeks, and when I drew in a startled breath, I tasted salt water.

"No," I whispered. He'd untied my hands, and now I shifted so that I could lift a hand and wipe away the tears. "No, I'm fine. I'm more than fine." I rolled over in his arms, saw the unease in his eyes, and wanted to cry for real. "They're not bad tears," I promised, then pressed my lips gently to his. "I feel wonderful. *You're* wonderful."

His brow furrowed, as if he was debating whether or not to believe me, and the raw emotion I saw there was so sweet and genuine it made me smile. More than that, it made me laugh, then lean in and press a wet, salty kiss to his lips.

"Thank you," I whispered.

Now the concern just looked like confusion. "For what?"

For caring. For being here. For everything.

I didn't say any of that, though. Instead I just brushed another kiss over his lips, drew in a breath, and gathered the courage to tell him the one thing that I had never shared with another living soul.

"I haven't—you know—with a guy in, well, never."

That wasn't entirely accurate, but I wasn't ready to tell him the entire truth.

"Slept with?"

"Come," I said, as my cheeks burned. I focused on his shoulder. On the ink work on that stunning dragon wing. Because I damn sure couldn't meet his eyes. "You know. Climaxed. Had an orgasm." I lifted a shoulder as if this were no big deal and I wasn't utterly and completely mortified.

But I still didn't look at him.

"Tell me," he said, in a voice as gentle as a breeze.

"I just did."

"Tell me why not."

I shrugged, then looked away so as not to let him see the lie on my face. "It's just the way I'm wired."

He was silent for a moment, his huge hand gently stroking my hair. And despite the awkwardness, in that moment I felt cherished. And when he finally spoke, I felt desired. "Whatever men you've slept with have been missing out. You're beautiful when you come."

"You're going to make me cry again." My smile was tremulous but completely genuine. "I think that may be the most romantic thing anyone has ever said to me."

He chuckled. "If that's the case, I'll have to do better. You deserve more romance than that."

My chest tightened, and I grappled for words. I couldn't find them, though. No combination of sounds could adequately express what was in my heart. Because how could I tell him that he filled me up? That there was so much more to him than what I'd seen over the years.

He was a mix of hard lines and angles, of soft colors and tenderness. He was like some of the art that hung in his gallery—a blend of so many elements that you're surprised you like it because it almost seems like too much. And yet it all makes up the whole, and if you took any part away, the entire image would fall apart.

"You're staring," he said to me, his eyes narrow and mocking.

I grinned, feeling foolishly giddy. "Maybe I like looking at you."

"That makes two of us," he said. "Turn around."

I did, and he pulled me close again, spooning against me as we lay on the thick, warm rug.

He traced his finger over my bare hip, then along my waist. The sensation made me tremble, and I sighed as my body fired under his ministrations. Slowly, deliberately, he stroked the curve of my breast, then teased my nipples until both were tight and hard and begging to be touched.

He didn't satisfy, though. Instead, he continued upward, finally tracing my bottom lip and then, ever so gently, urging my mouth open.

I closed my eyes and drew him in, sucking hard, teasing his finger with my tongue even as the desire spilled through me, as if his finger were on the pulse of all my erogenous zones.

I heard him moan, felt his cock twitch against my ass. "Someday," he said. "I'm taking you here, too."

"Yes," I said, even as my body tightened and warmed at the thought. "Anything," I said. "Everything."

"And just so we're clear," he added, his mouth so close to my ear that I felt the tickle of his breath against me, "if I'm fucking you, you're not fucking anyone else. Do you understand?"

"Of course," I said, and felt a small pang of pleasure at the realization that, at least for the moment, Cole August had claimed me as his own.

"Good."

I realized I was smiling so broadly my cheeks hurt. I rolled over to face him again, then pushed him onto his back.

"Feeling playful?" he asked.

"Hush," I said. "I have a plan."

I straddled him, feeling decadent as I settled myself so that my sex rubbed against his crotch, his wiry pubic hair teasing and tickling in a way that was seriously designed to drive me crazy.

And when I felt his cock twitch in obvious interest, a burst of feminine power shot through me, too.

"Something on your mind, baby girl?"

"I told you I could handle it," I said smugly. "Could handle you."

"So you did." He slid his hand down so that his fingers were at my sex, then started to idly play with me. Since that seemed like an absolutely delicious plan, I shifted my hips to give him better access. Immediately, he stopped.

I lifted a brow.

"Go ahead," he said, the corner of his mouth twitching.

"Go ahead? You're the one who stopped."

"My hand is still right there, all ready to be put to good use—unless you'd rather use your own?"

I squinted, not entirely sure what he meant.

He laughed, obviously amused by my confusion.

"I want to watch you make yourself come," he said. "I want to watch the flush on your skin as you get yourself off. My hand. Your hand. Hell, you can use a vibrator if you have one tucked in your purse. . . ."

"Cole!"

"Now," he said, but his voice had turned sharp. There was no playfulness left. This was the voice of command. A voice that got what it wanted. "Get yourself off, baby. I told you, I want to watch."

I shook my head, something tight twisting inside me. "No."

He lifted a brow. "What did you say?"

"Cole, please. I don't—it was so great earlier. But I'm not going to be able to, you know, and I don't want to totally destroy that memory."

"You won't."

"You don't understand the way I'm wired. I—"

But he didn't let me finish. Instead he grabbed my sex, pinching the smooth, bare flesh around my clit and sending waves of both pain and pleasure coursing through me. "You won't destroy the memory," he said, "because you're going to come for me. And do you know why?"

I shook my head, too distracted by the sting of that intimate pinch and the way my body was reacting to it—my nipples suddenly tight and needful, my sex clenching with a desperate desire to be fucked. I felt wanton and needy and on the verge. And oh, holy hell, what door had I opened when I had set my sights on Cole August?

"Kat." He twisted a little, and electric sparks seemed to sizzle over me, a billion tiny snaps and pops. "Are you listening?"

"You're making it really, really hard."

If he was sympathetic, I didn't hear it in his voice. "Very hard, actually," he said with a chuckle. "But you're going to touch yourself now, and I'm going to watch. And, Katrina, you are going to come for me."

"How can you be so sure?"

"Because I'm telling you to," he said in the kind of voice that brooks no argument. He shifted slightly, raising his knees as if to make a backrest for me. He was hard, his erection tucked in between my ass and his legs. "Lean back," he said, and when I complied I saw the tension in his face as my body rubbed provocatively against his cock.

"Now spread your legs wider."

I swallowed, thinking of the very intimate view that would provide him. "Cole . . ."

"Argue again and I'll spank your ass." He propped himself up on his elbows. "Do it, baby. I want to see that beautiful cunt."

I wanted to protest—wanted to clamp my thighs together in some sort of misguided attempt at modesty. I knew damn well I wasn't going to come like this—I was too self-conscious. Too aware.

But at the same time, I heard his voice. Heard his desire. And there was something about the command in his voice that made me want to comply. He was turned on—that much was an absolute certainty. And there was both power and excitement in knowing that it was my body and my reactions to him that were pushing him toward that edge.

"Legs," he repeated, and I kicked modesty to the curb and slowly pushed my knees as wide apart as they would go.

"Oh, baby," he said. "I like you waxed. You're slick and wet and I can see just how turned on you are. Tell me."

"Very turned on."

"You're so wet, baby. Slip a finger inside your cunt and see how wet you are. No," he added, when I closed my eyes as I complied. "Eyes on me. There you go," he said, his own gaze dipping down to watch me slide my forefinger into my slick, wet heat.

"Are you wet?"

"You know I am."

"I want to taste you," he said. "I want my mouth on you, my tongue inside you."

"Yes," I murmured, starting to shift so that he could do just that.

"No," he said. "Don't move."

"Cole, please."

"Put your finger on your lip, baby. I want you to see how good you taste."

I hesitated, then did as he asked.

"That's it. Suck your finger, Katrina. Hard. Pretend it's my cock in your mouth. No," he added, "don't close your eyes. That's it, baby. Dear god, that's hot."

It was, too. I was looking right into his eyes as I drew my finger, slick and musky with my own desire, in and out of my mouth. It was naughty, erotic, deliciously sexy, and I sucked harder, never looking away from his face, as the heat between us built and built to such a frenzy I could practically see the atoms spinning in the overheated air.

"Now touch yourself." His voice was raw, as if it was taking all his effort to remain in control. "Keep sucking, but use your other hand. Pinch your nipples—hard, god, yes, just like that," he said as I took my hard nipple between my fingers and pinched it tight.

I sucked in air, overwhelmed by the maelstrom building inside me. Power and heat radiating through me. My breasts, my belly, my sex.

"Oh, baby, you want to be fucked," he said, and I blushed, realizing that he could see the way my sex clenched and tightened in a desperate, driving need.

"Go ahead," he said. "The finger in your mouth, slide it down, thrust it inside—no, two fingers—oh, holy hell, Kat, I swear you're going to be the death of me," he said as he watched me touch myself in time with his words.

I never thought I could do something like this—could display both my body and my own arousal so intimately—but with Cole the fact of being on display made me more excited, not less. I wanted him to see the effect he had on me. I wanted the feeling to grow. And as he told me what to do—to fingerfuck myself, to tease my clit—I did as he directed, letting my vision go glassy and my body tense. Feeling the sensation build, the desire grow.

Then, when it got to be too much—when just one tiny push would send me tumbling over the edge—I forced myself to focus on his face. On his eyes.

And I watched the hot burn of desire reflected there as his words and my touch made me shatter into a million pieces.

When my body quit shaking, I collapsed against him, breathing deep. "Do you want me to go down on you?" I asked, murmuring the question against his chest.

"No," he whispered.

"But you haven't—and I want you to—"

He kissed the top of my head. "I'm content."

"You're hard as steel," I said, because there was no ignoring his erection that tented his sweatpants and pressed insistently against my thigh.

"I like it," he said. "You make me hard, Kat. I don't see any reason to change that just yet."

Considering how guys talked about blue balls, his words surprised me. Then again, I wasn't a guy, but I could understand how delicious the sensation of simply being turned on could feel. Besides, at the moment all I wanted to do was lie there, my body against his, his fingers lazily stroking my back.

"I think I've died," I said after a moment. "I think this must be heaven."

He trailed his fingers from my sex up over my breasts and to my lips. "Feels like heaven to me."

He brushed my hair back from my face. "I'm three for three," he said, making me laugh. "I assume you won't doubt me again."

"There's something magic about you, Cole August," I said. "But I guess I always knew that."

"Did you?"

"Sure," I said playfully as I stood up to stretch. I moved to the couch and curled up against the soft leather cushions. "Why do you think I picked you? Certainly not for your money or the fact that you can speak Italian. But give a girl a good orgasm . . ."

"How did you know I speak Italian?" He'd stood and was heading toward the wet bar in the corner of the room.

I frowned, trying to remember as he opened a small fridge and pulled out a bottle of wine. "I'm not sure. Maybe Angie said something once. Or Jahn," I added, referring to her uncle, and the man who had been a mentor to all three of the knights.

"Toss me my clothes, would you?" I added, after Cole brought over a bottle of Shiraz and two glasses. "Feel free not to bother with your shirt. I like the view."

"As do I," he said, eyeing me thoroughly before retrieving my shorts and top for me. "But this way I get to enjoy watching you take it all off again."

"I always knew you were clever." He grinned, then came over and poured us both some wine. He handed me a glass, then took a seat next to me.

"How come you never talk about it? Italy, I mean."

He swirled the wine in his glass as if considering the question. "I don't talk about a lot of things," he finally said.

"No, I guess you don't. Why not?"

"I like to look forward, not back. And that was just another time in my life that's over and done."

"Bad?"

"No. Good, actually." The way he said it made me think that the realization surprised him. As if there were far too few good periods lurking in his past.

"I've always thought it would be exciting to live in another country. Italy's not on my list, but I have a fantasy of living in Paris for a year. I want to see all the seasons change on the Champs-Elysées."

"And are you alone in this fantasy?"

I took a long sip of my wine, my eyes on Cole. "No," I said simply.

He leaned back on the couch, then patted his legs. I stretched out, my feet on his lap, a glass of wine in my hands. I glanced at the rug where he'd made me come, and couldn't help but think how quickly things had shifted from scorching hot to sweet.

"You have to pay attention around here," Cole said, apparently reading my mind. "Things move awfully fast."

"They do indeed."

"I'll tell you about Italy someday."

I peered at him. "I thought you didn't look back."

"I thought you wanted to know."

"I do," I said. What I didn't add was, *I want to know everything.* But I think he heard that last part, anyway.

We sat that way for a moment, all soft and comfortable. He held his wine in one hand and stroked my calf with his other. It felt warm and sweet and I should have known it was too good to last.

It wasn't obvious—I'm not even sure I could point to a particular thing. But the pressure of his touch changed, and the tenderness took on a hesitant quality. I got the feeling he was a man who believed that a storm was coming, and feared that it would rip the ground out from under him.

"Will you tell me what's the matter?"

He'd been looking at his hand on my leg, the contrast of his dark skin and my too-pale legs. By the end of summer, I'd be the same golden brown as a waffle, but this early in the season I was still winter white. Now he lifted his head to look at me directly.

"This is nice," he said.

"I can see why that would bother you."

"I like seeing you this way, the contentment so thick around you I could paint it. And I like touching you, being close to you."

"I like it, too." I couldn't manage to hide the wary note in my voice.

"You were right when you said you could handle it. Tonight— all this. Everything since you walked through my door. You've been everything I wanted and more than I could expect."

I licked my lips. He was saying all the right things, and yet cold fingers of fear were creeping up my spine.

"You handled it," he said again. "But what about the rest of it?"

"Don't do that. Don't assume you know things. You don't."

"Don't I?"

My temper flared. "No, you don't. You tried to scare me away earlier—talking about wanting the pain, wanting to hurt me."

"I meant it," he said, and his voice was low and dangerous and firm.

"I know," I said as I set my wine aside. Then I tugged my legs off his lap and shifted on the couch so that I was on my knees in front of him. I took his wine and set it on the coffee table. "In case it escaped your notice, I liked it, too."

"Vanilla," he said. "Tonight was watery vanilla."

"And you think I can't handle mocha almond fudge?"

"I'm not joking, Kat."

"Do you think I am? Dammit, Cole, I liked what we did. It made me wet when you spanked me, and when you tied my arms back . . ." I drew in a breath, shocked to realize that just talking about it made me aroused all over again. "Don't you see? Being helpless to you—it turned me on. It was new and it was incredible. It was like you showed me some wonderful secret about myself."

I tossed back the last of my wine. "So if you think I'm going to walk out of here and not look back, you're wrong. Instead, I'm going to beg you for more."

"It's the more that scares me," he said, and I think it was the only time I had ever seen hard, honest fear in those eyes.

I shook my head, not understanding.

"Christ, Kat, don't you get it? I'm not afraid you're going to want to walk. I'm afraid I'll take it too far. Do you have any idea how hard I have to work to keep my grip? How easy it is for me to just lose it?"

I thought about the glass I'd heard shattering at the gala and about all the stories I'd heard about Cole's famous temper.

And then I thought of the tender way he'd touched me and brushed away my tears. The softness in his voice.

"You won't," I said.

"You don't know me that well."

I do, I thought. But what I said was, "Maybe not. But I want to. And I know what I've seen so far."

I searched for some reaction on his face. Pleasure. Relief. Anger. Right then I really didn't care. But there was nothing. It remained passively blank.

He stood. "I'm going to take a shower."

"Dammit, Cole." I got to my feet as well. "I'm not afraid," I said as he started to leave the room. "I'm not, dammit, but if you are then don't touch me. Just call me."

I'm not sure where the inspiration for those words came from, but they worked. He paused in the doorway.

"Call you?"

"You kept backing off and backing off. Pushing me away. But then on the phone, when you called, you didn't hesitate. Not at all. Not really."

I remembered the strength in his voice. The certainty. "That's it, isn't it?" I asked, my voice gentle. "It was easy to call me because there was no risk. No reason to be afraid of hurting me because I wasn't there."

I could understand that. Hadn't it been easier for me, too? I had no problems getting myself off, but with Cole hadn't I actually come under a man's touch—albeit an imaginary one—for the first time since, well, since forever?

He'd opened a door for me, and dammit, I wanted to do the same for him.

He said nothing, but I saw him draw in a breath, then close his eyes for a moment too long.

I took a step toward him. "But I *was* there," I whispered. "I felt every touch, every sensation. You were right beside me, Cole, and everything was fine. Hell, it was more than fine. It was incredible."

I waited for him to say something, and when he didn't, I pressed on, determined to make him understand. "You want to spank me? To tie me up? Do you want to use a whip on me or, I don't know, something else entirely?" I finished lamely, because I really didn't know what the something else could be. "Then call me. Tell me. Describe it to me. Every lash, every mark. Lose yourself in it, Cole. Take me, hurt me. Don't you see? I'm giving myself to you—wholly and completely. You can have me any way you want me."

I pressed my palm to his bare chest and felt the pounding of his heart, so hard, so fast. "Start like this, and then you'll see. And maybe then you can take me the rest of the way. Because I want to go with you, Cole. I really, really do."

I tried to read his answer on his face, but his expression was shuttered and he closed his eyes. Desire and hope warred inside of me, and I wanted to drop down onto my knees and beg him.

Instead, I simply waited. One moment, then a moment longer.

Frustrated, I released a slow, soft sigh, then took my hand from his chest.

Immediately, he grabbed it, then put it back exactly where it was. Only once I was touching him again did he open his eyes, and the pure longing I saw there made me want to pull him close. To kiss him. To burst into song.

Instead, I stayed perfectly still, afraid that I was seeing too much. Expecting too much.

"Kat," he finally said, his voice so full of heat and tenderness that I was certain I would melt.

"Yes?"

"Two things."

I nodded.

"From now on, answer your phone when I call. I don't care what else you're doing, if it's me, you answer the phone."

My heart fluttered. "Yes." And then I remembered the books I'd read, the movies I'd seen. "Yes, sir," I added, and was rewarded with an amused curve to his lips. "And the second thing?"

"I want you in my bedroom," he said. "And, Kat? I want you naked."

I grinned. "Funny. I want that, too."

twelve

When he came into the bedroom with the wine and our glasses, I was sitting on the end of his bed naked, my fingers lightly stroking my sex. He paused just inside the doorway, then slowly raked his gaze over me, starting at my toes and then moving up to meet my eyes.

"How very bold you've become, blondie."

How right he was. I was shameless with this man. Wanting everything, and more than willing to play dirty to get what I wanted.

Right then, I was playing as dirty as I knew how. I arched my back, spread my legs just a bit wider, and slowly thrust two fingers deep inside myself. "I was hoping to give you ideas," I said. "Like subliminal suggestions."

His mouth twitched. "Oh, really?"

"I want you to fuck me, Cole. I want your cock inside me."
I moved my hips in time with my fingers, and saw the way that
he watched the show—and the way he was watching got me
even hotter. "I intend to get what I want. I promise you, I can be
very persuasive."

"I bet you can," he said. He put the wine and the glasses on
a nearby table and took a single step toward me. "I believe I told
you to come in here, get undressed, and lay down on the bed
while I went and got some wine."

"You said that," I admitted. "I think I mentioned that I've
never been very good at following the rules."

"I assume you know what happens to girls who are naughty?"
He gave the drawstring on his sweats a tug, then let them fall
from his hips to the ground. He stepped out of them, then
walked naked toward me, fully erect, huge, and intimidating as
hell.

I swallowed, then shifted my gaze up from his cock to his
face. I stood up and walked toward him. "Just so you know, I
intend to be even more naughty."

I put my hands on his hips, then sank to my knees in front of
him. Slowly—so deliciously slowly—I ran my tongue along the
length of his erection, pausing to pay special attention to the tip.

He shuddered, then moaned, then said my name, his voice
hoarse and full of longing. I didn't reply. Instead, I drew him in,
then tasted him, teased him—took him as far as I could.

I clutched his ass with my hands, felt the way his hands
twined in my hair, the way he took control of my head and the
rhythm of my thrusts, making me go farther and deeper than I
had been.

I liked it—knowing I was making him harder. Hotter. Knowing that he wanted this and that it was me who was making
his pleasure grow, making this tension and passion build up
so hard and so fast. He was close—so damn close. I could tell

from the tightness of his body and the way his fingers tightened in my hair. I could tell from the tempo of his breath and the way small shudders burst through his body, radiating all the way through me.

He was going to come—and damned if knowing that didn't make me even hotter. I was so wet, so turned on that I thought I might come, too, simply from the pleasure of knowing that I took Cole August over the edge.

And then, without warning, he stepped back, pulling me off him so that I was sitting on my heels, gasping and wet and desperate to finish him off. To feel him explode and know that I did that—that I brought him there.

"On the bed," he said, his voice all command and sensuality.

I must have hesitated, because he took my arm and lifted me to my feet, then slid his hand between my legs to stroke my sex. My knees went weak, and I sank onto his hand, so it was only the pressure of his palm cupping my sex that kept me from falling.

"Mine," he said, then thrust two fingers inside me. "Christ, Kat, do you know how much I want you? How hard I'm going to fuck you?"

"Show me," I said, and he lifted me up and put me on the bed. I lay on my back, but he made a circular motion with his finger. "Knees and elbows. Legs spread. I want to see your cunt. I want to see how wet you are, how much you want me. And I want to see your ass turn red when I spank you."

I felt something shift and tighten inside me as I complied. Anticipation, yes. Longing, most definitely. But a little bit of fear, too. Because there was an intensity in his voice that hadn't been there when he'd spanked me earlier, and that hint of fear—of not knowing what was coming or what he had planned—made me all the more excited.

"Oh, baby." His hands stroked the globes of my rear, and I

bit my lower lip as he spread me wide then slid his hand down to find me drenched and wanting. "Right here," he said, teasing me with his finger. "I'm going to fuck you so hard, baby. Tell me that's what you want."

"Yes." I could barely get the word out past the storm of emotion rattling through me.

"Tell me," he said. "I want you to say it."

"I want you to fuck me, Cole. Please."

"I think you can do better than that," he said, sliding his fingertip down to flick lightly over my clit. I gasped, as sparks and shocks raced over my skin. My nipples burned they were so hard, and my sex throbbed with a need so desperate I wasn't sure that he could ever fuck me long enough or hard enough to satisfy.

"Kat," he urged, thrusting his finger back inside me, then trailing his drenched fingertip up to tease my anus.

I sucked in air. "I want your cock. I want you to hold me tight and thrust into me. I want it hard, Cole. I want you to pound inside me, over and over, until I can't stand it anymore. And then I want to explode."

"What else?"

"Oh, god, isn't that enough?"

He chuckled. "Frustrated, baby?"

"You know I am."

"Then stop teasing, and tell me."

I realized what he wanted me to say. What he'd told me he wanted to do. And, yes, what I wanted as well. "I want you to spank me."

"Why?"

"Cole . . ." I shifted, feeling open and exposed, and not just because I was naked with his hand between my legs.

I waited for him to say something else, but he stayed silent, and I knew that this was part of my punishment, too—exposing myself to Cole. Not my body, but my whole self. My desires. My everything.

"I liked the way it felt," I admitted, my voice so soft I knew he was having to work to hear it. "There was pain, but it was so sharp and so pure—and I was already so turned on that it was like—like it was bigger than pain. Like it was electricity, and it was sparking through me, making the whole experience bigger and fuller. I don't know," I finished lamely. "I just know I liked it. And," I added before he could ask, "I want more. I want harder, Cole. I want to go farther. I want to go there with you."

I waited for his reply. For him to tell me that I'd said what he wanted. Or, god help me, for him to demand I reveal even more of myself to him.

But Cole was done with words. Instead, his palm lightly stroked my rear. I sighed, relishing the pleasure of his touch. But I tensed, too, because I was certain that I knew what was coming.

He didn't disappoint, and soon his hand landed on my rear with a hard smack. As before, I felt the sting, and gasped in surprise and pain. But then his hand smoothed out the rough edges and those sweet sparks buzzed through me. And then he did it again and again, alternating his blows to get both of my ass cheeks, finding a rhythm that soon had me almost floating and gasping—and my sex throbbing in demanding, unfulfilled longing.

"Now," Cole said, when the sparks had so consumed me that I felt like I was made of nothing more than electricity. He took my hips and tugged me toward him so that he was standing at the foot of the bed, the tip of his cock pressed against me. "I'm clean," he said. "I've been tested. But do you want me to use a condom?"

"No. No, I want to feel you." I was on the pill, so I wasn't worried about pregnancy, and I knew I was clean, too. But I appreciated his control, especially considering I hadn't even thought about protection, I'd been so caught up in the haze of desire.

"Good," he said. "You're so wet, baby." And then, as if to prove it, he thrust inside me. Slowly at first, and then, when he was buried to the hilt, he drew out and then slammed hard into me, just the way I'd asked.

I gasped, losing myself to the sensation of him filling me. Of his hands on my hips guiding me. Of the way his body exploded against mine, making my undoubtedly red ass fire even more with each thrust.

"Touch yourself," he said, his voice tight with the effort of holding back what was surely a rising storm. "Touch yourself and come with me."

I shifted my weight to one elbow so I could comply, then slipped my hand between my legs and teased myself with small circles, letting the sensation build, knowing that he was claiming me totally and completely—and losing myself to the pleasure of that sweet and decadent reality.

He exploded then, his fingers digging hard enough into my hips to bruise—and that was just enough to send me over, too. He waited for the shudders to die down, both his and mine, then pulled out and slid onto the bed, pulling me into his arms as we both lay there and looked into each other's eyes, our sated bodies touching and his fingers stroking idly over my naked and sensitive flesh.

"You're amazing," he said.

"You make me feel amazing."

His lips brushed my forehead, and before my sleep-heavy eyes finally closed, I saw satisfaction in his warm, dark eyes.

I laid on my back on the warm sand, feeling the surf rush up to my toes, then recede, cooling my overheated flesh.

My eyes were closed, and Cole was beside me, his fingers drawing lazy patterns on my skin, teasing my breasts, sliding down to my sex.

One finger slipped inside me, and I drew in air as heat from the sun and this man consumed me.

A shadow fell over me as he shifted, momentarily blocking the sun. Then he gently spread my legs apart, his palms stroking upward, the movement slow and teasing.

And then I felt the smallest flick of his tongue over my sex, but enough to make me arch up, wanting more. Needing more.

Dear god, he didn't disappoint.

His mouth closed over me. His tongue teasing and tasting. Laving me, playing me, bringing me closer and closer and closer until—

It wasn't him—oh, Christ, it wasn't him.

Not Cole but Roger. Sixteen years old, with dark hair and droopy eyes and soft fingers that played with my sex, groping and exploring, as I lay there, frozen and scared and turned on, with all the sensations building and building inside me, but I had to hold them back. Had to keep quiet and still. Had to keep the secret because—

Because—

Because if I didn't, then—

I came awake with a gasp, but kept my eyes closed.

I was on my back, my legs spread, and I could feel the warm heat of Cole's tongue on my clit, teasing and playing. I wanted to pull him up, to cry out for him to stop.

I wanted to do that, but I didn't want to explain. Didn't want him to see the secret on my face.

And oh, dear god, as he played and teased my clit with his tongue, I couldn't deny that I didn't want to stop him because it felt too damn good.

So I stayed there, legs spread, Cole's mouth so intimate upon me, his expert tongue doing amazing things, and the whole world reduced to this tiny point of pleasure that began as a single spot between my legs and would soon grow and grow until it had no choice but to explode.

And I would explode. I knew it. Hadn't Cole taken me there already? Over and over and over?

I waited, letting it build, relishing the sparks, the growing culmination of this ultimate passion. I clenched my hands at my sides, silently willing myself to go over, because it was too big now to hold in.

And yet, just like in my nightmares, the explosion wasn't coming.

I writhed against his mouth in silent demand, wanting, needing, and yet not finding. And god help me, I wanted to cry, because this was it—this was me right back again. Unable to get there. Unable to achieve. Unable to experience that last, final rush of pleasure.

Most of all, unwilling to explain to Cole.

So I did the only thing I could do. Something I knew how to do because hadn't I done it with every boy I'd dated? Every boy who had wanted to get close?

I cried out. I arched up. I let my body shake and quiver. I brought my thighs together, as if in an effort to ward off the near-pain of too much pleasure.

In other words, I put on a hell of a show.

And then, when the performance was over, I gasped and sucked in air and rolled over on my side saying, "Oh, god, oh, god, that was—shit, that was incredible."

"I'm glad you thought so," Cole said, pulling me close.

I rolled over and buried my face in his chest, then snuggled close.

He kissed the top of my head. I stayed as I was, not wanting to raise my lips for a kiss, because I didn't want him to see the lie—or my disappointment.

I'd thought I was cured, for lack of a better word. That being with Cole was all I'd needed to fix what had been broken since childhood.

Apparently I'd been wrong, and I hated myself for having gotten my own hopes up. Hated myself even more for caring so much about a goddamn orgasm.

But I did. Damn me, I did.

"Am I that much of an asshole?"

His words, so soft in tone and harsh in meaning, pulled me from my thoughts.

"What?" I looked up at him, saw the hard lines of his face and the hurt in his eyes.

"You heard me."

I propped myself up on my elbow, confused, because surely he couldn't know what I'd done. "What are you talking about?"

"You don't have to fake an orgasm to keep my ego in check. I promise you, I can handle it."

"Oh." Apparently he did know.

A little numb, I laid back down, then rolled over so that I was facing the wall rather than him.

"Why?" he asked. "Why not just tell me to stop? That you weren't in the mood? Did you think it would piss me off?" he asked, and there was no disguising the harsh tone of self-disgust in his voice.

"No." I spoke firmly, then rolled back to meet his eyes because he had to understand that it wasn't him. "No," I said again.

"Then why?"

"Because you made me feel it."

His brow furrowed. "I'm not following you."

"Everything you did—everything you were doing—it felt amazing. Being awakened that way. The sensuality of it. The eroticism. I loved it."

"But?"

I forced myself to go on. "It kept building and building, like light and color converging on a point. Like what I imagine a star goes through before it turns into a supernova—everything being pulled inward and then getting tighter and tenser and fuller until it has no choice but to explode in this crazy-wild splash of light and energy."

I drew in a breath and shrugged. "At least, that's what it feels like for me—an orgasm, I mean."

His lips twitched. "I got the orgasm part. Go on."

"I felt that—all of that. With you, I mean. It was all there, every feeling, every sensation. Huge and wonderful and—I don't know—earth-shattering. Except I couldn't get there."

His brow furrowed again, and I knew he must not understand.

"It's as if I'm one of those donkeys wearing the bridle with a carrot dangling in front. And I'm chasing that carrot, and I want it so badly. Only I don't realize that there's no way that I can ever reach it."

I licked my lips. "Except I *do* realize that. Because I've chased that carrot before. I've felt it all get bottled up before. And I know that I could chase the carrot all night and I'd still never catch it."

"And so you faked it."

"I'm sorry. I—I guess I wanted to give you the part you were supposed to have. Because you really did make me feel amazing. And if I just told you to stop, you'd never know that. And I wanted you to know." I hesitated. "Does that make any sense to you at all?"

He reached out and stroked my cheek, his expression so tender it made me want to cry all over again. "Yeah," he said. "I get it."

I exhaled, relieved. "But I am sorry. If I'd known that you could tell I was faking, I never would have." I frowned. "For that matter, how did you know? Oh, god, can all men tell?"

He actually laughed, which went a long way to making me

feel better. "I don't know about all men. I don't even know if I could tell with another woman. The topic doesn't come up often. But with you I can tell because I watch you. Because I've seen you come three times now." He lifted a shoulder in a shrug. "You matter to me, Kat. And so I pay attention."

I blinked back tears, feeling somehow both humbled and special. "Oh."

He brushed the pad of his thumb under my eye. "Tell me why."

"I thought I just did."

"No, not why you faked it. Why you had to. Tell me what happened to you."

I looked away, focusing on the orange glow of the morning light that was just starting to seep through the window. "Nothing happened. I told you. That's just the way I'm wired."

"Bullshit." He cupped my face with his palm and turned me back to face him. "For something that has the potential to give us so much pleasure, sex can sure as hell mess us up. Tell me how it messed you up, Kat. And don't lie to me."

I drew in a deep breath, not sure that I could talk about it. But this was Cole, and once I started to tell the story, it flowed easily.

"I guess when I said I'd never come with a guy, that wasn't entirely accurate. I have once before." I sucked in a breath and kept my eyes on his face. "I was ten," I said, and saw him wince before he was able to hide the sting of emotion.

"Yeah, I know, right? When I was ten and Roger was sixteen, we spent a lot of time together. Our parents were dating—working the grift together, really—and so when we traveled, they'd share a room, and put me and Roger in a connecting room. They'd lock the door, of course. I didn't really understand what they were doing, but Roger knew. And it got him worked up."

"What did he do to you?" Cole asked, the words so precise they scared me with their clarity.

I didn't want to remember. Didn't want to go there. But it needed to be said, and Cole had a right to know what was wrong with me. And so I clenched my hand tight at my side, and began.

"I was clueless the first time it happened," I said. "I'd gone to bed and Roger had stayed up to watch a movie—we didn't usually stay in hotels where you could rent movies, and he'd been poking around in the R-rated titles. I don't remember what he found. I don't even know if it matters. All I know is that I'd fallen asleep. And then I'd awakened to this sensation—it was Roger's fingers in my underwear."

"What did you do?" His voice was slow and even.

"Nothing," I said, my voice low. "I was confused and scared and I just sort of stayed there. I was on my back, just sleeping in a long T-shirt and underwear, and so I just pretended to still be asleep."

Cole said nothing, but his body had gone tense, and I knew the signs of his temper. If Roger had been in that room with us, I'm not entirely sure he would have been able to walk out of it.

"Go on," Cole said, once the silence had hung between us for what seemed like forever.

"He—well, you know," I said. "He touched me."

"Did he penetrate you?"

I shook my head, drawing strength from the way Cole was keeping his own temper in check. I could talk about this, yes. But only if I could keep emotion out of it.

"No," I said. "But he did other stuff. He played with me. Explored me. I'm not sure if he was just curious or if he was trying to get a reaction, but I kept my eyes closed and kept my breathing steady, and just pretended I was asleep. But I wasn't." I drew in a shuddering breath. I hated these memories. Hated going there. But I wanted Cole to understand.

Beside me, Cole took my hand. He said nothing, but that steady pressure was enough to urge me on.

"I could hear him breathing. And it started coming faster and faster, and the bed shook just a little. And then he gasped and sighed, and then finally he went back to his own bed."

I pressed my fingertips to my eyes. "I didn't realize until later that he was jacking off, but I do remember that I was scared. Not that he'd hurt me—not scared like that. But terrified that he'd know I was awake."

"You don't have to go on," Cole said. "If you don't want to talk about it—"

"No," I said firmly. "I do. I mean, I don't. Not really. I wish I could tell you without telling you. But I want you to know. I want you to understand. And—and in some weird way it feels good to get it out."

"I'm glad," he said, then squeezed my hand.

"Anyway, the next night we were still at that hotel. And I tried to stay awake. I like to tell myself that I planned to scream at him to keep his paws off me, but that wasn't the truth." I pressed my lips together, then sucked in air for courage. "And this is the part I really hate, because the truth is that I was ten and that meant that I was a walking petri dish of hormones."

"And what he'd done was horrible, but it felt good."

I looked at Cole in wonder. "Yes," I said. "Oh my god, yes. And as I laid there faking sleep, part of me was scared he'd do it again—but I think a bigger part of me was scared that he wouldn't."

"That doesn't make you bad," Cole said. "You were a little girl."

"I know. I do. But . . ." I trailed off with a shrug.

"I'm guessing he didn't keep his hands off you."

"You guessed right," I said. "The next night he got into my bed again. And he touched me and teased me, and this time my

fear was less. And that meant I felt more of what he was doing
to me. And it felt pretty amazing, you know? All this incredible
sensation that just flowed through me, building and building
like roses climbing the wall of a sensual garden."

I looked at Cole, but he said nothing.

"I liked the way it felt," I admitted. "And I liked that this
was what grown-ups did. And I liked that it made me feel special. But I also knew that it was bad. Shameful. And that he was
bad. But that I was worse for liking it."

"Jesus, Kat," Cole said when I confessed that.

I shook my head. "I was a kid. I was just figuring stuff out.
I'm telling how it was, not how it is." I clutched tight to his
hand. "But thank you."

I slid back into the memories. Back into the story. Whether
by plan or luck, Roger never got me so worked up that I reached
orgasm. But the nights became a ritual, and damned if I didn't
look forward to it.

"And then there was this one night. I don't know why, but he
touched me longer, and it all kept rising up, the way it does
when you're building, you know? And I was right there, and I
could tell that it was different this time. And part of me was terrified and wanted it to back off. But another part of me wanted
the feeling, because I could tell something was happening, and I
wanted to know. I wanted to *feel*."

"You came," Cole said, and I nodded.

"I tried to hold it in, but there was no way. I cried out, and
my body shook, and when I opened my eyes, Roger was staring
down at me." I squeezed my eyes shut in defense against the
memory. "He looked horrified. Disgusted. And I swear I'm surprised that his look didn't reduce me to dust right then."

"Kat," Cole said, then raised my hand to his lips and kissed
my palm. That was all he did, but it was enough. It gave me the
strength to finish.

"That was the last time he touched me," I said. "If we hadn't been traveling together, it would probably have been the last time he spoke to me. As it was, they were only with us for a few more months. I've never seen him again. I don't even know his last name. But I guess technically, before you, I did come once with a guy. Thank you, Roger." I shrugged, as if to suggest that this was all in the past and had no more effect on my day-to-day life than the price of Oreos in China.

Naturally, Cole wasn't buying it. "Baby," he said, then pulled me to him. He stroked me, telling me he was sorry. Making me feel cherished and special.

And, damn me, I started crying again.

"Sorry. Sorry," I repeated, wiping the tears away. "I get weird when someone takes care of me. It's not something I ever got used to."

"Your dad?"

"I love him, but he was more of the self-sufficient variety."

"I've got you now," he said, and made the tears start to flow all over again.

"It's fear, I think," I said, thinking about Roger and how he messed me up. "Fear that if I come, whoever I'm with will leave. Except maybe not," I amended. "Because you're the only one I've ever truly cared about staying."

"I'm flattered."

I met his eyes. "It's true," I said, because I was going all in and putting my heart on the line.

"I'm right here," he said, stroking my cheek. "And I'm not going anywhere."

I closed my eyes and breathed in deep, then turned my face so that I could kiss his palm. I felt warm and safe, and for the first time I was glad to be talking about all this junk in my life.

"Part of it's guilt, too, I think," I said.

"You have nothing to feel guilty about."

"But I do," I countered. "Because I liked it. I liked the way it felt when he touched me. I even . . ." I trailed off, then gathered my courage. I wanted this out. I wanted to slay these demons once and for all.

I sucked in a breath. "There were even nights when I told him I was afraid of nightmares and asked if I could crawl into his bed. He always said yes, and I always went because I hoped—"

"You wanted the feeling because it's a good feeling. But you knew he was doing something wrong, taking something without permission and taking it from a child who had no business consenting anyway."

He stroked my hair, twirling a blond curl around his finger. "You were a little girl whose body was awakening, and I know that you understand that. I know you don't really think you have anything to feel guilty about."

"I do know that," I said. "But knowing and feeling are two completely different things. And my body hasn't really caught up with the program. It doesn't matter, though," I continued. "Not anymore. You've got me past it over and over. That's pretty amazing."

"You humble me, Kat. But don't lift me too high. I assure you, I'm fucked up in some extraordinary ways."

"So maybe we're both broken," I said. "Maybe we make each other whole."

He looked at me for so long, I thought he was going to stay silent—and I started to get scared. Those were relationship words, and I wasn't entirely sure where they came from.

Except that was a lie. Maybe I'd told myself and Sloane that Cole was simply an itch to be scratched, but I'd never really believed it. Who's better at lying to herself than someone who's spent her entire life spinning lies?

And that particular lie had been a balm against a broken heart.

But Cole hadn't broken my heart. Just the opposite. And

now I was waiting—and not too patiently—to find out if he felt the same way.

"Cole," I said. "Please say something."

"I don't need to," he said, then wrapped me in the circle of his arms. "You've already said it all."

We held on to each other like that for a while, and I think I would have liked to have stayed that way forever. But I couldn't escape the one nagging thought. "Why was it so easy for me before, but when you woke me up just now, I was all bottled up?"

"Because I was taking," he said matter-of-factly, "and earlier, you were giving."

I shifted in his arms so that I could see his face—and so that he could see the confusion on mine. "Come again?"

His mouth curved into an ironic smile. "You're a submissive, Kat."

I blinked at him, trying to wrap my head around both the word and the concept.

"I don't like labels," he continued, "but I think the idea is true. Whether you always would have been or whether what happened to you as a kid shifted something inside of you, it's true now. It's part of you. Someone takes, and you close up. But if you give yourself to someone, then you've not only freed yourself but given them the best gift possible: all of you."

"You're saying I relinquish control? I don't think so. Even with you I was always—"

"Yes," he said. "That's my point. You were always. You're not giving up control. You're grabbing control by the balls. You're saying *this* is what you can have. Me, my pleasure, my body, and my heart."

His words rang over me, clean and true and pure. Except for one small thing. "You're wrong," I said, then pressed my finger to his lips when he started to argue. "Not someone, Cole. *You.*

You're the only one I trust. The only one I could hand it all over to."

I couldn't read the expression on his face. "Why?"

"Because you matter," I said, echoing the words he'd said to me. And then, as I watched the smile ease slowly across his face, I knew that not only were the words true, but they were the perfect thing to say.

thirteen

Since Cole's cooking skills ranked somewhere below mine, we had coffee and frozen waffles for breakfast. They actually tasted pretty good, and I liked the domesticity of eating them in his well-lit kitchen, sharing the newspaper, and occasionally brushing hands just for the hell of it.

I even offered to clean up, since that required little more effort than loading the dishwasher and throwing away the empty cardboard Eggos carton.

I poured myself a fresh cup of coffee, then checked my phone. "I should get going," I said. "I need to change before my shift starts at ten, and I want to go see my dad first."

He looked up from the Business section. "No," he said, and then went back to the paper.

I held out my spoon and knocked the top of the paper down again. "You want to say that again?"

"You heard me. No."

"No," I repeated. "I hope you're telling me that Glenn called and my shift doesn't really start at ten. Because if you're telling me I can't go visit my father, I'm going to be more than a little ticked off."

"You can't go visit your father."

I shoved back from the table and lunged to my feet. Cole thought *he* had a temper? Well, he hadn't yet experienced mine.

"Sit down, Kat," he said, his voice almost bored. "Sit and think. You know I'm right."

"I want to see my father."

"Do you really? Because every time you go there, you add to the risk that someone has learned the connection between you two. That they're following you. That they'll find him."

I sat down. I wasn't going to admit it out loud—not until he forced me to, anyway—but he was right.

"Ilya Muratti is not the kind of man you fuck around with. And I don't care how careful you and your father have been over the years, Muratti has resources."

"You're right," I said. "I'm just worried. I want to see him. Talk to him."

"Then call him on the burner. Let him know we have a plan."

"Do we have a plan?"

"We will," he said. "And until we do, your dad doesn't need to worry."

"You're good at this," I said.

"I've had practice," he said, then picked up his coffee cup.

"I believe that." I got up to get the coffee carafe, then refilled both our mugs. "What exactly do you do? Other than forge Da Vinci manuscripts, I mean?"

"Let's just say that I have my fingers in many and varied pies, and not all of them are legitimate."

"Still?"

"Evan's the only one who's gone completely straight. He's marrying a senator's daughter. And there are other reasons. He gets as much thrill out of running a straight business as he does planning a heist or con."

"And you?"

"The third degree, Ms. Laron? Should I frisk you for a wire?"

"Frisk me if you want, but I'm just curious." I didn't say that I wanted to know every little thing about him—even though that was absolutely true.

"I promise you I have the experience and the resources to help your dad. And I'm not squeamish. Whatever needs to be done to keep him safe, it will be. Okay?"

I nodded, because that did help. I still wanted to know about Cole's background—what happened when he was a kid? How did he end up in the scared straight camp where he met Evan and Tyler?

But all that could wait. Right now, I needed to focus on my father. "So what is the plan for my dad?"

"I'm still considering the options. Give me a day to think. To talk with Evan and Tyler and—"

"Cole, no. I don't want them thinking . . ." I trailed off with a shrug, not sure what it was I wanted to hide.

He reached for my hand and twined our fingers. "Everyone has secrets. I think the three of us know that better than anyone. Four," he amended, "counting you, too."

"Are we counting me?"

"Of course."

I waited a beat. "Just keep me in the loop, Cole, okay? This is my dad we're talking about. This plan you say you'll have? I want to know what it is. Promise me," I said. "Promise me you'll tell me the plan."

"I promise."

I nodded, satisfied. Then I cocked my head and studied him. "You know, you didn't seem as astounded by my revelation that

I'm not a completely honest and upstanding citizen as I thought you would be."

The look he shot me was laced with heat. "It's not exactly a secret that you caught my eye. I've done a bit of poking around on you."

"Really?" I couldn't keep the surprise out of my voice.

"Really," he acknowledged. "You're good at covering your tracks. I couldn't find a thing prior to you showing up in Chicago. And that was the most suspicious thing of all."

"Hmmm," I said, my voice all innocence.

"I guess that makes you like Aphrodite, born from the sea. Or at least from Lake Michigan."

"Naked in a seashell? I don't think so."

"Katrina Laron," he said, as if my name was a chocolate soufflé, light and airy on his tongue. "Who chose the name?"

I'd lived inside a cloak of self-preservation for so long that I almost protested that I didn't know what he was talking about. But I remembered myself and answered the question. "I did. I picked Katrina because it's close to my real name."

"Which is?"

I smiled at him. "You should know."

"Catalina?"

"My dad likes that island, too."

"And Laron?"

"That one I picked because I liked the joke."

"All right. I'll bite. What's the joke?"

"It's usually a first name for a boy, and it's French in origin. It means thief. I thought it was fitting."

From his expression, it was clear he agreed.

I frowned, thinking of my name and identities and all the stuff that people did to hide—and all the other stuff that people could do to find them.

"Cole," I began, but he silenced me with a simple touch of his hand.

"They can't find you. Not easily. And even if they do, they won't find your dad. Trust me, Catalina. It's going to be okay."

And, because it was Cole who was saying so, I believed him.

About ten minutes after I left his house, my phone rang.

I glanced at the display, saw that it was Cole, and felt the sweet flutter of anticipation in my chest.

I reached over and punched the button to answer the call on speaker. "Hey, stranger," I said. "It's been far too long."

"It has indeed," he agreed. "I need you to find a place to pull over."

I frowned at the serious tone in his voice. "Is everything okay?"

"As far as I'm concerned, everything's perfect," he said. "Including you."

"Oh. But then what—" I remembered my suggestion about phone sex. *"Oh."*

He laughed, the sound full of heat and wickedness, and I knew I was right.

I maneuvered into the parking lot of a nearby grocery store, then went around the back to the area where the deliveries are made and the employees park. That might, I thought, give me some privacy.

I'd expected the calls to come when I was home—if they came at all.

But I wasn't in the mood to argue. Not if Cole was giving my idea a chance.

And more than that, I was already turned on. Just the sound of his voice—just the thought that he wanted me, that he was thinking about touching me and fucking me—good god, I was wet already and my nipples were tight and hard and pressing almost painfully against the lace of my bra.

"Where are you?" he asked.

"In my car. Behind a grocery store. A long way from where any other cars are parked."

"No, you're not."

"No?"

"You're in a bedroom. The walls are painted red. There's a bed in the center of the room with an upholstered headboard and a white satin duvet. Can you see the room?"

"Yes. Is it your room?"

"No," he said. "But right now it's ours. Tell me what else is in the room."

"Um, candles," I said. "There's no light, but there are candles mounted in sconces on the walls. Some are simply in glass jars along the floor. The room is dim, and seems to flicker with the flames."

"I see it," he said. "And something else, too. Two things. Do you know what they are?"

I licked my lips. "Tell me."

"A trunk. Old-fashioned. Leather. You walk to it and open it."

"What do I see?" I asked, imagining the interior of the trunk.

"Toys," he said simply, in the kind of tone that brought to mind all sorts of erotic fantasies. "It's the one on top I'm interested in. Do you see it? There's a handle, almost like a stick wrapped in black leather. There are flails attached. Loose, thin strips of soft leather. Over a dozen of them."

"It's a flogger," I said, and heard the catch of excitement and fascination in my voice.

"Very good."

"I told you I'm not innocent," I said huskily.

"Have you ever used one?"

"No."

"Good," he said. "I want to be your first."

"Cole—" I stopped, unsure what I'd intended to say.

"Yes?"

"I—what else is in the room?"

"Just one other thing. A St. Andrew's cross. Do you know what that is?"

"Not really," I admitted.

"Picture an X made out of smooth wooden beams. It's attached to a frame, and that frame is attached to the wall. Your torso rests where the beams cross. Your ankles and wrists at the top and the bottom. Bound, Catalina. You understand that, right?"

I swallowed, then nodded, even though I knew he couldn't see me.

"Bound and naked and unable to move. To do anything but feel. I want you to go there, Kat. Go there, take your clothes off, and position yourself on the cross."

I closed my eyes and imagined it. Imagined my steps, slow and hesitant. Imagined putting my feet in place, leaning in, thrusting my arms up.

"It's padded under your wrists and ankles and belly. Do you feel that?"

"Yes," I said. I shifted in the seat, spreading my legs. A slow burn was starting to ease through me, simply from the power of my imagination and the anticipation of the words that were to come.

"Do you know why so many submissives enjoy being flogged?"

"It feels good?"

He laughed. "In a nutshell, yeah. But it's deeper than that. And the truth is it doesn't feel good right away. Pleasure from pain, and you can't get to the one without going through the other."

"Oh." My voice sounded breathy, and just a little concerned. I reminded myself that I was in my car, with nary a flogger in sight. This was a test run. And this was Cole. And this would be fine.

"I'm slipping the straps around your ankles now," he said. "First the left, then the right. Sliding up your body, stroking your inner thighs, teasing your cunt with my fingers. Just a little. Just to make sure you're aroused. That you want it. That your body is primed."

"It is." I realized that my hand had slipped down between my thighs. That I was cupping my sex. And that my hips were gyrating a little, as if seeking just the right amount of pleasure.

"I'm tracing my hands lightly up, over the curve of your ass, then cupping your waist, your sides, then going higher to bind your arms on the cross. Can you feel it?"

"Yes," I said.

"Spread your legs," he murmured, and I realized that I already had. "And arms up and wide. Have you done it?"

"Yes."

"How do you feel?"

"Turned on. Curious. A little nervous."

"The pleasure you feel depends a lot on the buildup. On making sure you're prepared. I like to start soft. Sensual. And there's music, too. Are you familiar with 'Carmina Burana'?" he asked, referring to the soaring cantata that was based on medieval chants.

"Yes."

"It's playing in the background. Can you hear it?"

"Yes," I whispered, and I could. It's one of my favorite pieces, rousing and uplifting and slightly disturbing all at the same time. It was, I thought, fitting to the moment.

"I'm letting the flails trail over your back, your shoulders. Then lower and lower until I'm between your legs, and, oh, Jesus, Kat, you're already so wet."

"Yes," I agreed, because at the moment that seemed to be the only word I was capable of forming.

"I flick it up, the strips of leather catch your sex, tease your clit. It doesn't hurt, the motions are too soft yet, but it's arousing. It ignites you. It makes the burn start to flow."

I swallowed, because I felt it. The buzz of heat between my thighs. The tease of the leather flicking against my sex.

I wanted to lower my hand, to stroke and touch and tease the low pulse of sensation into something wilder and more needy, but I knew that was against the rules, and I kept my hands firmly on the roof of the car.

"I do the same along your upper back—and, Kat, that's where I'm focusing. But the sensation will shoot through you. You'll feel it everywhere. You'll—well, you'll see."

I kept my eyes closed, the better to imagine.

"Do you feel it? The soft rhythm of the leather against your skin? Your upper back, first on one side of your spine and then the other. I'm getting into a rhythm, baby, back and forth, a bit harder, then a bit more, and the flails are landing in the same spot each time so that the sensation keeps building for you, up and up until you reach a point where you're not only feeling it, but experiencing it. Where pain shifts subtly into euphoria. Where you start to float."

"I feel it—oh, god, Cole, I do." I had no way of knowing if it would be the same in real life, but in this imaginary world inside my head, I imagined my back turning more and more red. I imagined the pain rising, and then breaking just at the peak, replaced by something close to bliss. Something that spread through me, warming me, and even taking me outside of myself so that I could fly, tethered by the rhythm of Cole's hand and the knowledge that he wouldn't let me float away.

He kept it up, talking me through what I was feeling, taking me higher, and then just when I was on the verge of floating so high I was afraid I wouldn't be able to come back down, he slowed the flogging, then stopped altogether.

"You're primed, baby, and I'm right behind you now. I can feel the heat radiating off you, and I press kisses gently on the sides of your back even as I slide my hand between your legs and stroke you, my fingers teasing your clit, then sliding inside you. You're so wet, baby, so turned on. You're right on the verge of exploding, and I'm going to take you there. I'm going to help you fly off one more time."

"Please," I said, as I felt the pressure on my clit. As my sex throbbed and clenched, drawing Cole in, seeking satisfaction.

I kept my hands on the roof, but I wanted to touch myself. I wanted to bring myself over. At the same time, though, I wanted Cole to take me there, because he was so close now, and—

"Now, baby. Come for me. Let me feel that sweet cunt clench onto my fingers. Let me feel you explode."

And god help me, I did, my body arching and shaking with such violent release I'm certain I shook the whole car. It washed over me in wave after wave, and there was one strange, giddy, wonderful moment when I feared it would never stop. That I would simply be lost in pleasure for the rest of my days.

But then the shaking began to subside and I could start to breathe again. "Oh, god," I said, and realized that I'd been saying it over and over and over.

"Kat?" There was a hint of worry in Cole's voice. "Baby, are you okay?"

"I'm fine. I'm more than fine." I could still feel the after-effects on my body, warm and tingly, and I knew that I wanted to experience this in real life, too. I wasn't sure what that meant— I'd never really thought that would be something I would like. But I had. I did. "It was, I don't know. It was so much more than I expected."

"I've never," he began, and then stopped.

"What?" I urged.

"You're not even here, and that was one of the most intimate things I've ever experienced."

"But you've done it before, haven't you?"

"Not with you," he said simply.

I closed my eyes, shivering. Wanting to hold his words and the closeness to me. "Oh. Thank you."

Silence grew between us, but not uncomfortable. On the contrary, I felt deliciously close to him. "Can I ask you something?"

"Of course," he said.

"Do you know how it feels?"

There was the slightest pause, and then he said, "I do."

"So you don't just use it on women, you've actually—"

"Yes."

The thought eased me somewhat. I wasn't sure how I felt about the fact that I liked the sensation of being flogged. Granted, I hadn't actually been flogged, but Cole had made it seem so real. So vibrant, and I couldn't help but believe that I'd responded the way I would when I truly felt the sting of the leather.

Knowing that he understood the sensation as well made me feel less self-conscious about all this stuff I was learning about myself. "I'm glad," I said. "I'm glad you like it, too."

"I need it," he said, his voice flat and even. And then, before I could ask what he meant by that, he added, "Evan's here. I have to go."

The call went dead, and I leaned back against the seat, still breathing hard, my skin still stinging sweetly from the flogging. I felt aroused and deliciously used.

Most of all, I felt cherished.

I closed my eyes and said a silent prayer that whatever was happening between Cole and me would continue to grow. Because now that he'd gotten inside me, I wasn't entirely sure how I would manage without him.

I don't remember ever going to Perk Up in a better mood. Within fifteen minutes, Glenn had managed to completely bring me down.

"Do you really think the customers want to hear you humming?" he asked me as I filled two cups with coffee for one of the regulars.

"I don't know why they'd mind," I countered.

"Hot date last night?" Sarah—the regular—asked.

I just smiled, too much of a lady to kiss and tell.

Sarah winked as she took her coffee, and I returned to restocking the small fridge where we kept lemon slices and cream.

As soon as Sarah was gone and there were no other customers lingering within earshot, Glenn clomped to me and put his hands on his hips. "That is exactly what I'm talking about. No one wants to hear about your sex life."

I looked up at him, a little indignant, a little confused, and a whole lot pissed off. "I didn't say a word about sex," I countered.

"And you damn well better not." He pointed at the fridge. "Spotless," he said. "And I need you to open tomorrow."

I gaped at him. "I'm off tomorrow."

"Not anymore."

I stood up, accidentally kicking over a pitcher of iced coffee in the process.

"Aw, Christ, Katrina. Clean that mess up, too, and hurry up about it. We're gonna be getting all the students any minute now."

I ignored the growing puddle of coffee. "I'm closing on my house tomorrow. I've had tomorrow scheduled off for weeks now."

"Beth quit. Got a job filing at some law firm. That makes you the next in line."

"Dammit, Glenn, I can't."

He stared at me. "Fine. What time is your closing?"

"Ten."

"You come here, you open. I'll relieve you at nine-thirty. You come back by eleven-thirty." He raised his hands in anticipation of my protest. "Best I can do."

On the one hand, I wanted to kill him. On the other, I thought the fact that he remained alive said a lot about my incredible powers of self-control.

"Do you have any idea how hard I've worked to get this house? How much it means to me?"

"And you should remember that they don't give mortgages to the unemployed. Do your thing and then get your tush back here and clock in."

"Glenn," I said sweetly, "do you know what I like about you?"

His eyes narrowed slightly. "What?"

"Not a goddamn thing." And then, with as much flourish as I could manage, I yanked off my Perk Up apron, tossed it at his face, and marched out the door.

fourteen

I didn't have a reason to go by the house, but Glenn had pissed me off enough that I wanted to see it. Maybe I wanted reassurance that it was real and that tomorrow it would be mine.

I didn't know.

All I knew was that I let myself in again, then stood at the center of the dingy room with the dingy walls and thought about all of this hidden potential.

And there was so much, I thought. Like people, so much of a property lay hidden beneath the surface.

I'd tried to say as much to Cyndee on a day when she'd been dragging me all over the city, looking at dozens of cookie-cutter houses with neutral-tone walls, flowers in just the right places. Fresh paint, fresh carpet.

Pretty, but sterile.

And I couldn't help but wonder what evils those fresh coats

of paint hid. Or what gateways to hell lurked under the safely beige rug.

Maybe it's just the way I was raised, but the whole process of staging and showing, praising and selling seemed just one small step away from the grift. A short con that no one ever complained about. Set the stage, bring in the pigeon, and take the completely legitimate commission.

The process had a certain beauty that I admired, and the job had the kind of lifestyle that appealed. No countertop to trap you, no manager who smelled faintly of rotten milk yelling at you.

The possibility had been teasing me for a few weeks now, and the pull was getting stronger and stronger.

It was like what I'd told Sloane about Cole. Eventually, I was just going to have to go after it.

I grinned. Going after Cole had worked out well. Maybe that was a sign that a job selling real estate was where I should land.

"First things first," I said, with a quick pat to the floor. "Tomorrow morning at ten, you're mine." And why did I know for certain that buying this house was the absolute right move for me? Because I didn't feel even the slightest bit foolish talking out loud to it.

I spent another hour poking around the house, measuring, taking notes, thinking about all the things I had to buy—in addition to the house itself—simply to make my meager amount of stuff fit into this tiny space. I planned to hit both Home Depot and The Container Store after the closing tomorrow. And then I'd spend the afternoon in the blissful haze of that lovely state known as home ownership.

After that, I'd see about finding another job. My job at Perk Up might have been crappy, but I'd been counting on the minuscule paycheck to cover the mortgage.

I was going to go straight back to the apartment to pack a few more boxes, but once I got in my car, I found myself heading toward the Windy City Motor Inn instead.

I knew that I should call Cole, but I didn't. He would only tell me to stay away. That every time I went, I ran a risk.

He was right, of course.

But I knew how to spot a tail and how to lose one, and when I arrived at the inn after my incredibly circuitous route, I knew I hadn't been followed.

The inn was conveniently located next to a Taco Bell, and I parked in that lot, then went inside to buy an assortment of burritos and tacos. I took my bulging sack across to the motel, scoped out my surroundings, then headed to my dad's room.

I tapped three times. "Daddy. It's me."

No answer.

I frowned and tapped again.

I pressed my ear to the door, but heard nothing except the pounding of my heart as my fear grew and grew.

I'd kept a key for myself, and though I hadn't used it originally out of respect for my father's privacy, I put it in the door now, then gingerly cracked it open. "Dad, if you're in the bathroom, I'm coming in."

I pushed the door the rest of the way open, then froze.

He was gone.

Except that made no sense. How could he be gone? Where could he have gone?

I looked more closely around the room. Nothing in the drawers. No suitcase anywhere.

I felt the rise of panic and tried hard to tamp it down.

Had they found him?

No—no, because then the room would be wrecked. So he was safe. Or, at least, he'd been safe when he left the room. But where had he gone?

Did he not trust me to help him? Had he suddenly gotten spooked by this room? Had he seen someone watching him?

I didn't know—hell, I couldn't know—and the whole situation both pissed me off and scared me. This was my dad. *My dad*. And he'd gone into the wind on my watch.

Fuck, fuck, fuck.

I locked the place back up, then stalked down to the management office. A bored clerk who looked to be all of fourteen was playing games on his phone. He barely glanced up at me. "Help you?" he asked, between smacks of gum.

"There was a man in room 247," I said. "Do you know where he is now?"

"Lady, this isn't the kind of place where the guests leave a forwarding address. He was here, now he's gone."

"So then he's definitely checked out?"

"Not too long ago, actually. Took his stuff. Paid the bill for the movies he rented. Left."

"In cash?"

"Yeah, then he took off with two guys."

Fear cut through me like a blade. It must have been Muratti. His goons had let Daddy pack. Given him that false sense that everything could be worked out.

I swallowed, forcing myself to push back the fear and focus. "Tell me about the two guys."

The clerk's face scrunched up as he remembered. "Um, a pretty-boy type in a suit, and a black guy—maybe some Hispanic blood there, too, had that light-skinned look, you know? But who can tell? Big, though. He was in a suit, too."

"Did they say their names?" I asked, though I knew the answer would be no before he said so.

That didn't matter, though. I knew who the men were.

Evan and Cole.

Shit.

Cole had come up with a plan, all right.

But despite looking me in the eye and promising to keep me in the loop, he'd gone and moved my dad without telling me a thing.

He'd lied to me, goddammit.

And that, frankly, pissed me off.

I sat in my car with the engine off and the top down and worked the phone. Not that it made a difference. Neither Cole nor Evan were answering, and though I caught Angie at work, she didn't know a thing.

"Evan only said that he and Cole had something to take care of this morning. Why? What's going on?"

"Nothing." I felt guilty that Angie knew nothing about my dad. Hell, about my old life. But how could I tell her now? "Nothing," I repeated. "Long story."

"Does this have anything to do with you and Cole finally hooking up?"

I'd been eating one of the bean and cheese burritos, and now I choked. "Oh my god. What did he tell you?"

Angie's delighted laugh sparkled across the phone line. "Nothing, are you kidding? When has Cole ever overshared?"

"But—"

"He didn't tell me or Evan anything. Or, if he told Evan, then he's keeping it to himself."

"Like Evan would keep something from you," I said.

"I know, right?" She said the words matter-of-factly, like a given, and I felt a tinge of jealousy. How nice to know someone so well. To trust them so completely.

"I figure Cole is keeping quiet," she continued. "No, Kat, the sad truth is that you are the source of your own intelligence leak."

"Me!" My voice rose indignantly—at least until I figured it out. "Flynn," I said.

"I had breakfast with him this morning. He sends his love. And," she added airily, "he told me to tell you that the apartment did not burn down last night, in case you'd acquired some misinformation and that's why you didn't go home."

"You know I hate you both."

She laughed. "You do not. That's why you're my maid of honor."

I made a grunting noise of acquiescence. "All right. Maybe I love you. A little."

"Mutual, Kat. And I'm thrilled about you and Cole. I mean, that's been a long time coming."

"No kidding."

"Listen, I have a meeting in a minute, but tell me quick what's going on with your house."

"I close tomorrow," I said, unable to keep the excitement out of my voice.

"I thought it was tomorrow. That's so cool."

"I'm giddy," I admitted. "It's like a rite of passage or something." I hesitated, then pressed on. "Listen, about the house. There's something else—"

"What's wrong?" I heard the sharp note of concern in her voice.

"Nothing. I swear. It's just this thing I've been thinking about. You know, my ever-present plan to get rich quick. Only I'm not sure this would be quick."

"I'm intrigued. Tell me about it over drinks?"

"You get married in a week," I reminded her. "When are we supposed to do that?"

"Maybe before the bachelorette party? Or breakfast? Anytime really, if I can tear you away from Cole."

"Speaking of, I need to try again to track him down. And you need to go to your meeting. We'll figure it out," I promised, then we said our goodbyes and ended the call.

Angie was smart. If getting into real estate was a bad idea, she'd tell me. Mostly, though, I just liked knowing that I had a friend to share my plans with.

I sat in my car and ran my fingers through my hair, wondering when in hell I'd become so settled?

And how the hell could I be settled with a missing con man of a father, and two of Chicago's most wanted escorting him around the city?

The knights own a lot of businesses, and I called every one of them. No Cole, no Evan, no Tyler. And the more time passed without any word—without any report as to where they'd taken my dad or what the plan for keeping him safe was—the more my temper soared. And, yes, so did my worry.

I had no real reason to go see Sloane, but I did anyway. I told myself I wanted to know if she had a clue. And if she didn't, I wanted a distraction. But it was more than that.

I was about to buy a house, I was getting serious about a guy, and I was thinking about pursuing an actual career outside of the coffee-pouring arts.

I was putting down roots, just like I had told my dad.

In other words, I was looking dead center at Big Life Things, and coming clean with my friends was part of making those things happen.

This new life I was building—this life that I'd be starting tomorrow when I signed my closing papers—needed a solid foundation. But until I cleared up a few lies of omission, that foundation didn't exist, and I was terrified that one day everything that I'd built would crumble, and everything I wanted and loved would shake and fall and turn to rubble.

I didn't want to risk that. Not now. Not when I was falling in love with my life and my world. *And,* a tiny voice in my head added, *with Cole.*

I found Sloane destroying the punching bag in The Drake's gym.

"Getting a workout?" I asked. "Or working something out?"

"Both," she said, then landed a hard punch. "Or maybe neither. Shit, I don't know."

She got in one final blow, then stood back, breathing hard. After a moment, she held out her hands to me and I helped her off with the gloves.

"Are we ladies who lunch now?" She glanced up at the clock. "Correction. It's cocktail hour. Are you here for a drink?"

"I wouldn't turn one down."

"Come on."

I followed her to the service elevator and then into the ornate suite she called home.

"This really is primo," I said, looking around at the classy, well-appointed living area.

"It is," she agreed as she moved to a small fridge by a wet bar. "Although I'm starting to feel boxed in. I'd like a yard. Flowers. My old partner is actually refurbishing his house. It's pretty cool. I keep bringing it up with Tyler and he keeps changing the subject." She scowled a little. "It's starting to get on my nerves."

"He just sick of owning real estate?"

"I don't know. I'm letting it go for now. Our caseload is too intense to do the house-search thing anyway. But it's a conversation we're going to have to have eventually. The trials and tribulations of being a couple," she added with a sigh.

"You love it," I said.

"I do," she agreed, and smiled so brightly she lit up the room.

"Well, if you have a whim to paint, feel free to come over to my place. Anything I can do to contribute to the peace between you and Tyler."

"That's right," she said, bringing a bottle of pinot noir to the coffee table in the living room. "Tomorrow's the big day." She opened the wine, poured us each a glass, and lifted it in a toast. "To home ownership," she said, and I laughed.

"Thanks. I can't believe it's really tomorrow. It's a huge deal for me. This will be the first house I've lived in that wasn't a rental."

"Seriously? Did you move around a lot as a kid?"

"An insane amount," I admitted.

"That makes tomorrow all the more special." She took a sip of her wine. "So did you come over because of pre-house jitters? Or—oh, shit—did I forget something about the wedding?"

"No. Honestly, I just wanted to hang out and catch up." I shrugged. "And I was wondering if you knew where Tyler was. And if he's with Cole."

"Misplaced the new boyfriend already?" she said with a laugh.

"Did you talk to Flynn, too?"

"No, I talked to Angie. She talked to Flynn."

I rolled my eyes in mock irritation, but I had to secretly admit I was enjoying myself. My friends cared about me. About Cole. They were cheering for us.

That was pretty damn cool—and it reinforced my determination to tell Sloane the truth. Because the longer I waited, the more entrenched the lie would be.

And, frankly, I'd waited too long already.

"But to answer your question," Sloane continued, not realizing my mind had wandered off, "no, I don't think Tyler's with him."

"You don't think?"

"Cole called here this morning and they talked for a while, and I overheard Tyler ask him if he needed help. Cole must have said no, because Tyler said that was good because he had plans today. Which, frankly, surprised me because I thought he was just catching up on paperwork at Destiny today."

"What did he say he was doing?"

"I overheard the call," Sloane admitted. "I didn't feel right about asking."

I watched her face. "But you have an idea. What are you thinking?"

She sat back. "Nothing good, I'm afraid."

I cocked my head. "Are you worried it's something that's going to get the cops looking at them?"

Sloane glanced at me, surprised.

I rolled my eyes. "It's not like I don't know what they do."

"*I'm* supposed to know what they do," she said with a sigh. "I didn't insist Tyler go squeaky-clean, but I do want to be in the loop. And, honestly, he was laying low for a while, and I liked it."

"Laying low to avoid Kevin?" I asked. Kevin Warner was an FBI agent who had once dated Angie, and who now had a chip on his shoulder. His attempts to nail the knights for all sorts of nasty stuff he believed had been going on at Destiny had fallen through—primarily because the knights weren't the bad guys there, but the good ones.

But Angie had told me the rest of the story. It turned out that Kevin had continued to press, and he'd let Sloane know just how dirty he believed they were. And that he would push to take them down.

"He's backed off," Sloane said. "He was transferred to D.C., and so the guys are off his radar as far as I can tell. At least for the time being. With any luck, he'll get over his broken heart and forget Angie and Evan and all the rest. But to answer your question, yes. That's why the guys were more careful for a while. But now I'm pretty sure Tyler's got some sort of jewelry scam going—"

"Jewelry scam?"

"I found out that he's been spending a lot of time in the diamond district." She pressed two fingers to the bridge of her nose. "Just another issue we'll be talking about."

I frowned. "But you two are okay?"

"Are you kidding, we're awesome. I swear I walk through the world with a big, goofy grin. It's astounding that cartoon birds don't fly around me, encircling my head. But that doesn't mean he's not a complete idiot at times. What?" she asked. "You're laughing."

"You're funny," I said. "And that's just good to hear. I'm not very good at relationships."

"But you're getting better at them, I think," she said, and from the tone of her voice, it was clear she was talking about Cole.

"Maybe," I said. "Right now, I'm a bit pissed at the man in my life, too."

"Really? Why?"

I hesitated only a moment. Then I sucked in a deep breath and told her about how my dad had gotten involved in a business deal with Ilya Muratti, and that Cole was supposed to be helping out, but was just pissing me off.

"Did this all start because your dad pulled some sort of con?"

"What makes you say that?"

"Cop, remember? And you told me once that your dad had dealings with Tyler on some real estate scam. I didn't get the impression that either man was on the up-and-up."

"Fair enough. And yes. It was a con." And since I really couldn't have asked for a better segue, I took the plunge and told her what had happened with my dad and the forgery of the will. And then I told her about my life. The way I'd lived growing up. All the cons I'd brushed up against.

"I was on the grift, too," I said, and it felt good to tell. "For a long time, actually."

"I'm glad you told me," Sloane said. "To be honest, I've suspected something like that."

"Really? Why didn't you say something?"

"I figured you'd tell me when you were ready." She shrugged. "Guess I was right. And now you're putting it behind you?"

"Hoping to. Honestly, that's one of the reasons I came here. New house, clean slate. Stupid, maybe, but . . ." I trailed off with a shrug.

"It doesn't sound stupid at all. Have you told Angie?"

I shook my head. "You're easier. We're newer at this friendship thing, and even though I wasn't certain, I kind of figured you already knew some of it."

"I get that."

"Angie's a little harder. We've been friends for a long time now, but I met her because I was planning on scamming her. I'm not sure how well that'll go over."

Sloane's smile was immediate and real—and made me feel one hundred percent better even before she spoke. "This is Angie we're talking about. Jahn's niece. Soon to be Evan's wife. I think she can handle the irony."

"When you put it like that . . ." I finished off my wine, thinking about what she said. And agreeing that she was right. "Thanks. I'm still royally pissed at Cole, but I feel better about the rest of it. So I'm glad I came."

"Me, too. It's nice to have an excuse to end my workout early."

I started to stand, then sat back down again. "Listen, there's one other thing. I think I may have said something I wasn't supposed to."

"Oh. What?"

"I told Cole I knew about the Firehouse. And then afterward, I realized that you might not have wanted me to say. I mean, he'll have to figure I heard it from you, right?"

"Probably, but don't worry about it. I doubt he's going to

take out an ad in the *Tribune* announcing that he's a member there, but it's not a state secret."

"Good. I was worried I'd broken a confidence."

"Did he take you there?"

I shook my head. "No. But—" I cut myself off.

"What?"

"Can I ask a personal question?" I began, then continued when she nodded. "Is it your thing? What goes on there, I mean."

"Let's just say that Tyler opened the world to me in more ways than one. He pushes my boundaries, and I need that. Plus, I like it," she added with a very wicked smile.

I thought about that, then gathered my courage. "I want Cole to take me, but I don't know if he ever will."

"I don't know a lot about Cole, so I may be wrong. But Tyler never really spent time there. It was more of an aside for him, you know? Like one more thing in the toy box."

"But with Cole?"

"Whatever he gets there, he needs it. Maybe he's afraid you can't handle it."

I knew that what she said was true. But I was hoping that maybe—just maybe—Cole was starting to learn that I could handle more than he believed.

"I should get out of your hair," I said.

"I won't beg you to stay if you have stuff to do, but I'm getting light-headed. Why don't we go down to the bar and have some appetizers? Maybe even some sort of fruity, sugary, bad-for-you cocktail to really celebrate your upcoming closing in style."

"Can I ask you about the Firehouse?"

"Can I ask you about growing up in the grift?"

And since that seemed like a fair trade-off to both of us, we agreed. Sloane changed quickly into jeans, and we headed out.

We were randomly chatting about all sorts of things when

we arrived at the Coq d'Or. The wedding, my house, general plans to spend a day at the beach. But all talk stopped the moment we stepped through the door and saw all three of the knights sitting right there at the bar, just as pretty as you please, as if Cole and Evan hadn't caused me a shitload of grief—not to mention completely pissing me off.

"I don't fucking believe it," I murmured, my voice low.

I stalked across the room, then grabbed Cole's glass. He looked up at me, his expression at first confused and then conciliatory.

"Kat," he began, but I didn't let him finish.

Instead, I tossed the drink in his face, drenching his face and his shirt in the bar's finest whiskey.

fifteen

"And that's our cue to leave," Sloane said, taking Evan and Tyler each by the arm.

"You guys stay," Cole growled as he mopped his face with a cocktail napkin and grabbed my arm with his free hand. "We're going."

I jerked free as he steered me toward the exit, then came to a dead stop right outside the door. "Goddammit, Cole, what the hell? You promised you'd tell me the plan. And then you up and move my dad without even contacting me? Do you have any idea how livid I am?"

Around us, the after-work crowd was moving into and out of the bar, all of them shooting us wary glances as they passed by.

"Shit," he said, taking my arm again. And this time, when I tried to pull free, he held fast.

The ladies' room was just down the hall, and he slammed the door open, then practically tossed me inside.

"What the—" I began, then snapped my mouth shut when he followed me in.

A twenty-something woman who looked like she was fresh out of college gaped at him, then edged carefully around us to escape.

"In," he said, stalking toward me so that I had no choice but to either back the rest of the way into the ornate restroom or get run over by him.

I entered.

The restroom at The Drake is as elegant as they come, with a long marble counter with multiple seats to give the women plenty of space to take care of both primping and gossiping. But what really makes it exceptional is that every stall is fully decked out as a little room, complete with toilet, vanity, mirror, sink, and even a little upholstered stool to sit on. Moreover, the door is floor to ceiling, giving a woman complete privacy.

Cole pushed open the door to the first vacant stall, then dragged me inside.

"Are you crazy?" I whispered as he locked the door behind us.

He didn't answer the question. Instead he grabbed me by the waist, picked me up, and sat me on the vanity. I gasped, for the first time truly realizing just how much he had on me in terms of weight, size, and strength.

"Dammit, Cole," I said, but I'd deflated a little bit.

He shoved my knees apart and stepped between them so that he was pressed up against the vanity and right in my personal space.

"You threw a drink on me," he said, his voice so low and so firm that I knew he was fighting to control his temper.

"You deserved it."

"Why did you come to me about your dad?"

"You know why," I snapped. "Because I thought you could help."

"And just what the goddamn hell do you think it is that I'm doing?"

"You can't just muscle in and—"

"All or nothing, Catalina," he said.

"Bullshit. He's my dad; you can't cut me out of the scenario, especially not when you said you'd keep me in the loop. You told me I'm a submissive, and maybe you're right. But that's in bed, Cole. Not out here. Not in the world."

I watched his face, saw the hard lines and angles tighten and his eyes narrow as he focused on me. "I'm not interested in taking away your autonomy," he said. "But I don't do anything halfway, and I'm not going to spend time trying to second-guess what the rules of engagement are. I already know the rules."

"Is that a fact? What are they?"

"Mine," he said, and I could tell from the heat in his eyes that it wasn't just the rules about my dad that we were talking about.

I licked my lips, trying to stay on track. "Dammit, Cole—"

"Take off your clothes."

I froze. A little shocked and—damn me—a lot turned on. "The hell I will."

He took the hem of my T-shirt in his hands and pulled it up, revealing my bra. "Take it off, or I will."

I felt my sex tighten and my skin go hot. "Do it, then," I said.

He did, yanking the shirt up, forcing my arms to follow, then tossing it on the floor near the door. He reached down and cupped my sex through my jeans. I was breathing hard, so turned on I was surprised my jeans weren't soaked.

"Will you take off the bra, or should I just rip it off?"

I reached back and undid the clasp, then pulled it off and tossed it on top of the shirt. "What are you doing?"

"Exactly what I want," he said as he unfastened the button on my jeans then eased the zipper down. "My rules." He slid his hand inside the jeans and under my panties, then eased one finger inside me, his smug grin widening when he found me not just wet, but drenched. "Mine. Say it, Kat."

"Yours," I said, finding it hard to make a sound, much less form words.

"And once you're naked, I'm going to fuck you. So hard it makes you scream, and everyone in here will know exactly what we're doing."

"Cole, no." But the words were for propriety only, and he damn well knew it. I was too turned on by what he said, and no matter what protests I might form into words, my body told the truth. And the way my sex throbbed and tightened around his finger in anticipation of what he'd described was the most eloquent admission of all.

He didn't bother to argue. He just bent down and tugged off my shoes, then eased my jeans over my hips until they were in a heap on the floor as well. He left my panties on, though, then pulled me off the counter and turned me around so that I was standing up and facing the mirror.

I saw myself there, my hands pressed flat on the vanity, my breasts full and heavy, my nipples dark with arousal. My face was flush, my eyes a little glassy. And Cole loomed behind me, still fully dressed, all power and control and pure masculine heat.

I heard the musical sound of his zipper, then the press of his cock against my ass. "Spread your legs, baby," he said, but I already had. I wanted this—I might have started out angry, but Cole had turned it all around on me, and now the only thing I wanted was to feel him inside me. The only thing I needed was to do as he said—to let myself go and just feel.

He made a low noise of satisfaction, then reached down and

stroked me through my panties. "Oh, yes," he said. "You're ready."

"Yes," I whispered, then gasped as he yanked the thin strip of satin to one side. "Bend over. That's right," he said, and I felt the insistent press of his cock against me, and then the sweet, hard push as he thrust inside.

His hands were on my hips, and as he moved forward, he pulled me back. He filled me completely, and the look on his face—such passion, such intensity—made me almost come right there.

He hadn't taken off his pants, and the material rubbed my rear as he pistoned against me. The knowledge that I was essentially naked and he was clothed—that he was taking me in this stall, that he could take me anywhere he damn well pleased—shot through me, enticing and terrifying and oh-so satisfying.

He kept one hand on my hip, but the other snaked around to tease my sex. The sensations were almost more than I could bear. The tease of his fingers on my hard, sensitive clit. The rhythmic pounding of his pelvis against my ass. The almost painful way he filled me, going so deep inside me, and with such steady and relentless power.

And then—oh my god—then he abandoned my clit to reach around and pinch my nipples, holding tight and twisting slightly, so that the frenzy of heated fizzles that shot from my breasts to my sex added yet another sensation to the erotic symphony that was building within me.

"Does that hurt?" he asked, squeezing even tighter.

"Yes," I whispered, hoping that the truth wouldn't make him stop.

"Do you like it?"

"God, yes."

"Look in the mirror," he said, and I realized that I'd closed my eyes. I opened them and saw what had to have been the most erotic vision of my life. Cole's hands twisting my swollen nipples. My legs parted, my sex damp. My body rhythmically undulating as I took Cole deeper and deeper. And then, when he slid his hand down my belly to tease my clit again, my lips parting in passion and my entire body trembling with the insistent, building climax that threatened to sweep me away.

"Tell me what you see," he said.

"I'm yours," I said, my breath a gasp. "I'm at your mercy. I'm in thrall to you."

"Any time I want, any way I want. Tell me you like knowing that's true."

"I do—oh, god, I do."

"Do you trust me, Kat?"

"Completely."

"Could I do this to you—fuck you in the bathroom of the goddamn Drake hotel if you didn't trust me?"

"No."

"Then trust me to know what I'm doing."

I nodded. And then, because I couldn't stand it any longer, I whispered, "Please."

"Please what?"

I pressed my hand over his on my breast, then drew his other hand up from my clit until he held both my nipples again. "Harder."

"Oh, sweet Jesus," he said, and as he squeezed tight—as I cried out from the sweet, delicious pain that shot through me—I felt him explode inside me, his release ripping through both of us.

Ribbons of pain that felt like pleasure burst through me, growing and building until my own climax shuddered through me. In that moment, Cole released the vise-grip on my nipples, and the feeling rushed back so quickly it made me weak enough that he had no choice but to hold me tight or let me fall to the floor.

"How do you do that?" I asked, when I could once again form words. "How can I be so pissed at you and then you turn it around, and use it to make me explode? And not just explode, but—oh my god, Cole. That was insane."

The corner of his mouth lifted. "Still pissed?"

"Yes," I admitted. "You broke your word."

"I wanted to ensure he was safe sooner rather than later," Cole said. "And I didn't break my word."

"Bullshit. You—"

"Were intending to tell you the moment I saw you. I only promised to keep you apprised of the plan, Kat. I didn't say a goddamn word about whether I'd tell you before or after I acted."

"That's a truly pitiful argument," I said. "You knew what I meant." But at the same time, I deflated. Because damned if his heart wasn't in the right place. He had moved in—and fast—to protect my dad. And angry or not, that really did mean the world to me.

I lifted myself up on my toes and kissed him.

"I don't know what tomorrow will bring, Kat. But right here, right now, you're mine. And I will always take care of what's mine. And that includes both you and your father. Do you understand?"

I nodded, because I did.

He dampened one of the provided hand towels and then cleaned me up, tending to me so very gently. I sighed, then lifted my arms for him as he put my shirt over my head.

He was taking care of me, dressing me, cherishing me. There was control, yes, but there was also a sweet sensuality to the moment. I thought about that, about the dichotomy of this intense feeling of warmth and safety juxtaposed against the pain and pleasure of the spanking and the pinching.

And as I thought, I realized something else—Cole was like me. Not that he needed to submit, but that he needed to dominate. He hadn't just wanted to spank and pinch me, he'd needed to. Just now. Last night. Because without that, he couldn't have reached orgasm any more than I could.

Hadn't he told me as much when I'd come to his door, boldly demanding that he fuck me? *I like it,* he'd said, talking about inflicting pain. *I need it.*

I didn't know what, but I was certain that he was able to empathize with me because something had happened to him, too. Something that kept him from coming unless he could pull himself over by grabbing onto the red threads of pain.

I was tempted to ask him to tell me. I didn't, though. He'd tell me eventually, and right then, it was enough to simply understand him. And to know that somehow—through all the crazy shit that had made us who we were—we had ended up in each other's arms.

sixteen

I followed Cole out of the ladies' room, ignoring the curious stares from the two women who were entering as we were leaving.

"Oh. My. God," I said, but Cole just grinned.

"You ready to see your dad?"

"Are you kidding? Of course."

"Then let's go." He led the way down the hall, then to a service elevator.

I frowned as he punched the call button. "We're going up to see Tyler and Sloane? I thought you were taking me to my dad."

He stepped into the car. "I am."

The elevator let us off on the sixth floor, and I followed Cole down the hall toward a corner room. "The Jahn Foundation keeps a suite here for out-of-town visitors. It's ironic, but the more money you spend on someone, the more often they will donate to a cause."

The Jahn Foundation, where Angie now worked, had been endowed by Howard Jahn as a charitable foundation with a primary purpose of preservation, restoration, and education regarding all forms of art. All three of the knights sat on the board of directors, so it didn't surprise me that Cole had access to this suite.

"What about security?" I asked as we paused in front of the door. "There are surely cameras in the elevators and halls."

"The odds of Muratti checking those are slim. But," he added before I could voice my protest, "we took precautions anyway. Wig, mustache, lifts in his shoes. We aren't new to the game, Kat. Remember that."

"I do," I said. "But it's my dad."

He took my hand and squeezed it. "I know."

"What about maids?" I asked as he tapped three times on the door. "Room service?"

"Taken care of," Cole said. "No one sees him." The door opened, revealing a perky girl in her early twenties who looked vaguely familiar.

"Hey! Come on in," she said, stepping back so that we could enter.

"Darcy, you remember Kat? She's Maury's daughter."

"He's such a nice man," Darcy said, holding out her hand for me to shake. "And we've met at Destiny. I used to dance there."

"Darcy's going back to school in the fall," Cole said. "She's taking a few college prep courses now, so we made a deal. She hangs out with your dad, answers the door and keeps him out of sight, and she can get paid for spending the rest of her time studying."

"Not bad," I said.

"It's a great gig," Darcy said, looking at Cole with something close to hero worship.

"Um, can I see him?"

"Huh? Oh! Right. Come on." Darcy led the way into the

suite, a still elegant but much smaller version of the one Tyler and Sloane occupied. "He goes into one of the bedrooms when anyone comes—maids or room service or maintenance. Hang on." She bounced across the room, then disappeared down a short hall. I heard her tap on a door and call for him. A moment later, my father walked into the room, a wide grin spread across his face, and his arms held out wide for me.

I hugged him tight, then stepped back to look at him. He looked calm and rested—the fear I'd seen on his face when he'd come to my apartment had all but been erased. I eased closer to Cole and took his hand in a silent thank-you, because he'd played a huge part in erasing that worry.

We settled in the living room, me perched on the arm of the couch so I could be close to my dad, and Cole standing near the window, looking out at the city. Darcy played hostess, offering coffee or wine or something stronger.

I went for the stronger.

"You're doing okay, Daddy? Not getting restless?"

"You know me, I'm always restless. But I'm content to stay put until your young man here tells me otherwise."

"Good," I said. "He's gone to a lot of trouble, and he knows what he's doing. You listen to him."

"I am. You've got a good man there, taking care of me. Taking care of you. I didn't want to put you at risk, kiddo, I really didn't. But I'm glad I came."

I sighed. "I am, too, Daddy. I just want you to stay safe."

I made him promise a dozen or so more times that he'd follow all the rules and not do anything stupid.

"I did a bit more poking around," Cole said, leaving the window to join us. "The property is prime, and although Frederick Charles doesn't want to sell to Muratti, that's not because he's looking to develop the property himself or expects his niece to after she inherits."

"He just doesn't want to sell to a mafia guy," I said.

"Exactly. Which gives us an advantage."

"I get what you're thinking, but even if Frederick sells the property, won't Muratti hold a grudge?" I asked.

"He's that kind, yes. But he's also about to retire, and his son, Michael, is starting to take over the organization. Michael's not as old-school mafia—no horse heads in beds—and he doesn't see the point of flying off the handle if it's bad business."

I caught my dad's eye. So far, that sounded promising.

"So once we're clear, I think Michael will simply write your dad off as a bad bet and everyone will go on their way."

"You think," I repeated.

"There's an element of wait and see, I won't sugarcoat it. But unless you want to call in the Feds—and then we'd be talking about witness protection—this is the best we can do."

"I got myself in deep, sweetie," Daddy said. "I can take it."

I nodded, then drew in a breath. "All right, then. So how are we getting him clear?"

"I have an idea," Cole said. "Let me work out the details and I'll let you know."

I started to argue, then decided to stay quiet. I trusted this man, after all.

And that felt pretty damn good.

"So am I forgiven?" Cole asked when we were in his Range Rover.

"Let's see," I said, making a show of counting things out on my fingers. "You've got my dad under control, I have my closing tomorrow, and we just had really amazing sex. If you take me by my house so that I can gaze longingly at it, then yes, you'll be forgiven."

"I can do that," he said, then reached over and stroked the back of my neck, a sweetly intimate gesture that sent shivers through me. "I like seeing you happy," he said.

"Convenient, since I like being happy."

It didn't take us long to get to the house, and I once again unlocked the door using the combination I wasn't supposed to know.

"Naughty girl," he said. "But useful to have around."

"This is the last time I get to live dangerously," I said. "Tomorrow I'll own the place, and letting myself inside will be completely legitimate."

He followed me over the threshold, then took my hand. With one quick tug, he pulled me close, hard and fast, so that I ended up crashing against him, then laughing as he cupped my ass. "I'm more than happy to provide the danger if that's what you're craving."

"I like the sound of that," I said, then curled myself around him for a long, slow kiss. "And I like doing that."

"Once again, we're in sync." He drew back, then waved his arm to encompass the house. "Show me everything."

I did, of course, dragging him through the house. Showing him every room, every closet, every nook and cranny. I told him where I planned to put my furniture, why I was certain I was going to need to add extra shelving, and exactly what kinds of vegetables I was determined to grow in my tiny backyard.

I showed him my bedroom, too. "I plan to spend a lot of time here," I said. "And I don't plan to be alone."

"Lazy mornings reading the paper in bed?"

"I'm more of an aerobic kind of girl. I was thinking wild, hanging-from-the-chandelier sex. But we can relax with the paper afterward if you want."

I saw the amusement flash in his eyes before he tilted his head up to the ceiling.

"Yeah," I said, "I know. Buying a chandelier is at the very top of my to-do list. But despite that little flaw, what do you think?"

"I think you got an exceptional deal. Whoever owned it could have sold it for at least ten percent more—maybe twenty—if they'd bothered to do just a little bit of cosmetic work."

"That's what I thought. And since I no longer work at the coffee shop, I'll have plenty of time to spend doing all that cosmetic stuff."

He cocked his head. "When did this happen?"

"About the time my boss showed his true asshole colors and tried to screw over my ability to go to my closing and then enjoy my house." I lifted a shoulder. "Fuck him. I can do just fine without him."

"I don't doubt it," Cole said. "But if you need a paycheck, I believe you're already technically employed at the gallery."

I smirked. "Careful, or I'll take you up on that."

"I'm serious," he said. "If you need help making ends meet, you know you can come to me, right?"

"I do," I said earnestly. And the fact was that I knew more than that. I could go to him about my life. About my hopes and my dreams. And not just *could go,* but *wanted to go.*

I wanted to share with Cole. Because this thing between us was more than just sex. It was life. It was us. It was everything.

"Hey," he said, peering at me. "Contemplating the horrors of having me for a boss?"

"Hardly," I teased. "Thinking about how little work we'd get done."

He grinned, but it faded quickly. "Is everything okay? You got suddenly pensive."

"Everything's great. I have enough money to cover the mortgage and my expenses for at least six months."

"That should give you time to find another job. Want me to talk to Tyler about sending your resume out through the placement office?"

"Thanks, but no. I have something in mind, actually." I glanced at his face, saw his attentive expression, and hurried on.

"I've been thinking about it for a while, now. Ever since I started house-hunting. I think—I think I want to get my real estate license."

"Do you?" He nodded slowly, as if he was seriously weighing my words. And then an easy smile crossed his face. "I think you'd kick serious ass in real estate."

Tension I hadn't even realized I'd been holding drained from me. "Do you really think so?"

"It's the perfect job for you. You're good with people, you know how to sell a thing and a concept. You can bullshit with the best of them," he added with a cocky grin. "Yeah, I think it's good."

"You are just raking in the brownie points today."

"I'll be sure to cash them in soon." He turned a slow circle in the room. "Yeah, this place was a great find. It has a ton of potential."

"In other words, it needs a lot of work."

He laughed. "That, too."

"Will you help me?"

The answer was there in the way he looked at me, his words only underscoring the truth. "You couldn't keep me away."

I took a moment to simply look at him and soak him in and wonder why it had taken me so long to go after what I'd wanted. Because now that I had Cole beside me, all those empty days before seemed even emptier. And I was determined to fill to overflowing all the days that were still to come.

He tapped the end of my nose. "You've checked out again," he said. "Where to this time?"

"Away," I said with a grin. "With you. To fantasyland."

His grin was bright and wicked. "I'm happy to make your fantasies a reality."

"And I am going to take you up on that. After I get your opinion on the rest of the house," I said, then laughed as I grabbed his hand and led him toward the second bedroom. "I'm just going to do a basic paint job in here. I figure Flynn can decorate it however he wants."

"Flynn's moving in with you?"

"He's my roommate now, and he'll be my roommate when I move. He needs one, and I always appreciate saving money. Especially since he'll be helping build my equity."

"I'm really not sure I like that."

"No?" I folded myself into his arms. "Then I guess you'll have to spend a lot of time right here to make sure I'm being a good girl."

"Kat . . ."

I'd been teasing, of course, but Cole's expression looked anything but amused. "Don't be jealous," I said, and though I tried to keep my irritation out of my voice, I don't think I succeeded. "You know there's nothing going on with me and Flynn. And honestly, if either of us has cause to be jealous, I think that would be me."

The minute I said it, I regretted it.

"Really?" He spoke in the overly polite tone of a boardroom executive.

I cocked my head and crossed my arms over my chest. "Come on, Cole, seriously? We're not playing this game. I know about the Firehouse, remember? And I have an idea of what goes on there. And I know that you fuck that girl, Michelle. And," I added, because I'd gotten myself worked up and was on a roll, "I don't even know if you've been with anybody since me. Because you told me that I had to be exclusive, but you didn't say a thing about yourself."

"Is that what you think?" he asked in that dangerously flat voice. "That I'm with someone else when I'm not with you?"

"Oh, hell, I shouldn't have said anything at all. I'm sorry. Truly." I drew in a breath. "I'm not sleeping with Flynn. I've never slept with Flynn. But he can't afford to live alone and I'm not leaving him high and dry. And no," I added, "I don't really believe you're with anyone else."

That was the truth, but it didn't matter, because my mind had skipped ahead to Michelle and the Firehouse and leather and—and that was the problem. I didn't know what the *and* was. And, damn me, I hated the idea that he couldn't—or wouldn't—get everything he needed from me.

Because even if he wasn't going to Michelle anymore, I knew that he was leaving something on the table. That he was afraid to push me to the edge. That despite how far we'd come, we still had a long way to go. And we weren't going to get there until he got over the fear that he was going to go spinning out of control.

"I'm sorry," I said again. "I shouldn't have mentioned her. I'm completely and totally jealous of her, but if you say you're not still seeing her, I believe you. You just pissed me off about Flynn. He's a friend. That's all."

"You don't have any reason to be jealous of Michelle." There was nothing flat about his voice now. It was smooth and soothing and full of tenderness.

"But I do," I said, as he took my hands and pulled me close to him. "Don't you get it? I want what she had. You shared something with her—something I don't understand because you haven't even shown it to me—and maybe it's petty and stupid, but whatever you did with her—whatever you got from her—I want you to get that from me."

"Oh, baby," he said, then claimed me with a wild, violent kiss full of teeth and tongue and power and heat. My head went spinning, my thoughts turning into a jumble, my worries fading to nothing more than mist. And when he cupped my ass and thrust me hard against him so that his erection teased me mercilessly, all I could think was that I had to have him—had to touch him—because then I would know that he was real and that he was mine.

He moved his hands to my shoulders, then pushed away from me as violently as we'd come together. "There is nothing—nothing—that I don't get from you. You fill me up, Kat. Don't you see that? Don't you understand that?"

"I do," I said, my words coming on a gasp. But that wasn't the truth. Not really. I still feared that I didn't fill the dark spaces inside him. That he needed more than he was taking from me.

At the same time, I remembered the phone and the car. The way he took me with such wild passion in The Drake just a few short hours ago. I remembered, and I hoped. And I decided to bide my time. I'd waited so long for this man, I could wait a little longer for the whole of him.

He hooked his finger under my chin and tilted my head so that I had no choice but to look into his eyes, hard now with purpose and heat. "Tell me what you want," he said, the gentleness of his voice in sharp contrast to the hard angles and lines of his face.

Everything. But I didn't say that. Instead I said, "Take me here. Hot and hard and wild. And in every room in this house—tonight, before it even belongs to me, just because the idea excites me."

Humor lit his eyes, but there was heat in his movements when he dropped his hand and stalked toward me, one step and then another. I matched him, backing up until he'd trapped me against the wall and he stood there, a solid barrier of masculine power.

My pulse had increased and my breath was coming unevenly. He was so close I could see the movement of his T-shirt as his heart beat inside his chest. I could smell the scent of lust. And there was no mistaking the violence I saw in his eyes.

With any other man, it would have been terror that cut through me, sharp and cold.

Instead, I burned for him. I was wet and open for him. And

when he grabbed my wrists and yanked them roughly above my head, it was a cry of passion I released. A wild, desperate moan of pleasure and need that, even without words, begged him to touch me. To fuck me.

"Is this what you want?" he growled, thrusting his knee between my legs so that it was hard against my crotch. "Wild and rough?" he demanded as he curled his huge palm around both my wrists to hold me in place, then used his other hand to rip open my T-shirt at the collar. The violence of the action made me gasp—and it made me wet. And when he then yanked apart the tiny piece of material that held together the two cups of my bra, I really thought I would come right then.

He cupped my breast, then squeezed hard, making me groan. Relentless, he focused next on my nipple—on taking it and rolling the erect nub between his fingers before adding more and more pressure until I felt it not just in my breast but in my sex, and I ground shamelessly against his knee, wanting to feel more. Hell, to feel it all.

"Oh, yeah, you like it rough. You should see your skin, Kat, so pink and flush. Tell me you want me to fuck you."

"I do. I want you to fuck me."

"Tell me you want my cock inside you."

"Yes, Cole. Please. Deep inside me. Hard inside me."

"Tell me you're mine," he said, releasing my nipple, then grabbing a chunk of my hair and twisting it tight in his hand. "Tell me you're mine," he repeated. "And then tell me what that means."

"I'm yours," I said. "Whatever you want, however you want it."

His eyes burned with the kind of passion I felt, and he used his grip on my hair to force me down onto my knees. "I want your mouth on my cock, baby."

Yes, I thought as I fumbled at his belt, then his fly. *Oh, god, yes.*

I was so wet, my body humming, my power to think reduced to a primal, passionate lust that only Cole could fulfill.

This was what I'd wanted to see. A wilder, more dangerous side of him. I wanted to go there with him, because I'd never been and there was no one else in the world I trusted to take me there. No one else in the world I'd want to slide down into the darkness with.

He was so hard and so thick, and I wanted nothing more than to taste him and tease him and take this man who'd opened the world to me right to the edge. I started slowly, trailing my tongue down the length of him, but Cole was having none of it, and he moved my head so that my lips were curled around his cock and I slowly drew him in, sucking and tasting and teasing with my tongue.

He tasted of male and lust and power, and I wanted to take him all the way. Wanted to be the one who made him break, and when he moaned and thrust into me, fucking my mouth, I concentrated on breathing and taking him deeper and deeper, even as my body fired with the knowledge that his passion was building.

His fingers were still tight in my hair and as he got closer, he thrust harder and controlled my head more, taking what he wanted, but also shifting off my natural rhythm and forcing himself just a bit too far back in my throat.

It was a little bit uncomfortable, and I felt tears prick in my eyes, not from pain but from that odd physical reaction that makes you tear up sometimes, like when you're dicing an onion or deep-throating the guy you love.

But those were minor things, and completely buried under the pleasure that fell over me like a blanket—the pure, sweet satisfaction of knowing that my mouth, my touch, had taken him to the edge, and was about to push him over.

But then he increased the tempo, thrusting harder into my mouth so that I had to shift my head so as not to choke. He was lost in the moment, though, and tugged hard on a shank of my hair to get me back where I was—and the violence of the motion sent unexpected needles of pain digging into my scalp.

I cried out as I flinched, and that made me choke. I tried to steady myself and control my breathing, but then I felt a hard shove. All of a sudden, I was falling backward. I reached my hands back to steady myself, but still managed to whack my shoulder blade hard on the windowsill before landing flat on my ass with a startled, frustrated yelp.

My sad little noise, however, was totally overshadowed by the look of complete horror on Cole's face.

"Kat," he said, his voice as ripped and destroyed as his expression.

I tried to stand and go to him, but he'd knocked the wind out of me when he shoved me backward, and I couldn't make a sound. All I could do was reach for him, but he stared at my hand as if it would bite him.

Slowly—like a man fighting for every ounce of control—he shook his head. "I should never have—Jesus, Kat, I told you. Didn't I goddamn fucking tell you that I'd go too far? That I'd hurt you?"

"No." The word came out hoarse, my breath still off and my throat raw.

He looked pale, battered, and when he lifted his hand and saw strands of wavy blond hair still twined between his fingers, I thought he was going to throw up.

He backed away from me, and I couldn't seem to move. It was as if I was trapped in amber, watching some horrific moment in history.

Then he was zipping his fly and buckling his belt. He reached into his pocket and tossed his keys onto my floor. "I have to go."

"Cole, no!" That time, the words burst out of me, and there was no disguising my fear. Not of the man, but of him walking out that door.

Cole, however, heard only the fear.

"Take the Range Rover. Get yourself home. And here," he added, pulling off his shirt and tossing it at me. "I fucking destroyed the one you were wearing."

"Don't go," I said, and when I reached up to brush away an escaping tear, I realized that I'd been crying all along.

He paused in the doorway, and there was nothing for me to read on his face—nothing at all.

He looked at me for one long moment, and then he left the house and walked out into the night, leaving me numb and alone and terrified that somehow the universe had shifted and we'd lost each other even before we'd really had a chance to begin.

For most of the night, I'd been numb.

I'd called his cell phone at least nine times during the night, but I'd gotten no answer. I'd gone to his house. I'd gone to Destiny. I'd gone to the gallery. I'd gone to every other business the knights owned, and every bar I knew that Cole ever frequented.

I'd called Angie and Sloane, but neither they nor the other knights had seen him.

I'd slept for a few hours, but not well. Now it was past seven and I still couldn't track him down. My closing was at ten and I was going a little bit out of my mind.

I knew that I'd end up making Angie late for work, but I needed company and reassurance, and so I headed to her condo, stopping for donuts along the way.

I wasn't worried that he was hurt or injured. Instead, I was worried that something inside him had broken—something I didn't understand but knew that I had to soothe or else risk losing this man forever.

"Hey," Angie said, once she'd buzzed me up. "You look like shit."

"And hello to you, too."

"Still no word?"

I shook my head. "No. He hasn't checked in with you guys, either?"

"Not as far as I know. Evan went out for a run. You can ask when he gets back, but he knows you're worried. He would have told me—or just called you—if he'd heard something."

"Shit," I said, then ran my fingers through my hair, because I really didn't know what else to do.

"Do you want to tell me what happened?"

"What I want is to just wish it away. But the bottom line is that he thinks he went too far. He thinks he hurt me."

"Did he?"

"No," I said. "No, he really didn't. But before this thing started he told me that there couldn't be anything between us. Because he was certain that he'd cross a line and somehow injure me. Honestly, Angie, it really worried him."

"Self-fulfilling prophecy."

"He's an idiot. I swear he has more self-control than I do. I don't see why he can't see it."

She shrugged. "Sometimes it's hard to see yourself, you know?" She glanced over me. "Speaking of seeing yourself, I'm guessing you haven't changed clothes since yesterday."

I glanced down, saw that she was right, and shrugged.

"Go take a quick shower. Then find something in my closet. You don't want to look wrecked when you see him, even if you are. He's the one who's wrecked, right? You're the one who's supposed to be strong."

"You sure?"

"Positive. And I'll go make some coffee for when you get out. You look like you need the jolt."

"I don't want to make you late for work."

She waved my words away. "What's the point of being the director if you don't go in late from time to time? Besides, I want to be here when Evan gets back. Just in case he's heard something."

"You think he has?"

"I don't know. But maybe Cole called during his run. Those three are in each other's pockets, so maybe." She glanced at her watch. "What time is your closing?"

"Ten."

"You have time," she said, then waved toward her bedroom. "Go. I'll meet you in the kitchen."

When I emerged fifteen minutes later, I did feel better. Not by much, though. And Evan still hadn't come home.

I forced myself to push it away. I told myself to take deep breaths, de-stress, and trust that it would all work out. It had to. Because I needed Cole in my life, and damn the man, I was certain he needed me, too.

"It's going to be fine," Angie said when I slid onto one of the chairs at her breakfast table.

"Keep saying that," I said. "Maybe the universe will listen." I devoured a donut, then licked the sugar off my fingers. "Listen. There's something else I want to talk to you about."

Her brow furrowed, and she sat down beside me. "Is something wrong?"

"No. No, it's just—" I sucked in a breath. "It's just that I've got this secret, and—oh, shit," I said. "I'm not exactly who you think I am."

"Oh, really?" Her brows lifted as she leaned back in her chair, and to my relief she looked more intrigued than pissed. "I'm listening."

"Right," I said, then told her everything. How I'd grown up. The mess my dad was now in. Even the Big Truth about how I'd originally tagged her as a mark.

"Oh my god, seriously?"

"Well, yeah." I dragged my teeth across my lower lip.

"So why are you telling me this now?"

"Because I'm about to go buy a house."

She laughed. "We must be really good friends, because that makes total sense to me."

"You're not mad?"

"Why would I be? You know my secrets—and god knows I have them. Now I know yours." She narrowed her eyes. "Unless this is some sort of long con? Am I going to wake up tomorrow and find out that I've deeded this condo to you?"

I laughed. "I wish."

"Well, there you go. We're even. We're good. I love you. And," she added, reaching across the table to give my hand a squeeze, "we'll figure out what to do about Cole."

And that, I thought, was why she was my best friend.

seventeen

I stood just outside the hangar and stared at the sleek silver jet owned by one of the knights' various corporate entities. I knew Cole was inside, and in a moment, I would be, too. He hadn't invited me—didn't even know that I was standing outside—and I could only hope that the emotion I'd see on his face when I stepped onto that plane would be pleasure. And not anger or fear.

Or, worst of all, regret.

"He's going to Los Angeles," Evan had said.

"Los Angeles? Why?"

"For you."

"What? How?"

"You'll have to ask him."

"I damn sure will. If he's going, I'm going."

"Good," he'd said. "I wouldn't have told you if I didn't think you should." He'd taken my arm. "You're good for him, Kat. He knows it. Don't let him forget it."

"He's good for me," I'd countered, and Evan's mouth had curved into a slow, sad smile.

"I believe you," he'd said. "But Cole's going to be harder to convince. I love him like a brother, but of the three of us, he's the most fucked up. Honestly, he has the most reason to be."

"I don't care about the reasons. And I'm not giving up on him."

"Good," he said, then kissed my forehead.

Now I drew in a breath for courage, then walked inside the hangar, knowing that the crew was holding the plane for me, making excuses about mechanical issues per Evan's instructions so Cole wouldn't wonder why they weren't already underway.

"Welcome aboard, Ms. Laron," a petite flight attendant said as I began to climb the stairs leading into the main cabin. "Mr. Black requested that you stay in the crew section until we're underway, and then you can move to the main cabin."

She said all that as if it wasn't the world's strangest request, and I had to admire her professionalism. The plan had been Evan's, but I'd easily agreed. Because there was no way that Cole could kick me off this plane once we were cruising at thirty thousand feet.

The attendant, who introduced herself as Jana, offered me a glass of wine before takeoff, which I gratefully took. Then, once we were airborne, she offered me another, and I downed that as well. By the time the plane had reached cruising altitude and I was allowed to stand up and move through the door that separated the two sections, I'd bolstered my courage enough to think that I just might survive the wrath of Cole.

I drew in a breath, then another, then slid the door open, stepped inside, and closed it behind me. I saw him immediately, of course, as he was the only person in the cabin. He was seated in one of the chairs that surrounded a small table. He was leaning back, a White Sox baseball cap pulled low over his eyes.

He hadn't noticed me, and I took a moment to look around. I'd never been in a private jet before, and this small room seemed more like a hotel lobby than the interior of a plane.

There were three other chairs around the table at which Cole sat, making a small conversation area. On the opposite side of the cabin, a sofa sat beneath a row of cloud-filled windows. A small coffee table filled the space in front of it. Finally, two plush recliners filled the area in the rear.

The entire cabin positively gleamed with polished wood and bright metal trim. The upholstery managed to look both comfortable and expensive. Honestly, I could get used to this.

And, of course, I was stalling.

I took one step toward him, then another, then another after that until I was standing just a few feet away, my hand on the table for balance.

I started to say his name, but then he lifted his head. I couldn't see his face because of the cap, but after a moment, it was clear that he was slowly letting his gaze travel up the length of my body, and when he reached my face, he pulled the cap off and tossed it onto the chair beside him.

"Kat," he said, and though there was sadness in his voice, I thought that I heard hope, too.

"Hey," I said. "Fancy meeting you here."

His mouth quirked up into a quick, tight smile. "I heard the door, then your footsteps. I thought, dear god, that can't be her, because that would be a miracle, and I don't believe in miracles."

He reached out a hand for me, and I took it, letting him tug me closer. His knees brushed my legs, and that connection—that spark of light and arousal that I always felt when I was with him—burst through me, making me feel warm and happy. Making me feel like I'd come home.

"I believe in miracles," I said. "I believe in you, too. Cole, you shouldn't have gone."

"You're right," he said, and I felt as though wings had burst free on my heart. "I shouldn't have left like that. But, Kat," he added gently, "I was right to leave."

The words hit me with the force of a slap, and I knew that I had let myself believe too quickly. That I'd let hope settle inside me, and it had gotten the better of me. Like Icarus, I'd allowed those damn wings to draw me higher and higher—and all I got for my reward was to come crashing back down to earth.

"You son of a bitch," I said, my voice as tight as wire because right then it was me who was having to work to control my temper. "I never took you for a coward or a fool, but you're both. I can't fucking believe it, but you're both."

"Dammit, Kat, don't do this."

"Don't do what? Don't fall in love with you?" The minute the words were out of my mouth I wished I could suck them back in. "Dammit," I said, then pushed away from him, needing space to think and to move.

I stalked to the couch at the back of the cabin and fell upon it, then bent over, my head in my hands. Goddamn him. *Goddamn him to hell.*

I felt the pressure of his hand on my shoulder, but I didn't look up. I knew I couldn't. Not yet. Not without crying. I'd shown too much of my heart, and I really wasn't in the mood to have it trampled.

The cushion shifted as he sat next to me, then took my hand, twining his fingers through mine. "You're missing your closing."

"Yeah," I said. "I know."

"Baby . . ."

I sighed. "I talked to Cyndee. The sellers will do their thing, and then I'll do mine and eventually I'll get the house."

"That's not the point," he said gently. "It's the ritual. The being there. In that tiny room scrawling your name on all that official-looking paperwork. Besides, don't you have movers coming on Saturday?"

I turned my head so that I could look at him. "Some things are more important."

He held my gaze for a moment, then ran his hands over his head. He stood up, paced to the end of the cabin, then turned around and came back again. I knew he was looking at me—I could feel the weight of his gaze—but I was focused on his hands. On the fists he made and released. On the battle he was waging.

Finally, he stopped in front of me. "I sat in that room at The Drake and listened to your father praise me for taking care of you. And what a goddamn load of bullshit that was."

"Cole—"

"No. I practically forced you in that ladies' room. Pinched you. *Hurt* you. And then at your house I almost ripped your hair out, and then I fucking made you cry. I was so wrapped up in what I wanted, what I needed—in my own fucking need to just shoot my goddamn load—that I didn't even realize I was hurting you. Choking you. Jesus, Kat, do you know how much it killed me to see you like that? Sprawled on the floor, tears streaming down your face? Do you have any idea how much I hated myself?"

Now I really was crying, and I brushed the tears away and then stood in front of him. I pressed my hands to the sides of his face, then brushed the softest of kisses over his lips. "For a man who is so smart—who has made so much of himself—you're a damn idiot, Cole August."

"Catalina . . ."

I pressed my finger to his lips. "My turn," I said, then brushed away a fresh spill of tears. "Forced me in the ladies' room? Are you kidding me? I was so hot I'm almost embarrassed to admit it. That was an incredible moment, Cole, don't you get that? Naughty and sensual, and just public enough to be a bad girl turn-on. I mean, come on. It was like acting out a fantasy, and it was amazing."

He started to speak, but I just shook my head. "No. Not finished. Did you mention pinching me? Did you say that it hurt? Well, guess what, mister, I have a secret to tell you."

I pressed a hand to his shoulder for balance as I leaned in close to his ear. I felt a tremor go through him, and a corresponding wash of heat shot through me, brought on by nothing more than a simple touch and our proximity.

"It did hurt," I said, as his body tensed beneath my hand. "It hurt, and then it felt amazing, and dammit, Cole, it made me so fucking wet. You hurt me? Maybe you did, but I loved it. Hurts so good, right? Isn't that what they say? That's how you made me feel."

"Kat. Oh, baby."

I eased back so that I could face him again. "You keep interrupting me. Stop that." I pointed to the couch. "Sit. Before we hit an air pocket or get lectured by Jana for not wearing our seat belts."

He sat, and to my relief I saw that some of the pain on his face had been replaced by humor.

I perched on the table in front of him, my eyes trained on his face.

"Made me cry, you said? If I remember right, I was having one hell of a good time getting you off. I liked it, Cole. I was into it. I was into you."

I knelt in front of him then gently pushed his knees apart so that I could ease in closer. Very deliberately, I moved my gaze from his crotch to his eyes, and as I did, I reached out and pressed my hand over his cock, then felt it stir beneath my palm.

"I wanted to taste you, to suck you off, to take you in as deep as I could because it turns me on to know that I'm giving you pleasure." I stroked him as his erection hardened under my touch and with my words. "But guess what? There's this whole physiology thing working there, too, and let's see you try to deep-throat a cock as impressive as yours and not have tears prick your eyes."

A flicker of a grin touched his mouth. "I'd rather not."

"Yeah, well, you owe me. I was damn close to taking you all the way, and you bolted on me, you bastard. And as for yanking my hair," I continued before he could interrupt, "yeah, that hurt. You yanked, I wasn't expecting it, and it hurt."

I saw him flinch as if I'd slapped him.

"BFD, Cole. Big. Fucking. Deal. So you accidentally yanked my hair. One of these days you'll probably roll over in bed and whack me with your elbow and I'll have a black eye for a week. It's not like you lost your temper and beat me to a pulp."

"What if I had?"

"You didn't, and you wouldn't. You're not capable of that. Of losing it, sure. But you couldn't hurt me if you tried."

"Kat, you don't understand."

"The hell I don't. What have I just been telling you? There was no reason to go, but you did. Hell, you ran. And *that* was what hurt me, Cole. Not the rest of it."

He looked away, and I bit back a curse.

"God, you're thickheaded. You say I don't understand, but you're wrong. Don't you get it? You've showed me a new side of myself, and I love it. I'm not scared of what you'll show me about yourself." I reached for his hand. "The truth is, I understand more than you think."

"Bullshit."

"You need pain," I said softly. "You need to inflict it. Turns out I rather like it. Seems to me like we fit together nicely. A perfect set. Like salt and pepper. It's what I should have told you last night in the house, but I didn't know how to say it. I *want* it, Cole. When I said I wanted you to get everything you need from me, that's what I meant. And I'm not scared that you'll go too far. Because you can't. You won't."

His eyes flicked to mine, but he said nothing. *Please,* I thought. *Please let me be getting through that damn thick skull.*

"You think you don't have control, but I'm telling you that you do. Everyone loses it occasionally. Hell, you've got an edge up because you've worked at it for so long."

He scrubbed his hands over his face, then dragged them back over his scalp. Then he just looked at me while I sat there, my stomach twisting in anticipation of his answer. "How do you do it?" he finally asked.

"What?"

"Make me believe that maybe I'm not as fucked up as I think I am."

I lifted a shoulder. "So what if you are? At least we won't be bored."

He almost laughed, and I felt a swell of relief that maybe—just maybe—the storm had passed.

"Seriously, Cole. Who isn't fucked up? I think we all are. I sure as hell am. Maybe the trick is to make your fucked-up-edness work for you. For us."

He said nothing.

"Cole. Please." I closed my eyes and took a breath, debating what I wanted to say, knowing I was showing more of my heart than was smart or careful. But maybe around Cole I didn't have to be either. Maybe I just had to let him know how I felt.

"I need you," I said simply. "I thought at first that I just wanted you. That you were an itch I had to scratch so that I could get you out of my system. But it's more than that, and I can't stand the thought of losing you. I honestly don't know if I could survive it." I drew in a breath. "And right now, I really need you to say something."

I sat frozen, praying he would do just that, but also terrified of the words he might say. After a moment, he stood up, then crossed to the far side of the cabin. He stood with his hand on one of the armchairs, his back toward me, his head turned in a way that made me think he was looking out the window at the world spread wide beneath us.

"I've always been able to get by," he began, his voice low but firm. "Slide in with the gangs. Mingle with students, with professionals, with artists, with anyone. I was able to easily pick up the way men with money talk and walk and act and behave. I blend, and it's easy, and I make it look good."

He turned then to face me. "But at the core, I'm just one more motherfucking gangbanger."

"Bullshit," I said, the response immediate and firm.

He shook his head. "No, it's true. It's true and I'm not ashamed of it. It is what it is, you know?"

"It's not. You got out of that life."

"Fuck yeah, I did. I got out because I'm smart. And I became successful because not only am I smart but I made the right friends."

"And because you three cheated a little," I said, and made him laugh.

"There is that." He took a deep breath. "I can put paint on a canvas in a way that sucks people in. That makes them feel right here," he said, thumping his chest over his heart.

I wanted to say something, but I didn't know where he was going with this, and I was terrified of knocking him off track. So I simply sat, breathing in his words, and silently praying that when he finished speaking, the message would be something I wanted to hear.

"I can paint love and pain and honor and longing and any goddamn emotion you want to name. But saying it? Showing it? I'm not good at that, baby."

My heart twisted with the realization that all of those beautiful words had been leading back to me.

"I don't need eloquence, Cole. I just need you."

He nodded, as if in understanding. "Here's the bottom line. I'm fucked up, Kat. But you're fucked up, too."

I smirked. "Told you."

"So you did. So maybe instead of fighting this thing between us, I should embrace it." He held out his hand, silently calling me to him.

I went, then folded myself into his arms, which was just where I wanted to be.

He kissed my head, then murmured, "Maybe you're right," he repeated. "Maybe we should just be fucked up together."

I tilted my head up to smile at him, feeling lighter than I had in hours. "I told you I was smart."

"And ballsy, too. If we hadn't already been in the air, I would have kicked you off this plane."

"I still don't know why you're on this plane," I admitted, letting him draw me with him back to the couch. He sat, then pulled me down to straddle him. As I did, a wash of happiness came over me, so intense it seemed to sweep away all the pain and fear I'd been feeling.

I'd come to the plane intending to get Cole back. And dammit, that's just what I'd done.

I hooked my hands around his neck and leaned back so that I could see his face. "Even when you were scared and angry, you still thought of me. You're going to Los Angeles because of me. Because of my dad."

"Yes," he said as he took his finger and slowly traced my lower lip. "I can't not think of you, Kat. Even if you hadn't come to me—even if I'd never touched you again—you would still fill my days and my nights and my imagination. I'd sketch you if I couldn't have you, and I would mourn the loss of you in my arms."

I blinked, and a tear trickled down my cheek.

He brushed it away. "I need you now, Kat. Here and now and hard. Because I need to know that you're here and that you're real—and that you're really mine."

"You know I am," I said, my voice breathy because of all the emotion trapped in my throat. I leaned forward and our mouths collided, teeth banging, tongues warring. I felt overwhelmed, taken by him—and damned if I wasn't taking right back.

His hand was inside my shirt and mine fumbled at his zipper. I have no idea how he managed it, but somehow my shirt and bra ended up on the floor, and I was straddling him, my hand inside his pants, his erection hot and hard under my hand.

"Christ, I need to be inside you," he said, as he cupped his hand over my sex, stroking me through my jeans as if we were two horny teenagers in the backseat of a car.

"I want you in my mouth," I said.

"No." He shifted his hands so that he was gripping my hips, then yanked my jeans down. "I'm going to fuck you, Kat. I need to be inside you. I need to feel you tight around me."

I felt my body clench in time with his words, and my breath came shallow and hard. "Whatever you want," I said, my body melting under the knowledge that however he wanted me, I would happily submit. "Whatever you need." Frantically, I struggled to get out of my jeans, then my panties, until I was naked and on his lap, my fingers fumbling at his waistband as I tried to shove his jeans down.

They didn't come all the way off, but once his cock was free, I didn't give a flying fuck about his jeans—I just wanted him. Inside me. Hot and hard and thick. And I held on to his shoulders, straddling him, reaching down to find his cock and position the thick head at my center.

"Now," he said, gripping my hips and pushing me down, hard and fast, so that he filled me completely. Pain and pleasure shot through me, red streaks brought on by the violence of the motion. The wonderful, desperate intensity of it that had me crying out, "Yes, oh, god, Cole, yes!"

My words echoed in the small cabin, and as the sound surrounded us, my eyes went wide. I'd forgotten where we were, and I saw the twitch of his mouth when he realized what I was thinking. And then, very slowly and deliberately, he reached up and pressed the privacy button near the lightswitch on the ceiling.

"She heard that," I whispered.

"Does it bother you?" he asked, as he lowered his hand to tease my clit. "Does it bother you if she knows that I'm fucking you? That I'm deep inside you? That you're naked and hot and that I'm going to make you scream when you come?"

"No." I could barely force the word out from the pleasure his words and his touch were shooting through me. "No," I repeated. And then, because I wanted him to know just how much I meant it, I leaned forward and hooked my arms around his neck, putting my body at an angle and lifting my ass off his legs as I impaled myself over and over in a sensual rhythm that made both of us just a little crazy.

"Spank me," I said, and felt his cock harden inside me with the whisper of my words. "Make my ass red, Cole. I want to feel the sting of your hand, even after you're done with me. Spank me because the thought that Jana knows what we're doing makes me so damn wet. Spank me," I murmured, "because you know you want to. And because, dammit, I want to feel you come."

He groaned in response to my words, a pure, sensual sound full of need and longing. And just when I was afraid that he was going to ignore my demand, I felt the sweet sting of his palm against my rear. I cried out, the sound silenced when he captured my mouth with his.

"Now," he demanded, when he broke the kiss, then landed another sweet spank to my ass, making my body arch up in a way that not only teased my clit, but forced his cock deeper inside me. "Come for me now, Catalina."

And then, because I was his and knew that I always would be, I gave myself over to him, let myself go, and shattered in the arms of this man who had claimed me.

eighteen

"I don't have to tell you how much I appreciate you squeezing us in today," Cole said to the positively gorgeous man who sat across the table from us, his stunning wife at his side.

Of course I'd recognized both of them the moment the waiter had led us through the cozy Malibu restaurant to the patio dining area. Not only was Damien Stark a former tennis star turned billionaire entrepreneur, but he'd also been all over the news not that long ago. Sex, scandal, murder. The kind of stuff that the tabloids ate up—especially when you were as photogenic as Stark and his now-wife, Nikki Fairchild Stark.

I'd gotten over my awe quickly enough, though. Damien was casual and friendly and completely down to earth in a plain T-shirt and black jeans. And when Nikki insisted she and I share an order of cheese fries—which is so not the usual fare for model-beautiful LA women, I'd developed a little bit of a girl crush.

"Today's no trouble at all," Nikki said in response to Cole's comment. "Our flight's not scheduled until much later tonight, so this is the perfect pre-trip dinner."

"And the gallery's right next door," Damien added. "We can swing by there after we're done."

"I'd like that," Cole said. "This trip isn't about checking up on any of the Knight Holdings properties, but if we can squeeze in a quick run-through, that would be great."

"An art gallery?" I asked, confused. Cole had yet to explain to me how this trip to LA was supposed to help my dad, and I was doubly confused now that we were dining with Damien Stark. If an art gallery was now involved, I was starting to get a little nervous. Not that I didn't trust Cole, but this was beginning to feel like he was setting up a long con in order to get out from under a short one.

Cole squeezed my hand. "Nothing to do with the casino property," he said, apparently reading my mind. His words also told me that whatever he was planning here in LA centered around the land at the heart of Daddy's problem. And that it wasn't a secret—or at least not much of one. Otherwise, he'd be keeping quiet about the land around Damien.

"I never did learn how you two know each other," I asked.

"I've known Cole for years," Damien said. "We met through one of his business partners, Evan Black, and then got to know each other better in the last year or so."

"Evan bought a few galleries from Damien about a year ago," Cole added. "He transferred them to Knight Holdings, and I've been overseeing their operation for the last six months."

Our meal arrived, and the conversation shifted to the kind of random tidbits that people talk about on a beautiful spring evening. Plans for the next day, for the summer. Movies, cars, the absolutely incredible cheeseburger the waitress had put in front of me.

I'd finished off my dinner and was debating between apple

pie or the slightly more sane bowl of berries, when a messenger arrived at our table. He delivered a package to Damien, who took a quick look at it, then passed it to Cole. "I think you were expecting this."

The envelope was thin, with the exception of some bulk in the middle. He reached inside, pulled out a smaller padded envelope and tucked that into the leather backpack he'd brought with him. Then he pulled out a sheaf of papers. "For you," he said, then handed them to me.

I glanced down, confused at first, then a little giddy when I saw what they were. "My closing documents?"

"I arranged to have them scanned and sent to Damien's office."

"And I'll get them returned tonight by courier so that you'll have access to your house tomorrow," Damien said. "Congratulations, by the way."

"Oh my god," I said, looking between the two men. "Thank you."

Cole squeezed my hand. "It's your first house. It's important."

"Your first?" Nikki repeated, and I nodded, foolishly teary-eyed, and not even caring. "Then we need to make a toast," she said, then lifted her half-empty glass of wine. "To your new home. May it always be filled with love and happiness."

"Thank you," I said, as we all clinked glasses.

There was some more general discussion about the house, and I probably bored Nikki to death with my musings about where I was going to put my furniture. She was, however, polite enough to look interested. And considering she made a few suggestions, maybe she genuinely was.

"Now that Katrina's signed her papers," Damien said, turning toward Cole, "I should tell you that all of the documents you'll need to sign will be ready in the morning. I'm sorry I'll be out of town, but Charles will meet you at my office, and he'll push everything through. And then Nikki and I will see you in Chicago for the wedding."

"Looking forward to it," Cole said. "And I appreciate you going out on a limb like this."

"I'm not," Damien said. "It's a good investment, albeit a bit tricky in the details."

Nikki rolled her eyes. "Next he's going to say that's what makes it fun."

Damien shrugged. "Well, it is." He stroked his fingers over her shoulder, but spoke to Cole. "I'll check in from Tokyo. But if you need anything, Charles will take care of it," he added, referring again to his attorney.

"Tokyo?" I said. "Business?"

"As a matter of fact, yes, but not mine."

"It's my first international trade show for my software development company," Nikki said. "Thank goodness Damien's going to be there to hold my hand."

They had, I noticed, been holding hands or otherwise touching throughout the evening.

It had made me happy to see it. For that matter, it had made me want that, too. But even as I was wishing for that very thing, I realized that Cole had held my hand most of the afternoon. And now, his fingertips were resting on my thigh. During the meal, he'd brushed his thumb over my lip to catch a bit of mustard. And more than once he'd fed me a bite of dessert off his fork.

I reached over and took his hand, then met his eyes.

What? he mouthed.

But I just smiled, thinking of how much I already had, and how lucky I felt simply being with this man. And how, at least for the moment, everything was right with the world.

When Cole suggested that we take a quick stroll through the gallery, I'd expected to see colorful paintings that featured the sea. Wyland-style images that were so often popular in coastal communities.

What I saw instead, was me.

Not just me, of course. But there was an entire wall featuring portraits similar to the ones that I'd seen at the Chicago gallery. All anonymous, true, but now that I knew the subject of the portraits, it was easy enough to recognize myself.

"I had no idea," I said, taking Cole's hand. "How many of these have you painted?"

His mouth quirked up. "How many hours have I lost watching you?"

"Lost?" I teased.

"Invested," he said. "Treasured. Enjoyed."

I leaned in close and kissed him. "Better," I said. "And I really am flattered. Awed." I shook my head, not quite able to find the words. "Each time I see myself on a canvas and know that it was your brushstrokes that put me there—I don't know, Cole. It makes me feel warm inside. It makes me feel special."

"That's because you are," he said. "That's because I can't see you any other way."

Nikki and Damien had come with us, and though Damien had moved to the far side of the room to admire some colorful glass sculptures, Nikki was close enough to have overheard our conversation. When Cole kissed my cheek, then headed across the room to join Damien, she moved to my side.

"I didn't mean to eavesdrop," Nikki said, "but I couldn't help but overhear."

"It's okay," I said. "I love these images. I fell in love with the first one I saw even before I realized it was me."

"Really?" She lifted a brow. "And when you realized that Cole had painted it?"

I pressed my lips together. "It's like what I told him—it made me feel special." What I didn't add—what I still couldn't say out loud—was that it made me feel loved.

Beside me, Nikki nodded, and I saw understanding on her face.

"Damien didn't paint your portrait," I said. "But I'm guessing you felt the same way."

"You know about that?"

I lifted a shoulder. "It was kind of all over the news." Damien Stark had paid a million dollars for a nude, erotic portrait of Nikki. She'd been anonymous in the portrait—her face hidden. But when her identity had been revealed—along with the fact that she and Damien were a couple—the press had gone on a feeding frenzy.

I'd felt bad for her at the time. Now, knowing her, I despised the press even more. "That must have been hell," I added. "I'm sorry you had to go through that."

"So am I," she said. "But I survived it. It wasn't easy and it wasn't fun, but in the end I think it made me stronger. It sounds clichéd, but I really mean it. And one absolutely good thing came out of it."

"What's that?"

"Damien, of course. We came through it, and we came through it together. And when we did, we proved to the world what we already knew."

"What's that?"

"We fit each other." She shrugged. "Simple, but true." She smiled then, broad and happy. "I look at you and Cole and that's what I see. Am I right?"

I glanced across the gallery to where he stood with Damien, two gorgeous men who outshone all of the art that hung around them. "Yeah," I said. "I think we do fit." And I could only hope that Cole thought so, too.

nineteen

"You're sure you don't want a night on the town?" Cole asked as we stood in front of the Beverly Wilshire hotel and watched Damien's driver, Edward, pull the limo back into traffic. "Los Angeles. A limo. That's a lot of potential to pass up."

"The only potential I want is you," I said. "In our room. Preferably without clothes."

He grinned. "Well, when you put it that way . . ." He took my arm and led me inside the hotel that, though I'd never been in it before, seemed so familiar from all the times I'd watched and rewatched *Pretty Woman* as a teen. At the time, I'd been more interested in the musical shopping montage than in the romance plot. But I did remember that in the end, Vivian had gotten both the clothes and the man, though there'd been a few moments when it had looked like he and his issues were going to blow it for them.

I looked at the man on my arm, and couldn't help but smile. I hadn't seen it coming, but I couldn't deny that I wanted the fairy-tale ending, too. And I was going to do whatever it took to make that happen.

"What?" Cole asked, catching me eyeing him.

"Just thinking about this hotel," I said, as we moved through the exquisitely appointed lobby to the bank of elevators. "A lot of celebrities come through here. Some pretty hot men, too."

His brows rose ever so slightly. "Planning to snare yourself a movie star?"

"Hardly." I linked my arm through his. "I was just thinking that the man on my arm is so much hotter."

"Funny," he said, pulling me to a stop and kissing me fast and hard and deep. "I was thinking the same thing about the woman on mine."

We'd registered before having Edward drive us to Malibu for dinner, so now we headed straight to our room on the eighth floor.

"You still haven't asked me what we're doing here," Cole said as the elevator opened onto our floor. "About what the plan is for your dad."

"No," I said lightly, as I walked a few steps in front of him. "I haven't."

He caught up with me at the door, then stilled my hand before I could put the key in. "Katrina."

"I'm just playing by your rules," I said. "I seem to recall you were very insistent on getting that point across to me in the ladies' room of The Drake. Or was I mistaken?"

He shook his head, obviously amused, then took the key from my hand. "Not mistaken."

"Good."

He opened the door for me, then followed me over the threshold. As soon as the door closed behind him, I eased up against him and started to unbutton the pale blue shirt he'd paired with faded jeans. "The truth is, I'm really hoping that being a good girl is going to be even more rewarding than being punished was." I lifted myself up on my tiptoes and nipped at his earlobe. "Otherwise, why not just be bad?"

"You raise a good point," he said, tucking his finger under my chin to lift my mouth up for a kiss. "And I do like to punish you. . . ."

"I can be bad," I said, cupping my hand over his already hard cock. "And we have a nice long night in a gorgeous hotel ahead of us with nothing else to do but for you to punish me for being naughty."

"Or reward you for being nice."

"Or both," I said, then squeezed his cock and made him groan.

"Stay there," he said, leaving me standing just a few feet from the door. We had a regular room, not a suite, and I liked the fact that it was small and intimate, with little more than a bed and a desk and a chair.

It was as if the room was stripping away all other possibilities, leaving nothing else for us to do except take off our clothes and enjoy each other. That was fine by me. The way Cole had bolted in Chicago had left me feeling edgy. I'd recovered a bit on the plane and even more with Nikki and Damien. But I wasn't going to feel completely right—I wasn't going to feel completely *his*—until I'd spent hours in his arms. Until he'd claimed me again and again. Until he'd taken me every way imaginable and then some.

And until he stayed with me afterward.

Now he sat on the edge of the bed and looked at me. I remained still, knowing that was part of the game, but wanting badly to move because my legs were starting to cramp. Just when I thought I could take it no more, he said a single word. "Strip."

I didn't speak. I didn't smile. I did nothing, in fact, except take four long strides toward him, bringing me all the way into the room and putting me right in front of him.

I'd had no time to change before racing to the plane, and that meant I also had no luggage. Fortunately, I'd known from my repeated viewings of *Pretty Woman* that it was easy to solve a wardrobe crisis on Rodeo Drive—at least, it was if you had money. Now I wore a stunning Dior wrap-style dress in pale blue. And since Cole had paid for it—all the way down to the lace panties and push-up bra—I figured he was entitled to watch it come off.

I untied the sash, then unwrapped the dress until it hung on me like a robe, revealing the bra, very tiny panties, and stunning blue stilettos.

"You like?"

"I think I like this view even better. Maybe this is how you should wear the dress from now on."

"Okay," I said, teasing. "But let's see if we can manage an improvement." I slowly slid my hand down my stomach until my fingers disappeared under the lace band of the panties. I was wet and hot and I arched back a bit as I stroked myself, my fingers sliding over my bare skin and teasing my clit enough to send tingles of sensation running all through me.

I kept my eyes open, locked on his, and when I heard his low, guttural moan, I knew that I'd just won a round in whatever game we were playing at the moment.

I withdrew my hand, then sucked on my finger. I was rewarded with another groan and a soft, "You're killing me, Kat," which made me laugh.

In one fluid motion, I pulled the dress the rest of the way off, then let it fall to the floor. Then I unclasped the bra and tossed it casually aside. Next came the panties, until I stood in front of him, completely naked except for the fuck-me heels.

I moved closer, then simply stood there, mere inches from him. "If we were at Destiny, there'd be a no-touching policy."

"Good thing we're not," he said, then reached out to run his fingers lightly over me. Up and down my arms, over my thighs, lightly along my breasts. The caresses were gentle, almost casual, but the sensations he stirred in me were anything but.

I'd been standing with my legs together, but his touch had sent such a flurry of sensation through me that my body was now throbbing for release. I shifted, spreading my legs a bit, then I leaned in and put one hand on his shoulder, both for balance and to bring me closer to his ear. "I'm so close," I whispered. "Make me come."

I leaned back enough to see his face and the heat reflected there. I saw the way a muscle in his cheek twitched as he fought for control. And I heard that single, unexpected word—"No."

I lifted a brow, frustrated both by the tension in my body and the amusement I saw in his eyes.

"Fine," I said, then moved my own fingers to my sex, because this was a problem I could take care of on my own.

"No," he said. "My rules tonight. You don't come until I tell you to. And you do what I tell you to."

I lifted a brow. "Sir. Yes, sir."

He smirked, then glanced at the floor. "I think I'd like to see you on your knees. And I know I'd like to see your lips around my cock."

I forced myself not to reveal anything when I looked at him. This was full circle, right back to where we'd been before when he'd bolted from my house, and I couldn't deny that I was nervous.

But the bottom line was that I wanted this night—not drama or regrets—and I knew that Cole wanted it, too. I might be a little nervous, but I trusted him. More than that, I knew better than to disobey.

I dropped down to kneel in front of him. I put my hands on his knees, then gently eased his legs apart and moved closer until I felt the press of the mattress against my lower body.

I hesitated, expecting him to unfasten his jeans and tug down his fly. But all he did was lean back, putting his hands slightly behind him for support. He looked at me, and for a moment the only thing I felt was the heat that seemed to shimmer in the air between us.

Then he broke the connection by tilting his head back and drawing in a long breath.

I got the message. This was for me to do—to free him, to suck him, to take him all the way.

I had the control—except I didn't. Because right then I was doing Cole's bidding. I was the girl on her knees and we both knew it.

And damned if I didn't like it. Because he was right—there was power here. Power and submission. That duality excited me. And what excited me even more was that it had been Cole who'd seen that side of me. Who'd so clearly seen all of me.

Slowly, I tugged his zipper down, then freed his cock. I traced a fingertip lightly along the length of him, then closed my hand around the base, stroking him slowly up and down, my own body growing hotter and tighter as I felt his erection grow under my touch. I wanted to drive him crazy—to make him go wild. I wanted to take us both to the edge and then leap into the chasm with him.

I wanted the man. And I wanted everything that came with him.

I drew in a breath, feeling suddenly overwhelmed. I tilted my head back a bit, wanting to meet his eyes. But his were closed, and the expression of pure pleasure that colored his face gave me such a rush of feminine power that one touch to my clit would have sent me tumbling over the edge.

I used my tongue to tease the head of his cock, lightly stroking his glans, then using the tip to circle the head in a way that all those intimate magazine articles swore would drive your man crazy. If his deep, guttural groan was any indication, those articles were dead-on perfect.

He shifted his weight, using only one hand to support his body as he leaned back. With his other, he threaded his fingers through my hair. I tensed, then forced myself to relax. I wanted this. And even more I wanted Cole to know how much I wanted to give him pleasure—however he deemed to take it.

With the pressure of his hand to the back of my head, I took his cock deep, then drew back, sucking and licking, my head bobbing in time with the sound of his breathing and with the rhythm of his hand upon me. He was hard and tight and so damn close, and with each thrust of his hand to my head he made me take him deeper, harder, until I was certain that he would come right then, right there, and I really wasn't sure that I could handle the force of his explosion, but god help me I wanted to try.

But then he stopped, pulling my mouth off him, then scooting back onto the bed.

I looked up, afraid that he'd once again feared injuring me. But it wasn't worry or fear or anger I saw in his eyes. It was bold, hot, blatant need.

"On the bed," he said, his voice raw and edgy. "On the bed and on your knees."

I complied, not sure what he had in mind, but willing to go wherever he wanted. I was so wet I could feel my arousal between my thighs, and even the brush of air between my legs made sparks shiver through me.

I did as he asked and got on the bed on my knees with my legs slightly spread. My upper arms rested on the bed so that my back was flat, like a table. My breasts felt thick and heavy, and I desperately wanted to touch myself. To stroke my nipples. To lift a hand and slide it back between my legs. To feel how wet I was and know that it was Cole who'd brought me to such heights of arousal and pleasure.

The bed shifted as he stood, and I turned my head to see him looking at me. "This is the picture I keep in my head," he said. "You on your knees, open and ready and desperate for me."

"Yes," I murmured.

"Do you remember the first time you were like this? My house. You'd stormed in all wildness and bluster."

"Of course I remember."

"I'm amazed I've had any other thought in my head since the first moment I touched you. You fill me up, Kat, and I can't stand the thought that you're not yet mine completely."

"But I am."

"You're not," he said. "But you will be. Do you trust me, baby?"

"You know I do."

"Good. Because I'm going to fuck you hard tonight. I'm going to claim you. I'm not going to leave even the slightest doubt in your mind that you belong to me." He leaned over me, stroking his hands along my bare back, and that touch ricocheted through me, making me feel connected. Complete. And very much alive.

Somehow he'd stripped his jeans and briefs all the way off, and his erection pressed hard against me, the tip teasing my sex as he thrust just slightly into me. Just enough to make me gasp and want. Then the bed shifted as he got on to kneel behind me and I felt the press of his cock at my ass, hard and insistent and just a little terrifying.

I must have sucked in air, because he shifted away, and I heard myself moan with disappointment.

"My girl wants me to take her there," he said, reading me perfectly.

"Yes," I said, voicing a desire I hadn't fully understood.

"Good," he said, then bent to whisper in my ear. "So do I."

Three simple words, and yet the heat from them spread through me, making me even needier than I already was.

"Stay," he said, then left the bed for a moment before coming back with the padded envelope that had been delivered with my closing documents. He'd come around the bed so that he faced me now, and with a little bit of a flourish, he ripped open the envelope, then reached in and pulled out something that looked like a small vibrator, only more conical and with a flange on top.

"Do you know what this is?" he asked, setting it on the bed in front of me.

I nodded.

His brows rose. "Really? Tell me."

"It's a butt plug," I said, shooting for a matter-of-fact tone but failing miserably. "I already told you I'm not innocent."

He laughed. "So you did. But have you ever used one?" He moved beside me, then trailed his fingers softly down my back and over the swell of my ass. "Has anything ever penetrated this sweet, tight ass?" Gently, he spread my butt cheeks, then pressed his fingertip to the rim of my anus.

I sucked in air, surprised by the shock of the contact and the jolt of pleasure that seemed to shoot through me, like a preamble of things to come. "No," I said. "I told you. Never. No one. Nothing."

"Exactly what I wanted to hear."

He reached around me for the bag, then pulled out a small bottle of lube. He flipped the lid, put some on his fingertip, and then slowly stroked the sensitive skin between my ass and my vagina, each tender movement making the storm that was building inside me rage wilder until I wasn't sure how much longer I could stand it.

"Cole." I ground out his name. "Please."

"Please what?"

"I—you know."

"Please this?" he asked, then slowly inserted his well-lubed fingertip into my rear.

I gasped, then bit my lower lip, astounded by the wash of pleasure that crashed over me. "Yes," I said. "Oh, god, yes."

He reached for the plug, and as I watched he spread lube on it. I was still on hands and knees. Still vulnerable to him. Still wide open. And everything about the moment turned me on. I wanted to feel everything he had to offer—I wanted him to take me as far as I could possibly go. I wanted everything.

I wanted Cole.

I tilted my head up, then turned so that I could meet his eyes, certain that he could read my thoughts. For a moment, that's all there was, that connection between us, then he bent over and pressed a kiss between my shoulder blades even as his hand slid down to my ass and he teased me with the plug, not putting it in, but touching me just enough to rile me up.

"I'm not going to fuck you here—not tonight. But I am going to fuck you with it inside you. I want you completely full. I want to watch you come knowing that I've taken you completely. That every sensation is at my pleasure and subject to my command. Do you understand?"

"Yes." The word was wrenched out of me, my body tense, my sex already throbbing with demand.

He slipped his finger inside me first. Slowly, almost teasingly, until my muscles relaxed. It didn't hurt—on the contrary, there was something wickedly erotic about being touched there, being fucked there. My sex clenched in time with his gentle thrusts, and my nipples had hardened to painful nubs.

With his other hand, Cole stroked my clit, teasing me by refusing to penetrate me despite my very desperate pleas. Worse, he tormented and played with me just enough to have me climbing toward orgasm. Then he backed off so that I was nothing more than passion and want and need.

I would have cursed him, but I was too destroyed to manage it.

"Frustrated?"

"Cole." His name came out part plea, part whine.

He chuckled. "All the way to the edge and back, baby. And only when I'm certain that you're teetering on the cusp am I going to bury myself in you and feel you explode around me. But right now . . ."

He trailed off, his voice taking on a teasing tone. Then he withdrew his finger from my rear as I moaned the loss of contact, of a sweet sensation that before this night I hadn't even realized I craved.

"Don't worry, baby," he said, with intimate understanding of my moods and desires. "We're not done yet."

Gently, his lube-soaked fingers stroked me, opening me, and then I felt the pressure—not painful, but still intense—as he slowly thrust the plug inside me. I gasped, feeling full and, dammit, wanting to be fuller. Wanting all of it. Wanting all of him.

"Cole." I tried to say more, but I'd lost words. I was too swept away by sensation.

"Imagine it's me. My cock, teasing you. Stretching you. Taking you as far as you can go."

"Yes," I said, the word emerging on a groan.

"Turn over, baby," he said. "Turn around and sit on the edge of the bed. Legs apart, hands on your knees. I want to see how turned on you are."

I did as he asked, my pulse quickening from the sensation of my body's weight against the plug working to thrust it deeper inside me. I sucked in air, steadying myself, then spread my legs even wider as I drew confidence from the look of pure, undiluted passion I saw in his eyes.

"Do you like it? The way it feels? The way it fills you?"

"Yes," I admitted.

"Tell me what you want."

"You," I said. "I want you inside me."

"Like this?" He moved to stand in front of me, then reached down to stroke my sex and thrust a finger deep inside me.

I groaned, so on edge it was a wonder I didn't explode. "Yes. No. Oh, god, Cole, please."

"Please what?"

"Please fuck me."

"It would be my pleasure," he said. "But not yet. I don't think you're quite ready yet."

"You've lost your mind," I protested. "I'm not sure I've ever been more ready."

He just smiled the kind of smile that suggested he had a secret, then picked up the padded envelope again. One by one, he took things out. A silver chain connected by two small metal clips. A coil of hemp rope. And, of course, he'd already removed the plug and the lube.

I licked my lips, unable to hide my amusement. "Seriously? You had these delivered with my closing documents?" I looked up at him. "I'm not going to ask why—that part I get. But how?"

"It's amazing what you can arrange on short notice in a town like LA if you're willing to pay for the service."

I lifted my brows. "I don't know if I should be impressed or mortified," I said, but the words were only for show. My skin was hot, my nipples tight. My sex burned with need of him, and the stretched, full feeling in my ass only made the desire burn that much hotter.

Cole glanced at my breasts, then lazily continued his inspection up and down my body. A slow smile spread across his face. "You're impressed," he said. "Shall I slide my finger into your cunt to prove it?"

I made a noise that was probably a yes.

He chuckled. "No, I don't think so. Not yet." He took the rope. "Shall I show you what I can do with this? Shall I explain in intimate detail just how this rope is going to make you come?"

I couldn't speak. Hell, I could barely nod. But the answer was yes. A huge, desperate, demanding yes.

He took my hand, then gently tugged me to my feet. I stood naked in front of him, my body on fire. I felt wild and wanton— as if he could fuck me all night and I still wouldn't be satisfied.

And then, as he began to take the rope and move around me—as I felt the rough brush of the hemp against my waist as he knotted the cord into a sort of makeshift belt, another set of emotions joined the mix. Curiosity. Eagerness. *Passion*.

There was no denying that he had a plan, and so help me I wanted to experience every sweet second of it. But I was on edge, too, not knowing what he intended. Not understanding why he had leashed me.

And that edge only added to the excitement.

"It's like a belt, you see," Cole said, running his finger around my waist where the double strand of hemp was nice and snug. "Right here is where I'm going to draw it under you," he said, and then proceeded to thread the two lengths of rope that had been behind me through my legs to my front.

He pulled it tight, making me gasp—and then making me almost come when he positioned each rope on either side of my vulva, so that the cording essentially rubbed against my inner thighs, but was also tight enough to keep some pressure on my sex.

"Tell me how that feels."

"It's strange," I said. "It's good. There's pressure, and there's awareness. It makes me wet. It also—" I cut myself off with a shake of my head.

"No," he said. "No secrets. I want to know everything."

"It makes me hot to know you're binding me," I said, not quite able to look him in the eye as I spoke. "To know that I'm completely at your mercy. I trust you," I added, meeting his eyes. "More completely than you probably realize. But that doesn't change the fact that this is still—"

"Dangerous?"

I nodded as heat flooded my cheeks. "And that just makes it

hotter," I finished, my voice little more than a whisper, as if revealing that most intimate truth would push me over the edge. That it was the final secret that would cost me everything and leave me totally open to him. Totally vulnerable.

But I wanted that—so help me, I wanted to be vulnerable to him. I wanted everything with him. I wanted to go as far as we could go together, and then I wanted to take it even further.

I knew that about myself with unerring certainty. But more than that, I wanted this man, fully and completely. I wanted to see what was inside him. To understand his needs and his desires.

I wanted him to open himself to me. And I could only hope and pray that by opening myself to him—by trusting him completely—that he would trust me in turn.

As my thoughts circled around, Cole adjusted the rope, tying a knot that brought the two separate strings together. Then he positioned that knot right over my clit before continuing to secure the end of the rope to the section that encircled my waist.

The end result was similar to wearing crotchless panties—if those panties were made out of rope and designed to stimulate with the slightest motion.

"You move, you even breathe, and this will drive you just a little crazy."

"It already does," I confessed. I felt the pressure of the knot rubbing against my sensitive flesh, and sending waves of pleasure rolling through me. But it was a frustrating sensation, because while it felt damn good, it also wasn't building, and I knew that the torment of this particular setup was to get a woman hot—but to never quite get her to come.

"It's a little evil, isn't it?" I asked wryly.

He chuckled. "Just a bit. What can I say?" he asked, sliding his hand down to cup my sex and making my body arch in response and demand. "I like you primed and ready—but you only get to come when I say."

"If I ever said you were a nice man, I take it back."

"I'm not a nice man, baby. I really thought you knew."

I almost grinned, but was quickly distracted by the way Cole had hooked his fingers under the rope just above my belly button and was guiding me back to the bed. In one fluid motion, he picked me up, then held me close in his arms. He murmured my name and then, before I had the chance to lose myself in the sweet sensuality of being held by this man, he put me gently on the bed.

Gently, however, wasn't gently enough, because as he laid me down, the cord that stretched so intimately beneath me shifted over my clit at the same time that the weight of my body pressed against the plug in my ass. I gasped, then clung to him. "Do you know what you're doing to me?" I asked, my voice heavy with arousal. "Do you have any idea how primed you've made me?"

"I intend to take you much further," he said, then reached for the two pillows at the head of the bed. He pulled them down, then situated them under my hips, raising me up while my torso angled slightly down to the mattress.

He spread my legs, and the motion caused that damnable knot to tease me mercilessly, sending heat coursing through me, making me wild and frustrated and itchy and so damned needy I wanted to scream. "Please." I forced my voice to stay level. "Christ, Cole, please."

He eased between my legs, his cock erect, and his face reflecting so much desire and adoration, that I thought I could come simply from the way he looked at me.

"Next time I want to bind your arms behind you, flip you over, and take you from behind. But tonight I want to see your face when you come, and when . . ." He trailed off, and I saw mischief in his eyes.

"Cole?"

"Tell me you want to go further," he said, his voice shifting to a new level of intensity that excited me all the more. "Tell me you liked my palm on your ass, my hand twisting your nipples. Tell me you liked it rough."

I felt my sex clench simply in response to his words and his tone. "You know that I did."

"Tell me," he repeated.

"I liked it. I liked it all."

"Baby, I want to give you every form of pleasure I know, but some of them aren't reached except by passing through the curtain of pain. I'm going to take you there. Take you high, I promise you. Do you trust me?"

"More than anything."

He reached beside us on the bed for the chain and held it up for me. The chain itself was gold, with two gold alligator clips at either end. Except they weren't really alligator clips because there were no teeth. Just a smooth, waxy plastic.

"The boundary between pleasure and pain shifts. What can be painful one moment," he said as he opened the first clip and secured it to my erect nipple, "can turn to pleasure the next."

As he spoke, fire seemed to shoot through my nipple, and I had to bite my lip to keep from crying out. It hurt—damn right it hurt. But there was something else underneath, and by the time he had fastened the clamp to my other nipple, the first was humming. A warm, wonderful sensation that made my whole body seem larger than life and desperately, wonderfully aware.

"Pain," Cole said simply, giving the clamp a little flick with his finger and making me groan as that warm sensuality ramped up, bringing heat and fire that maybe hurt but maybe didn't.

"And then there's pleasure," Cole said, as my body sank in response to the fading sensation, moving through that curtain Cole had described to the wondrous blanket of pleasure that waited beyond.

I sucked in air, awed by these reactions. By how sensitive my skin was. By how erotic the simplest touch had become, and by how even the caress of the air against my flesh held the intensity of a lover.

"I want to give you both," Cole said, his expression almost rapturous as he gazed at me, my legs spread, my back arched, my sex bound, my nipples clamped. I was an object for his pleasure—and for my own. And that thought alone sent waves of delight coursing through me, making my already sensitive clit swell and harden, so that each movement, each breath was torture as that damnable knot rubbed against me and the plug worked in tandem to remind me of just how completely I was his.

"More and more," Cole said. "Not tonight, but over time. I want to take you as far as you can go, Kat. Tell me you want that, too. Tell me you want everything I can give you."

"Yes," I moaned. "Oh, god, yes."

"I'm going to fuck you now," he said, and I almost wept with relief.

He lowered himself over me, and I almost passed out from the wave of intense pleasure when he positioned himself and then readjusted the rope so that it would stroke his cock on either side as he thrust into me.

He did just that, and I wasn't expecting how the movement of the rope with his cock would intensify the motion of the knot against my clit. Or how the impact of him thrusting so damn hard into me would shift the plug in my ass, setting off a riot of sensations in me. Or how the building pressure of the nipple clamp combined with every other sensation would shoot sparks through my body, making me electrically charged, so that even the slightest brush against my skin would totally light me up.

I was there—right there and ready to explode faster than I'd ever done in my life, and I gasped, calling for Cole. Needing and wanting and demanding. And through that gray haze of sexual drunkenness I became aware that he had taken hold of the chain. And as I arced up toward release, he yanked on the chain from the center with enough force to pull the clamps off my nipples in one violent, fluid motion.

Pain shot through my breasts, but that pain translated almost immediately to delight. And in that gap—that tiny gap between the two—the world exploded around me and I came more violently than I'd ever come before. I was desperate. Wild. My sex clenched around Cole's cock, bringing him right along with me to the hardest, fastest, hottest orgasm I had ever experienced. One that left me breathless and exhausted and completely astounded.

"Wow," I said when the world returned to me. "That was—that just was."

He chuckled. "Yes. It certainly was," he said, and then kissed me, hard and deep. The kind of kiss that marked a woman in a way that even wild sex couldn't manage.

He pulled me close to him and held me tight. I was still bound, and that made me feel more small and fragile. As if he were holding me safe, keeping me shielded from whatever awful things might lurk in the world.

I floated there a moment on a wave of contentment, but his words kept playing back in my head. "More, you said," I murmured. "Will you tell me what the more is?"

"Eager?" he said, with a tease in his voice.

"Maybe."

"I won't tell you, but I'll show you. Not all at once, but when you're ready. Trust me, Kat. Trust me to make this journey exceptional for you."

"I do." I hesitated, then asked, "Will you take me to the Firehouse when we get back to Chicago?"

It may have been my imagination, but I thought that he stiffened slightly. "Maybe," he said. "I haven't decided."

"Oh."

I'm not sure why his response disappointed me, but it did. "Is it because of Michelle? Why you're not sure, I mean?"

He eased back, then rolled me over so that I was facing him. "No," he said. "Not because of Michelle."

I nodded, knowing I should drop it. I could tell that much just from the tone of his voice. But somehow, I couldn't quite seem to back away. "Were you two together?"

"No."

"Oh." I licked my lips. "I saw you the night of the gala. That argument with Conrad. I don't know. I just thought . . ." I trailed off into a lame shrug.

"Conrad Pierce is a fucking asshole," Cole said. "He was trying to recruit some of my girls into prostitution. I made it clear that wasn't going to happen."

I recalled Cole's fury that night, and decided that it was perfectly understandable. "Was he trying to recruit Michelle, too?"

Cole exhaled. "No," he said. And then a moment later, he added, "Christ, Kat. She works in that trade, okay?"

"Oh. Right." I hesitated a moment, then pressed on. "Do you pay her? To fuck her, I mean."

I saw a muscle in his jaw twitch, as if he was trying hard to keep a grip on control. "Can we quit with the twenty questions?"

"I'm sorry." I rolled away, suddenly chilled by the gulf I felt growing between us. "Really. Never mind."

"Shit." I heard him exhale, then felt the press of his hand against my shoulder. "Shit," he repeated, this time more softly. "I'm the one who's sorry."

He drew in a breath, and the irony of the situation—me naked and bound with a plug in my rear while we discussed another woman—really wasn't lost on me. "I don't want to have secrets from you." He eased me over so that I was facing him again, and the intensity I saw in his face nearly did me in.

"But I do have secrets," he continued. "I won't lie to you. But I want to start chipping away at them. So let me start by saying that I don't pay Michelle, but I do fuck her. Or I did. I haven't touched her since you. Haven't wanted to. Haven't needed to."

He looked at me, and I felt that sweet ping in my heart. "Really?" The word tasted like hope. More, it tasted like love.

"I told you, Kat. You fill me up. It may take some time for me to figure out what that means, how it manifests. But I know that it's true. Can you be patient, baby? Can you let me find the words my own way, in my own time?"

"I can," I said, because at the heart of it the past didn't matter. The Cole I'd fallen for was the one I saw in front of me. All the rest was just backstory and gossip. And all of that could wait.

twenty

"Cole?"

"Mmm." He sounded far away and yet right beside me.

"Before you fall asleep, do you think you could untie me and, you know, all the rest?"

I heard the low rumble of his chuckle. "I don't know. It's tempting to just keep you like this, bound for my pleasure, mine to take whenever I want."

"I already am," I said. "You don't need the ropes for that."

I saw the emotion in his eyes in response to my words. And when he removed the plug and gently untied me, I thought that I'd never known anything more erotic than the simple experience of being tended to by this man.

Once I was unbound, we lay atop the covers, legs twined so that we were facing each other. I traced my fingertips over his chest, enjoying the way his skin felt against mine. "Thank you,"

I finally said. "For showing me this. For showing me that I like it, too."

"Oh, baby." He brushed my cheek, and though there was no mistaking the tenderness in his voice, I couldn't help but see the storm clouds in his eyes.

"What did I say?"

He sat up, leaning over in the bed as he took two long, deep breaths. "I'm glad you like it. There's nothing I want more in this world than to give you pleasure."

He stood up, then turned back so that he was facing the bed. I was sitting up now, wary because of the measured tone of his words. I wanted to beg him to explain what the trouble was, but I also knew that he would. He just needed to take his time, and I just needed to be patient.

"It's not a question of *like* for me. It's a need. A requirement. Hell, it's my goddamn sustenance." His eyes were locked on my face, and I don't know what he saw there. Understanding? Maybe a little. Mostly, I wanted to simply hug him, because no matter what I did or didn't understand, I knew that he was hurting. And all I wanted—all I would ever want again—was to see this man happy.

"I want to help," I told him simply. "I want to understand."

"I know," he said. "I want that, too. I told you I didn't want secrets, and I meant it. But that doesn't mean it's easy."

"No," I said. "It doesn't. I think the hardest thing I've ever done was tell you about Roger."

"You're stronger than me, Katrina Laron. But then again, I've always known that."

"And that's just bullshit," I said. "Just tell me. No matter how hard or how horrible or how complicated, just find the beginning and start there."

He looked at me for a long moment, then pulled me close and kissed me hard. Then he sat down on the edge of the bed, and I scooted over to sit beside him, one leg tucked beneath me so that I was at an angle to face him.

"You have Roger living in the shadows of your life," he began, his matter-of-fact words somehow managing to drip with pain. "I have Anita."

I reached out and took his hand, then held it tight in mine. I said nothing, but I knew that he'd continue when he was ready.

"I didn't think I'd ever talk about her. I wanted to forget her. To pretend the bitch didn't exist."

"But she did exist," I said softly. "And even if you could forget her, it wouldn't change whatever she did to you. But it helps to talk about it." I managed a small, supportive smile. "In case you were wondering, I have it on good authority that talking about childhood shit with someone you care about helps a lot."

He held tight to my hand for a moment, then released me and stood up. After a moment, he moved to the window and spread the curtains wide. It was late now, the sky pitch-black, the stars unable to push through the curtain of ambient light that rose like a halo to surround the city.

Beyond Cole, I could make out the silhouette of buildings, most just a few stories tall, that filled the view before ending abruptly at a dark expanse of ocean that seemed to reach up and merge with the deep black of the night sky.

"I was eleven when I got in tight with the gangs. Young, but not for that life. Especially not for a kid like me who needed cash. Because it was just me and my grandmother and my aunt, and it was me who took care of them. There was no other man, not who stuck, and I don't think I would have relied on someone else, anyway. How could I when my grandmother had taken me in and worked herself to the bone taking in laundry and sewing when my bitch of a mother had dumped me on her? And then was left with nothing when her mind started to go?"

"Where is your mother?"

"Dead," Cole said, without any emotion at all. "She was a junkie and a whore, and she died when I was five. And good riddance to the bitch. She'd already poisoned herself. Poisoned me. She drank, smoked crack, did god knows what when she was pregnant with me, and then gave birth to a scrawny, screaming baby who was as much an addict as she was."

I sat frozen, completely clueless as to how to respond to something like that. What I wanted to do was stand up and hug him. What I did instead, was simply give him space.

"Fuck," he said after he ran his hands over his head and sucked in air. "I didn't mean to get off on all that. Point is, my grandmother took care of me practically from the day I was born. Made me work, made me think, made me something better than I would have been. So when early-onset Alzheimer's started to kick in, I knew I'd be the one to take care of her and my aunt even though I was only eleven."

"Not an easy thing for a kid," I said.

"No, not easy. And damned near impossible if you want to come by the money legitimately. But if you're not too picky, then there's always the gangs. And since the gangs are there—right under your nose from the first moment you set foot in the world—they already feel like home. Hell, I was practically part of the Dragons from the moment I slid out of the womb, but when I was eleven I made it official."

"The Dragons? That was the name of the gang?"

He nodded.

"That's why you have a dragon tattoo."

"No. I have the tattoo because I got out." He turned so that I had a better look at his back. "The gang sign was a small dragon on the right shoulder. See it?"

I peered, then found an outline of a dragon hidden inside the bolder, wilder artwork of the beautiful creature that covered Cole's back.

"This one's mine. I drew it. I designed it. I hired the artist to do the needlework. And the most important part was covering up that mark. Making my own symbol."

"It's wonderful," I said, feeling absurdly proud that he had not only done that, but that he'd thought of it. "You took something horrible and made it beautiful."

"I tried," he said. "But the horrible still creeps in around the edges. I'm getting ahead of myself," he said, before I could ask what he meant. "I was talking about the gang. We were into everything, but drugs mostly. That and guarding our turf and all the bullshit that goes along with that life. Even then I knew it was bullshit," he said, meeting my eyes. "But I also knew it was the only option I had."

"It must have been so hard." I could picture him, so young, his innocence stripped from him. Tears pricked my eyes, and I brutally brushed them away.

"Wasn't easy," he said. "But I didn't mean for this to be a lesson in gang culture."

"You wanted to tell me about Anita," I prompted.

"She was my rite of passage," he said, in the kind of flat voice that made me want to pull him close and hold him tight.

"What does that mean?"

"It means that no one gets a cut of any real income without being fully inducted. And no one is inducted until they've popped their cherry. More than that, though. One night wasn't enough. No, you had to be fully initiated. And that's where Anita came in."

"She was your first."

"In so many ways." His voice was raw. Hateful. "She liked pain. Serious pain. Giving and receiving. Cigarette burns. Wire pulled tight around your cock. Knives. Straws jammed up your urethra. God knows what up your ass. She was a sadistic, masochistic bitch, and she tied every single goddamn orgasm to one of her fucked up games."

I shook my head, not really willing to believe that what he was saying could be true. "She made you—"

"There's a parabola of pain, you know. After a period of time, it turns to pleasure. Not just the kind of pain I've shared with you. But real pain. Torture pain. The kind of pain that pulls state secrets and turns spies. But you cross a line, and that torture doesn't work anymore, because the victim has slipped over into euphoria. So if you want to fuck up somebody's sexual wiring, then you take a kid—a kid who's barely had a hard-on much less an orgasm—and you wind him up and jack him off over and over. You make it hurt, then you make it feel good, then you make it hurt again—" His voice had gone hard, and now it broke. "*Shit,*" he said.

"You don't have to tell me any more," I said.

"But I do, because with me there was more than just the way her fucked up games messed with my mind and rewired everything that gets me hard. She pushed my limits with sex—and couple that with the shit my mother left me with—impulse control problems, anger management, all the bullshit that lingers when you've got that goddamn 'crack baby' label. Makes me like a goddamn bomb just waiting to explode and you can damn well bet that sex is one of the triggers."

He paced to the end of the room, then came back and started the circle again. I watched him, my heart breaking for the boy he'd been and the man he'd become.

Finally, he stopped in front of me. "Bottom line is I'm fucked up."

"No," I said, standing so that I could press my hands to his face. "The bottom line is that you're the strongest man I know."

"Kat—"

"No," I said fiercely. "Don't you dare argue with me. Maybe you are fucked up. So what? I mean, who isn't? But you're not screwed up like that. You don't take it that far. You don't explode—not really. You don't hurt yourself or me like that."

I could see that he wanted to interrupt, and so I pressed a fingertip to his lips. "You've defied your past in so many ways,

Cole." I kept my voice gentle, hoping he could understand how much I meant these words. "You're not the least bit like Anita. She's inhuman. But you're not. You're just the opposite," I said as I drew my arms around him and pressed my cheek to his chest. "I know, because you're the best thing that ever happened to me."

His body was stiff against mine at first, and then I felt his lips brush my hair and his arms go around my waist. He relaxed, his body molding to mine. "Christ, Kat," he said. "You unravel me."

My heart swelled, and I clung to him a moment longer, then pulled back so that I could see his face. "Come back to bed," I said. "I want you to hold me."

"How could I ever let go?"

I moved to the bed and drew him down, then lost myself to the simple feel of his arms around me and his skin against mine. "I like this. Just being next to you. It's nice."

"Yes," he said after a moment. "It is." He stroked his fingertips lightly over my shoulder. "The hard and the wild burns through you, so intense you never want to let it go. But these soft moments . . . they're what give you the fuel to burn in the first place."

I shivered, moved almost to tears by his words. "You really are an artist," I said, my voice soft. "You paint beauty not just in pictures but in words."

"Maybe. Or maybe it's just that you're my muse."

Since I liked that thought, I closed my eyes and tried to drift off. One question kept bugging me, though, and so I finally gave in to my curiosity. "Cole? Are you still awake?"

"Mmm."

"About the pain—do you need it, too? I mean, being on the receiving end?"

For a moment he was silent, and when he answered, his words were oddly flat, as if he feared he might scare me off if he made too much of the question, much less the answer. "I have," he said. "But that's not something I'd ask you to do."

I thought about that, then rolled over. I pressed my hand to his chest, wanting to feel the beat of his heart thrumming through me. I was awed by all he'd told me. Not only the bare facts but the emotions and need behind it.

"If you do need it," I whispered, "you only have to ask me. You say I'm yours, Cole, but you're mine, too." I drew in a breath, hoping he understood how completely I meant these words. "And I will always give you what you need."

"I know," he said. "Thank you."

I nodded, satisfied. He still hadn't said that he loved me despite my confession. But he'd told me his secrets. He'd trusted me with his past.

He'd opened his heart, and he'd let me claim it.

And with a man like Cole, who holds his secrets close, that was the essence of love.

twenty-one

I woke to Cole's large hands brushing over my naked body.

"Mmm. Good morning."

"Go back to sleep," he whispered. "I'm heading downtown to meet with Charles. I didn't want to wake you, but I couldn't leave without touching you."

I took his hand and pressed my lips to his palm. "I'm glad." I propped myself up on my elbow. "You sure you don't want me to come?"

"To come?" he repeated with a devious gleam in his eye. "Always, and about a thousand different ways. But if you mean to join me downtown, then no. It's not necessary. Not if you trust me."

"You know I do."

"I'll tell you the entire plan once it's firm. But I want to make sure everything is on track. That Charles didn't come across a snag." He reached out and ran a strand of my hair through his fingers. "I want to take care of this for you, Kat. I want you to know that you can come to me and say 'I need this,' and be certain that whatever it is, I will make it right for you."

I felt a tightening in my chest, a sweet sensation, like a hug to my soul. "I already know that." I rose up on my knees to kiss him lightly. "Now go do your thing."

I watched him go, sighing a bit because he was wearing a suit and, honestly, the man looked too damned amazing. Once the door clicked shut behind him, I considered going back to sleep, but the allure of Southern California was too much, and within the hour I was showered, changed, and full up on a bagel, cream cheese, and at least a gallon of coffee.

I didn't have a car, but I did have cash, and I asked one of the taxi drivers to simply drive me around Beverly Hills. It turned out to be even better than I anticipated, as he knew the flats intimately, and pointed out at least a dozen houses that had once been owned by various studio darlings from the Golden Age of Hollywood.

He went up into the hills next, and the drive was much less interesting, since most of the homes were behind massive stone fences or set so far back from iron gates that there was nothing to see. But once we reached Mulholland Drive, I was in awe. The day was unusually clear according to my driver, and I could see all of the west side spread out below me, not to mention the roofs of some homes that looked like they could house every resident of a small country, but were probably only occupied by one couple, one child, and a very spoiled dog.

By the time I returned to the Beverly Wilshire, I was deep in thought about real estate and the Chicago market, and how I could position myself to sell houses like that—the kind that could keep a commissioned agent living high for a solid year.

I half-regretted my plan to abandon the grift in favor of this new career. If I combined the two, I could probably make a killing.

The thought amused me, and I was grinning when I got on the elevator. My grin widened when I checked my phone and realized it was almost one. With any luck, Cole would be waiting for me in the room.

He wasn't, though, and I swallowed my disappointment as I stepped inside and tried to decide what I wanted to do. I was debating between going downstairs for a drink or taking a taxi down to the beach in Santa Monica and simply texting Cole to meet me there, when I noticed that the message light on the phone was blinking.

I knew it wasn't from Cole, since he'd call me on my cell. But I hit the button to play the messages on speaker just in case it was important, then went a little bit numb when I heard the soft, female voice.

"Hey, Cole sweetie! It's Bree. I can't wait to see you, but I need to change our plans up a bit. I left a message on your cell phone, too, but it keeps going straight to voicemail without any sort of greeting from you, and I'm afraid I wrote the number down wrong and I've been bothering someone else."

She laughed then, light and airy, and I felt a sudden need to punch her in the nose. Who the hell was this woman? And what plans was she talking about?

"Anyway, hopefully you'll get one of my messages. Call me back, okay? Love you! Oh, and here's my number in case you need it again," she added, then rattled off a number in the 310 area code, which I'd recently learned included LA.

I pressed the button to end the message, then just sat on the bed staring at the phone like it was a wild thing about to bite me. Then I played the message again. And then one more time after that.

It never changed. Never gave a clue who this woman was or why she was calling my boyfriend "sweetie."

And the message sure as hell didn't give me a hint as to why Cole hadn't said a single thing about her.

I told myself that Cole was not sleeping with this woman—he'd told me as much, right? No Michelle. No anyone else.

So it was ridiculous for me to be getting worked up.

Except, dammit, I was worked up. And even if this woman was a former fuck buddy, shouldn't he have told me?

And considering that my name was on the room registration just as big and as bold as Cole's, didn't that mean that I hadn't violated any major rules of etiquette by listening to it?

I banged the heel of my hand against my forehead in the hopes that I might actually knock some sense into myself. Because I could either sit there for another half hour and make up another dozen or so ridiculous excuses—or I could simply pick up the phone, dial the woman's number, and politely explain that Cole was at a meeting. And then equally politely ask who the hell she was.

I chose door number two—then almost choked when the voice that answered was Cole's.

"Kat," he said, his tone apologetic. "I'm sorry I'm late. And I'm sorry for what you must be thinking."

I opened my mouth to reply, realized I didn't have a clue what to say, and shut it again.

"Catalina?" The apology was gone, replaced by worry. "Are you there?"

"Yes." I cleared my throat and tried again. "Sure. Yes. I'm here."

"Come on down. There's someone I want you to meet."

"Down? You're here?"

"In the lobby."

"Oh," I said as the universe tentatively righted itself. Because surely he wasn't inviting me down to meet his mistress. "I'll be right there."

When the doors to the elevator opened, I saw Cole standing next to a stunningly beautiful woman with ebony skin, legs that seemed to go on forever, and a friendly, welcoming smile. She looked barely over twenty.

And Cole had his arm around her shoulders.

When he saw me, he shifted, sliding his arm off and replacing it with a proprietary hand to her back.

I stepped off the elevator, my eyes darting from him to her, and I'm certain that my confusion must have shown.

"Katrina Laron, I'd like you to meet my aunt, Bree Crenshaw."

Bree held out her hand, that amazing smile growing even wider. "I am so glad to meet you. Cole just won't shut up about you."

"Bree . . ."

She laughed. "It's true. And if she doesn't already know you adore her then you need to tell her. And if she already knows you should tell her more often."

"Bree's in nursing school," Cole said dryly. "She has a very excellent bedside manner."

I laughed out loud, my earlier angst having completely disappeared. "It's great to meet you, but I thought aunts were older." When Cole had described his gang years to me last night, I'd pictured him taking care of two older women. Now I realized that he must have been like a father to Bree. Or at the very least like a big brother.

Bree hooked her arm through mine as she led the way through the lobby to the elegant bar next to the hotel's signature restaurant. "Let me guess. Only child?"

"Um, yeah."

"I'm Cole's mother's sister. She had him when she was fifteen, then died about five years later." I nodded, remembering what Cole had told me about his mother. "I was born about five years after that." She shrugged. "My mom was really young when she had my sister, and she had complications when she had me."

"She had a stroke during the birth," Cole said. "They think that may have contributed to the Alzheimer's. She had Bree when she was forty-two and a few years later she was pretty much mentally gone."

"That's so sad."

"It is," Bree said. "And that's another reason I'm more like Cole's little sister than his aunt. He pretty much raised me and took care of my mom."

Cole caught my eye, then took my hand. "I should have told you she was younger, but it didn't occur to me," he said, obviously realizing that I'd been thrown a bit off-kilter. "Bree is just Bree, and I didn't think to explain that she was younger."

"Explain?" Bree asked, as sat down at one of the tables in the bar.

"Cole was telling me the story of his life last night," I said.

"Oh, really?" Her brows lifted. "I hope that's true. Cole keeps too much of that stuff to himself, and there's no reason to do that."

"Bree." The warning note in Cole's voice was unmistakable, and I couldn't help but wonder what family secret rattled around in his closet that Bree so fervently believed he should set free. Not Anita. Frankly I doubted that Bree knew *that* secret. But something else. Something that put that clipped, secretive tone in his voice.

"It's not a state secret, Cole. And you know that I think it should be out in the open."

"This isn't a discussion we're having. Not right now. Are we clear?"

She rolled her eyes, and I bit back a grin. Secret or not, I liked the dynamic between these two. It was normal and human and a little bit sweet. On impulse, I reached for his hand, then squeezed tight.

He looked at me, his expression mildly surprised. "Sorry. I love her, but she pushes my buttons."

"She's sitting right here," Bree said.

"You two are wonderful," I said, unable to keep the laughter out of my voice. "I'm so glad to meet you, Bree. Really, I am."

"See that?" Bree said, aiming a triumphant smile toward Cole. "I knew I'd like this girl." She cocked her head and looked at Cole. "Don't mess it up, okay?"

"I'll try my best," he said dryly.

"Don't worry," I added. "I won't let him."

"Good," Bree said. "Between the two of us, there just might be hope for him yet."

After two rounds of drinks and several more rounds of conversation about everything and nothing, Cole and I poured Bree into a taxi, then waved her off as the cab disappeared from view.

"I like her," I said, though I was certain he'd already picked up on that little fact. "She's great."

"She is," he agreed. "And I'm sorry I didn't tell you ahead of time that we might get together with her. I wasn't sure the timing would work out. But Bree's incredibly important to me. And since you are, too, I really wanted you to meet her."

"I'm glad," I said, though the words sounded thick with emotion.

"Don't tell me you didn't know how much you mean to me, Kat. It's hardly a secret that you fill me up." He held his hand out for me, and I took it, then came willingly when he drew me close. "You're my future," he said, "and Bree's my past. It made sense for you to meet."

"You're going to make me cry."

He brushed his thumb under my eye, wiping away an errant tear that had escaped as if to prove my point.

"Walk with me," he said, taking my hand as we walked down the sidewalk. "I wanted you to meet her first, but there's more to the story I told you yesterday. It's not something I talk about, but Bree's right. You need to know. No," he corrected. "I want you to know."

"All right," I said, twining my fingers with his as we started to walk down the pristine Beverly Hills street.

"You know about my rages, the impulse-control issues. You know about the crack and my bitch of a mother and how much it all fucked me up for sex."

"I know what you've told me," I said. "And I still don't think you're fucked up. I think you're you. You're the man I fell in love with, Cole. And that man is solid."

There I went, telling him I loved him again. And he still hadn't said the words back to me. But it didn't matter. He needed to know how I felt. More than that, I needed him to know. I wanted him to have my love to hold tight around him like a blanket when he told me these horrors. So that he could remember that no matter how bad it had been or might be, I would always be there.

And so what if he hadn't said the words back to me? Yes, I wanted to hear them out loud, but the truth was that he said them to me every day. Not in words, but in actions. In the way he talked to me. The way he took care of me. The way he treated me.

I thought of the wicked way that he'd fucked me last night. The myriad of ways in which he'd taken his pleasure. The things he'd done to bring me both pain and pleasure. And more than that, I thought of the reason why.

Because he wanted to take me higher. Because he wanted to mark me as his.

Cole August was in love with me whether he admitted it or not. And that simple reality not only made me happy, it made me proud.

"You didn't know me as a child," Cole continued. "I was wild. Anything would set me off. It was Bree who taught me control. It was Bree who kept me grounded. Not so much because she did anything—hell, for most of that time, she was just a baby. But it was the fact of her. The fact that there was this little person in my life, and I was responsible for her. Because by that time, my grandmother was broken. She was there—but she'd checked out. I was father and brother and best friend all rolled into one for Bree. And for the longest time, she was my world."

"She's great," I said. "I think she's a walking testimonial to your exceptional parenting skills."

"Or to her own exceptional personality."

"That, too," I agreed. "But there's more to the story than your mutual admiration."

He paused under an awning. "Yeah. There is."

I waited, giving him time. Then he reached out and touched my shoulder. Just a simple brush of a finger over the thin material of my shirt. But I knew that he was taking stock. Making sure that I was real and this moment wasn't going to evaporate. "I want to tell you everything," he finally said. "Kat, you have to know—there's no one else I've told all of this to. No one else knows everything that happened with Anita or everything I'm about to tell you. Not even Bree. Not even Tyler and Evan."

That fist that sometimes clenched around my heart started to close again, and I drew in a ragged breath as I nodded. And then, because I couldn't not kiss him, I leaned forward and brushed my lips over his. "Thank you," I said simply.

A small smile touched his lips, but it didn't quite reach his eyes. He'd gone back into memories, and his words when they came seemed far away.

"Bree was raped," he said flatly, without preamble. "Beaten. Worked over like you wouldn't believe."

"Oh, god. Cole, I'm so sorry."

"She was eight years old at the time. *Eight*. I was looking to find a way out. I'd pissed some people off, including a rival gang. Their punishment was for one of their new recruits to earn his stripes by raping that little girl." His voice broke. "They almost destroyed one of the best people you will ever know because of me. Because they wanted to punish *me*."

"It wasn't your fault. *It wasn't*," I repeated more harshly because I wanted him to hear me.

"Maybe not," he said. "But everything that happened afterward was."

"What happened?" I asked, certain that I could guess his answer.

"I lost it," he said. "I completely flew off the handle." He met my eyes. "I killed them. The fucker who raped her, and the co-captains of the gang who'd set him up to do it."

I swallowed, but I didn't say anything. What could I say? That I understood? I did. That the bastards who would do that to a little girl deserved it? I sure as hell thought so, but I knew damn well the courts didn't.

And I knew that Cole had to live with the consequences of his actions each and every day.

"I can't even remember making the decision to do it, but I can remember with absolute clarity how good it felt to smash my fist into their flesh. To feel their bones shatter. To snuff the life from each of them. I liked it, Kat. Hell, I sought it out. I needed it. Because that was the only way to turn off the rage that had burst out of me like a goddamn geyser."

"They tortured a child. You defended her. You stood up for her and went to the mat for her. And because you did, she's grown up to be one hell of a woman."

He didn't say anything, but he seemed to draw in my words like oxygen, as if simply having them there to hold on to made everything else just a little bit easier to handle.

"I was caught, of course. If I'd been even halfway in my head, maybe I could have figured out a way to cover up what I'd done, but I couldn't manage it in the state I was in. I was arrested. I was tried. I was convicted. And that's how I met Evan and Tyler."

"The scared straight camp? They sent you there even with three murder convictions?"

"I had the diagnosed impulse control issues—thank you, crack baby syndrome," he said with disgust. "And there was an experimental program running through the system then. They sealed my record because I was a juvenile and under the terms of the program, if a defendant is later arrested for homicide, the sealed file can be opened and used as evidence in the adult homicide case."

He shrugged. "In other words, I'll never shake my past."

"You don't have to shake it," I said. "You just have to live with it. Like everybody else on the planet. But it's done, and it's behind you. And didn't you once tell me you preferred to live life moving forward?"

"That sounds like something I'd say," he admitted. "That doesn't necessarily make it true or smart."

"Bullshit. You're not going to kill anyone. Your past is sealed up and gone, and it's going to stay that way. You just have to trust yourself to move forward. Or if you can't trust yourself, then trust me. Because I trust you completely, and I'm a very smart woman."

As I hoped, he smiled. But it faded quickly. "I can't imagine killing anyone intentionally now," he said. "But the darkness inside me hasn't gone away. The impulse control issues that nailed me as a kid—as a teenager. They're still all right there, and I know that any moment I can go completely off the rails. It's like spending your life walking on dynamite."

"But you don't go off the rails, Cole. Don't you see?"

"I'm fighting every damn day, Kat."

"But that's the point. You're fighting. You're winning." I slid my arms around his waist and moved in close. "You have more control than you give yourself credit for."

"Someday I'm going to lose that battle and seriously hurt someone." He hooked a finger under my chin and tilted my head up. "What if it's you?"

"Not possible. For one thing, you're not going to lose it. You may not see how strong you are, but I do. For another thing, the only way you'll hurt me is if you leave me." I swallowed, feeling suddenly overwhelmed by emotion. "Don't leave me, Cole," I said, knowing that those words were stripping bare my soul. "Please don't ever leave me."

"No," he said, pulling me close. And though the word that he said was "never," in my heart, I knew that the message was, *I love you.*

twenty-two

Katrina Laron—domestic goddess.

That's how I felt as I stood in the living room of my new house surrounded by pails of paint, drop cloths, brushes, and rollers.

The movers were scheduled for the next morning, and I was hoping to at least get the living room painted so that once the furniture arrived I could assemble one room and feel as though I had accomplished something.

Not that I'd be completely done with that room. I'd still need to deal with the floors, getting curtains, fixing the window panes that seemed likely to stick no matter what the weather, and all the other wonderful, happy, irritating quirks that came with home ownership.

I'd had the place for a grand total of three hours, and I was already desperately, hopelessly in love.

And speaking of desperately, hopelessly in love, I heard the familiar rhythm of Cole's footsteps crossing the front porch, and I turned in time to see him open the screen door and step inside.

He carried two wrapped presents tucked under his arm—one big and one small. His other hand held tight to a toolbox on top of which he was balancing a bundle of roses.

"For me?"

"No, I just like to carry presents and roses whenever I take my tools out. Makes the repair work seem more festive."

I rolled my eyes, and hurried to help him before he dropped everything—and to get a kiss.

"Congratulations," he said, after he brushed his lips tenderly over mine. "You look beautiful. Home ownership suits you."

Considering my hair was shoved up into a baseball cap and I was wearing ancient paint-splattered cargo pants and an old Disneyland T-shirt, I knew he was lying. But I still appreciated the thought.

"I don't have anything to put the flowers in yet," I said, looking around the room as if a stunning crystal vase would magically materialize. "But I think there's a soda cup from Taco Bell in the trash. We can use that."

He went to dig it out and fill it with water while I unwrapped the flowers from paper and plastic. We put them on the hearth, then stood back and admired them.

"Definitely makes the place more homey."

"There's more," he said, nodding at the other two presents that were now on the floor.

I grinned up at him, feeling like a kid at Christmas. "You didn't have to, but I'm thrilled you did."

He laughed, then pointed to the larger, flat one. "That one first."

I picked it up, easily able to tell that there was a framed piece of artwork hidden beneath the wrapping paper. "I hope it's a Cole August original," I said. "Those things are just going to shoot up in value."

"The man's got talent," he said. "Go ahead. Open it."

I did, then gasped when I saw the image on the canvas—the image of me. This one was different from the one that hung in the gallery, and I hadn't seen it in his studio. I was naked, my back facing the viewer, my hands flat against a red wall. My legs were spread just a bit, not so much as to be obscene, but enough to be suggestive. And there was no mistaking my tattoo. For that matter, anyone who might not be able to read it could easily pick the words up from the delicate script on the wall. *Ad Astra*. To the stars.

"It's amazing," I said sincerely. "Stunning and provocative. How on earth did you do this so quickly? I mean, when did you find the time?"

"It's not new. I painted it last year." He met my eyes, smiling slightly when he saw my obvious surprise. "It's been hanging in my office at Destiny. I thought it was better suited for here."

"A year? But—" I glanced back at the portrait, my throat suddenly tight with tears. "We wasted a lot of time, Cole."

He came to me, then drew me into his arms. "Then we'll have to be sure not to waste any more."

For a moment, he just held me. Then he kissed the top of my head. "I want you to open the other one, too, but first I have some news. The land deal's done, deeds filed, property away from Ilya Muratti's hot little hands and into the coffers of the newly formed Casino Building and Investment Trust, of which Damien Stark is the primary shareholder and I am the president and secondary investor."

"And Damien doesn't mind going head-to-head with Muratti?"

"We're not. We didn't double-cross him, didn't steal the

property out from under him. We bought it in an arm's-length transaction from a seller who had been reluctant to sell to Muratti."

He took my hand, then lifted it to his lips and kissed it. "As an added precaution, Damien asked his attorney to call Michael Muratti, Ilya's son. Stark has a lot of connections, so it was easy for him to say that he heard through the grapevine that Ilya's plan to forge the will fell through—not in so many words, of course—and to ask if there was going to be blowback. Because if there was, Damien might want to unload the property."

"And?"

"Michael's not remotely interested in playing the revenge game. They lost the property, we acquired it. End of story. And he's taking his father back to Italy for a family reunion. He's hoping to convince the old man to retire there. I want to keep your dad cocooned in The Drake for a few more weeks—at least until Muratti's out of the country—but I think this thing is about to blow over."

"Blow over?" I repeated. "To the tune of millions of dollars. Damien must have put in a fortune. For that matter, you must have, too. Good god," I said, as that truth settled fully over me for the first time. "I can't believe you did that for me. For my father."

"First of all, I would do anything for you. Second of all, neither Damien Stark nor I are in the habit of throwing money out the window. The price was high, yes. But the land is prime. To be honest, I expect that your father's poor judgment is going to end up adding another several million to my portfolio."

"Oh." I nodded. "I'm still not crazy about you guys taking such a risk, but that makes it better. Here's to you two getting even more stinking rich," I said, then held up an imaginary glass to toast.

He clinked an imaginary glass right back at me, then handed

me the second present. It was a solid rectangle wrapped in pretty pink paper, and when I shook it I heard absolutely nothing.

"I don't have a clue," I said.

"Then I guess you have to open it."

I did, carefully at first, but then losing patience and ripping the paper right off.

The rectangle, it turned out, was a velvet box with a stiff metal hinge. A jewelry box.

I looked at Cole curiously, but he was giving nothing away. I opened it, then gasped at the stunning choker that gleamed against the black velvet. It was made up of dozens of squares of gold, each of which had been pounded flat and were hinged together so that the ornament conjured thoughts of Egyptian princesses.

"Cole, it's stunning."

"I made it with the idea that it would be worn by you. I promise, it will be even more spectacular once it's around your neck."

"You made this?" I stroked my finger over the intricate necklace, a bit awed by the detail and time that had gone into it.

"I did. And now," he said, taking it gently from my hand, "I want to see it on you."

At his direction, I lifted my hair and turned so that he could fasten it around my neck. There was no mirror in the house yet, so I used the tiny compact I keep in my purse to take a look. Even from that awkward perspective, I could see that the necklace was more than a piece of fine jewelry. It was art. It was a statement.

It was a collar—and it was mine.

More than that, it meant that I was his.

I brushed my fingers over it, trembling a bit as I did because the gift had moved me. "Thank you," I said softly. "It's perfect."

"Wear it tonight," he said.

"To the party?" I asked, referring to the cocktail party on Evan's yacht.

"Yes, and then I want you to wear it after."

"After?"

"The Firehouse," he said, the words simple but underscored with heat. "If you still want to go, then I'll take you tonight."

Except for the water that surrounded us, the yacht that Evan kept docked at Burnham Harbor—*His Girl Friday*—might as well have been a luxury condo.

Granted, that was a slight exaggeration, but the truth was that the boat was huge and comfortable and more than capable of hosting this party of thirty to fifty guests, the number being in flux because it was an open-house style function, with friends flitting in and out to get drinks and offer wedding congratulations before heading out for their own exciting night on the town.

Then again, maybe I was projecting. Just because I expected my night with Cole to be exciting—what with the promise of the Firehouse—I could hardly be certain that my fellow partygoers had equally engaging plans.

We'd only been at the party for half an hour, and already I was getting antsy. Unfair, I suppose, considering this cocktail party was in celebration of my best friend's upcoming wedding, but I'd be lying if I didn't say that I wanted out of there. I wanted to explore this dungeon. I wanted to know its secrets.

I wanted to understand what Cole wanted and needed.

Most of all, I was just too damn curious.

And the two Cosmopolitans I'd already downed hadn't chilled me out at all. Instead I had a nice little buzz going. The kind that made me feel just bold enough that—if I wasn't careful—I'd sidle up to Cole and whisper inappropriate comments in his ear just to see if that got him moving faster.

It was a tempting plan—and one I was seriously considering—

when Flynn caught up to me on deck. "Hey," I said, throwing my arms around him. "I've missed you." Not that it had been that long, but I was in the house now, and he was still in the apartment. And the truth was that most of my time was spent with Cole, which meant that roommate time got pushed to the wayside.

Unfair, maybe, but thus was the bloom of new love.

"Are you almost all packed up?" I asked. "The lease runs out pretty soon."

"Yeah, I was going to talk to you about that."

I frowned. "What's wrong?"

"I decided to go ahead and keep the apartment. It's not that I don't love rooming with you, but I'd forgotten how much I enjoy having my own place."

Warning bells started clanging in my head. "Flynn, having your own place isn't worth—well, you know."

He shook his head, managing to look both amused and chastised. "I'm not. I swear. But with the new job, I can afford it."

"New job?"

He cocked his head, eyeing me strangely. "Cole didn't tell you? I'm managing the main bar at Destiny."

"Oh." I realized I was standing there, a little shell-shocked, then pulled him into a hug. "Sorry. I was just—anyway, that's wonderful," I finally managed. I meant it, too. Destiny was a great place to work, and I was sure that Flynn would make much better money. What had thrown me for a loop—and still had me reeling—was the fact that I wasn't as sure about Cole's motives. And considering he'd neglected to tell me this little tidbit of news, I had a feeling that his motives weren't entirely pure.

"We had an opening," Cole said simply when I cornered him a few moments later.

"Uh-huh. And that offer had nothing to do with the fact that you weren't happy with my roommate situation?"

"Seems like a win-win," he said to me. "Flynn gets better

pay and better benefits. And you," he added, running his finger over the intricate collar that I wore, "have a house all to your-self. Honestly, the possibilities are endless."

I tried to maintain my stern expression, but it wasn't any use.

"Speaking of," he said, tapping the necklace, "I think you and I should make the circle and say our goodbyes."

We did, pausing a bit longer when we reached Angie, not just to thank her for the party, but to wait with her while the harbor security escorted away a wiry little man she'd seen sitting on one of the benches along the pier.

"At first I thought he was a guest," she said. "But then he just sat and sat and stared at the boat. It creeped me out."

The security guard who escorted the man away called Angie right before we left to tell her that the man was a tourist from Kansas who apparently thought that watching a party on some rich man's boat was the kind of event that rounded out his bucket list.

"People are strange," Angie said philosophically, and since I couldn't argue with that, I didn't even try.

I was still thinking about that statement when Cole pulled the Range Rover into the valet slot at the Firehouse. He came around and opened the door for me, and I stood there for a moment, just looking up at the nondescript building that hid what I imagined were dozens of fantasies and adventures. The possibilities both intrigued me and made me nervous, and I looked to Cole for support.

He took my hand automatically, but I felt distance, not the support I craved. My stomach twisted unpleasantly, and I couldn't help but wonder if this was about me. If he was afraid that I couldn't handle whatever went on in there.

"Mr. August," a pretty young blonde wearing next to noth-ing said as we entered. "Welcome back." She smiled at me, then returned her attention to him. "Your usual room?"

"Yes," he said, and I had to bite back a frown because of the stiffness in his voice. A stiffness that seemed to increase once we were checked in and he pressed his hand against my back to lead me through a doorway and into a darkened corridor.

We'd taken two steps—and my eyes still hadn't adjusted to the dark—when he pulled me to a stop. "No."

That was all he said. And then he turned around, took my hand, and tugged me back toward the exit.

"Cole!" I said, once we were back outside, having blown past the baffled-looking hostess. "What the hell? What's wrong? Is it me? Is it Michelle?"

"This isn't the place for you."

"Dammit, Cole, I thought we were past that. I can handle it. I want to handle it."

"I know you do." The words were low and harsh and laced with anger. "But I don't want you to."

I took a step back. "Okay, back up. What did I do? Why are you mad at me?"

Even as I watched, his expression seemed to crumble. "Fuck," he said, then kicked the tire of the Range Rover that the valet had just returned from the lot. "Dammit, Kat, I'm not mad at you. I'm mad at me. Don't you get it? I don't want you here. And not because there's anything wrong with the Firehouse, or anything wrong with you."

He moved in front of me, then wiped away a tear that I hadn't realized I'd shed. "It's because of what you are to me," he said, his voice so gentle it almost made the tears flow freely. "It's because I came here because I needed something I couldn't get anywhere else. I needed a safety net. But I don't need that anymore. If I truly have you the way you say I do—the way I hope and believe that I do—then I don't need this place anymore. Do you understand?"

I nodded, a little bit humbled, a little bit amazed.

"Is that okay?"

Okay? With every word and every touch he was telling me how much I meant to him. How could it be anything but okay?

And yet—

He'd been examining my face, and now he frowned.

"Oh, baby, I'm sorry. If you want to go in, that's okay. I understand."

"No—no," I repeated quickly. "It's not so much that I want to go in—Sloane's told me a little bit about it, and to be honest, I'm not sure I'm keen on the public part."

"But?"

I shrugged, then looked away. "I guess I want the experience." I gathered my courage and met his eyes, finding them warm and understanding. "I want what I could get in there with you."

A muscle in his cheek tightened, and he nodded. "Okay. We'll go in."

I shook my head and grabbed his arm. "No, you don't understand. I just want you to take me there. I don't care if it's in the Firehouse or your bedroom or my house or in the back of your Range Rover. Does that make sense? I want it all, Cole. Everything you are and everything you have to offer. I'll admit I'm curious, but it's not a big deal. And if you don't want to take me here, that's fine." I reached up and fingered the necklace he'd given me. "I'll wear this anywhere you want me to. I just want you to take me all the way."

"I've been thinking about that," he said, with an odd gleam in his eye. "I was waiting for the right time to bring it up."

I cocked my head. "What are you talking about?"

"Instead of the Firehouse, I want to take you to our playroom."

I raised my brows. "You mean, like with sex toys and stuff?"

His laugh was pure delight. "God, Kat, you're wonderful. Yes, with sex toys and stuff."

I cocked my head and crossed my arms over my chest. "I

hate to mention this, but I don't think we have such a room. And if we do have one, I'm a little ticked off that you never bothered to mention it to me before."

"That's because it doesn't exist yet. But it occurs to me that you suddenly have a free bedroom. And I can think of one very interesting use that we can put it to."

I had to admit that he'd made an excellent point.

Over the next few days, we divided our time between Home Depot and Forbidden Fruit, the local sex toy store that Cole introduced me to and that I spent many fascinating moments perusing.

What I found the most interesting, though, was that Home Depot became our primary destination. I might be fascinated with the edible body paint—which I intended to let Cole put to good use, what with his innate artistic skill—but it was wood and pipe and brackets and bolts that he was focused on.

It was a little disconcerting how much hardware was going into that room. And, honestly, I had a feeling he was trying to outdo whatever setup they had at the Firehouse.

He was putting together a St. Andrew's cross—which was, frankly, the very first thing I wanted to try. But he also had something that looked like a tumbling horse and a piece of pipe with soft ankle restraints on each end that he told me was a spreader bar.

There was a wall with various hooks and latches to allow for different positions. An ornate chandelier that Cole told me would—once it was properly mounted—act as the top cross bar for a sex swing that he had ordered.

Considering how much I'd loved swings back when I was five, the very idea of combining a swing and sex made me more than a little giddy.

In addition to all those things, Cole had at least a dozen more gizmos and contraptions in the works, none of which he'd tell me about.

"Trust me," he said. And since I did, I left him alone to do the hardware thing while I worked on stocking the more intimate items into pretty baskets and picking out the colors for the room—which wasn't too difficult since I decided I wanted a deep rich purple, and if Cole wanted to veto it, he would just have to repaint the room himself.

I'd just finished rolling paint onto one of the walls when I turned to find Cole watching me. "You are not going to tell me I'm doing this wrong," I said. "Because all I'm doing is turning a wall purple. And even someone like me whose skill is limited to stick figures can handle that."

"Take off your clothes and stand by the wall."

I frowned. "Excuse me?"

"I have an idea."

I narrowed my eyes, but he stood firm, his brows lifted in silent demand.

"Yes, sir," I said archly, and then very slowly and deliberately stripped out of my shorts and tank top.

"Arms spread," Cole said. "Like you're doing jumping jacks. And here," he added, handing me some of the goggles he wore when he used the circular saw. "Just in case."

"What the hell?"

But Cole said nothing. And because I knew the score, I did what he said. I put on the goggles, I held my arms out—and then I laughed in delighted surprise when he flicked a wet paintbrush at me, splattering me and the wall, but in such a way that the splatter left the silhouette of a woman in a pose of what looked like exultation.

"Another," Cole said, as I laughed and moved into a slightly different pose. And on and on until the wall was covered with dancing, brilliant silhouettes . . . and I was covered in paint.

"Now that is lovely," he said, moving closer and tracing his finger over the splatters on my skin in a human game of connect the dots. "I do like to paint you," he said, his voice full of heat and promise.

"Right now it's my turn to paint you," I said. "Off with the clothes."

But I didn't splatter him. Instead I pressed against him, hot and hard, and transferred the paint from my body to his. He laughed, then pulled me down to the floor that was, thankfully, covered in drop cloths.

We slid over each other, moving and stroking and playing in the paint—and laughing like little kids—until the mood shifted, taking on more heat. More fire.

"What are we doing?" I asked, because I could no longer hold back the question. "What are we to each other?"

"Everything," he said, then pulled me in for a kiss.

And as his mouth captured mine—as I moaned from the sweetness of it all—I knew that he was right.

"What do you think?" Cole asked, taking his hands off my eyes so that I could see the finished St. Andrew's cross. It was mounted on a deep wooden box that was attached to a mirrored wall, which allowed for access around the cross itself, not to mention allowing whoever was standing to see the face of whoever was on the cross in the mirror.

As for the cross itself, the wood was polished to a shine, and the leather padding looked bright and comfortable.

I felt my body clench just looking at it. I'd been wanting this ever since Cole suggested this playroom. Hell, ever since he'd put me on that imaginary cross in my car and stung my back with the leather flails.

"Cole," I said, and heard the need in my voice.

"I know," he said. "Me, too. But I believe you have plans tonight."

I frowned, because he was right. In fact, I'd been just about to leave when Cole had pulled me away from the vanity in my bedroom where I was putting on my earrings to bring me into the playroom and show me the finished product.

"You just wanted to tease me."

"How well you know me," he said, moving behind me, and then sliding his arms around me. I was wearing a Lucky Brand miniskirt and V-neck T-shirt, and he slipped his hand into the neck of the shirt and into the cup of my bra.

With his other hand, he eased up my skirt, then slid his hand into my panties and thrust two fingers deep inside of me. "You're wet," he said. "Naughty girl."

"You got me excited," I countered. "Now I'm going to have blue balls all night."

"That really is naughty," he said, then pinched my nipple hard enough to make me yelp—and to make my sex clench tight around his fingers. "A preview," he said, "of just how hard I'm going to fuck you when you get home."

"That was an awfully short preview," I said. "Maybe you should make me come. Take the edge off before I go watch half-naked men gyrate onstage."

"Not happening," he said. "Besides, I like the idea of you coming back hot and bothered. All the more reason to spank that pretty ass."

He pulled his hand out of my panties then, stroking slowly over my clit as he did and making me moan with a combination of pleasure and frustration.

I spent the drive to Angie's worked up, and then the alcohol and mostly naked men at The Castle—our first bachelorette destination—really didn't help matters. Not that I was interested in the mostly naked men, but I would lose all street cred as a typical American female if I didn't at least appreciate the way those dancers were built—even if most of the time they faded away in my mind into a fantasy of Cole.

The party was an informal affair, because Angie had decided to ditch the idea of a big party and just hang out with me and Sloane. One last girls' night on the town before she became Mrs. Evan Black.

We'd started at The Castle because the drinks were potent, the guys were hot, and the owners knew our men, so we were able to wrangle a few extra special, totally in-your-face dances for Angie. All of which Sloane and I recorded with our phones so that we could show Evan.

Once we were sufficiently plastered, we had Red drive us to Forbidden Fruit. The idea was to buy Angie toys for her honeymoon—and we went a little crazy in that respect—but I had my own shopping to do, too, and before we piled back into the limo, I bought a present for Cole and me. One I very much hoped we would get some use out of soon.

The last stop, of course, was Destiny, where Sloane and I had deviously arranged for the dancers to pull Angie into the dressing room, get her decked out in a costume, and then let her give Evan his own private lap dance.

It was another iPhone moment, but Sloane was going to have to handle that one on her own. I was too intent on the man at the bar who was talking with Flynn but keeping his eyes on me.

"On a scale of one to ten, just how drunk are you?" Cole asked after I wrapped my arms around him and kissed him hard.

"Very," I said. "Very, very drunk. But I have a present for you."

"Do you?" he asked. "Nice to know you thought of me while you girls were out carousing."

I put the box from Forbidden Fruit on the bar in front of him, then leaned in to whisper in his ear, and as I did, I pressed my hand to his thigh, letting my fingers find and stroke his already hard cock. "You're all I thought about," I said. "Your hands, your cock, your mouth." I nodded toward the box. "Open it."

He did, pulling off the lid to reveal a black leather flogger that perfectly matched the one that he'd made come alive in my imagination.

He tilted his head up to meet my eyes, and I saw a gleam of anticipation in his eye that matched my own.

"Take me home," I said, brushing my lips over his ear one more time. "Take me home right now."

"Hell, yes," he said, and I swear we broke a dozen traffic laws getting back to my house in just over half an hour. A feat which pretty much defied the laws of nature.

"I'm going to fuck you," he said once we were in the room. "I'm going to take you every way possible tonight," he said. "But first I want you on the cross. I want your back red. I want your body to sing."

I nodded, my mouth too dry to form words.

Without waiting for him to tell me, I positioned myself. And as I did, reality meshed with the fantasy. I'd felt this before. The way the bindings at my wrists and ankles felt. The pressure of the padding against my skin.

And then—yes—the sharp sting of the first blow, and then the second, and on and on, with the pain rising, but the pleasure building, too. Growing from beneath the pain, pushing up like lava from a volcano that would soon burst forth and cover everything.

And it did. Adrenaline, endorphins, magic fairy dust. I didn't know the reason or care. All I knew was that I'd crossed a line, just as I had in the fantasy. And just as Cole had talked me through in the car, now he was leading me through in the flesh.

I was floating. I was lost. I was rapturous. And the fact that this kind of sex, crossing over from light kink to a little bit harder stuff, drew me in so fully, only cemented my certainty that Cole and I fit together perfectly.

A fact that he proved in a much more literal way when he took me off the cross. I moaned against him, feeling alive and intensely aroused. My body might be limp and languid, but my sex was hot and wet and my breasts were tender and sensitive.

He put me facedown on the bed, a position I thought was to spare my shoulders, still sore from the flails, but turned out to be so much more.

He drew his hand slowly over me, stroking me, then bending over to kiss me. He spread my legs, then thrust hard inside me, his hand on my clit making me spiral even higher and faster.

He felt warm and wonderful and familiar inside me—or at least he did until I felt the lube on his fingers and then the press of his thumb against my ass. "I'm taking you here," he said. "I need to have you every way," he said. "I need to feel you tight around me."

I nodded, wordless, because while he'd been talking, his thumb had been doing amazing things, teasing and stretching me, making me ready, so that when he pressed his cock to my ass, I was ready—at least as much as I could be.

He pushed inside me. Slowly, gently, but I sucked in a sharp breath anyway. "Does it hurt?"

"Yes," I said truthfully. "But it feels good," I said, also truthfully.

"I'll go slow," he said, "but oh, god, baby, you feel amazing."

"Don't stop," I demanded. "I want it all."

"Greedy."

"Yes," I agreed, and sucked in another breath as he pushed even farther inside me. Again I felt the pain, and then again—but after that something miraculous happened, because the pain shifted again to pleasure, just as it had on the cross. "Harder," I demanded. "Please, Cole, I want the rest of you."

"If you're sure," he said, and when I nodded, he thrust inside, sending swirls of pain and pleasure curling through me.

His own moan of pleasure matched mine, and he fucked me hard, just like he'd said he would. Hard and deep and fast until he exploded inside me, then collapsed against me, pulling me close and lazily stroking my clit to bring me over, too.

After, I lay curled in his arms. I was facing the cross, and I simply looked at it for a moment. "Thank you," I said to the man pressed against me.

"For what?"

"For everything," I said. "But right now, for that." I nodded toward the cross. "I felt things I never felt. I feel alive. I feel—" I cut myself off along with the word I'd intended to say. *Loved.* Instead I ended the thought with "special."

We stayed like that for a few moments, and then Cole shifted on the bed. He got off, and I watched him walk to the cross. He paused in front of it, then turned to look back at me.

"You're going to have to fasten the straps," he said, and those simple words made my body go weak.

"Cole, are you sure?"

"I want it," he said. "I want it from you. If you're willing to give it."

I nodded, though I couldn't deny that I was nervous. And when Cole moved into place, I hurried to fasten his ankles, his wrists. I looked in the mirror and saw him there, naked and bound, and felt something shift inside me, like the sensation of falling off a curb. This man—this strong, wounded man— was giving himself to me. His trust, his emotions, his soul, his heart.

I was humbled and just a little terrified, afraid that I wouldn't do this right. Afraid that somehow I would make this thing between us wrong instead of beautiful.

In the mirror, his eyes caught mine, and I saw understanding there.

I lifted a shoulder in what might have been an apology. "I don't want to do it wrong," I admitted, my voice soft to hide how foolish I felt.

"You won't, baby," he said. "Take it slow."

I did, trying to emulate what he'd done, wanting to give Cole the same pleasure that he'd given me. I held the flogger, then flicked it the way he'd showed me, wincing a bit at my first two attempts, which qualified as supremely lame.

But Cole's eyes met mine, and the passion I saw there gave me strength. I tried again, this time feeling the impact—and knew that I'd done it right from Cole's moan of deep, pure pleasure.

It took me a few more strokes to find a rhythm, and my strokes were nowhere as accurate as Cole's, but I managed it anyway. And as I did—as I watched the flails sting his skin—I felt a raw power build inside me, one that seemed to match the intensity of his moans and the rising of his own passion.

"Kat," he said after a while, his voice pulling me from the sensual trance I'd slipped into. I looked into the mirror, and his eyes met mine. And the demand I saw there stripped me raw, stealing the power and putting Cole back in charge, and that despite the fact that he was still strapped spread-eagled to the cross.

"Get me down," he said, and I hurried to comply. As soon as he was free, he pulled me to him, then picked me up and carried me to the bed.

"Do you have any idea how amazing that was?" he asked, his voice full of wonder.

I nodded, unable to speak. Certain that tears would fall if I tried. Because it was amazing, and so was this—this closeness that I felt with him now. This new intimacy that couldn't be supplanted even by the way he held me, the way he spread me, the way he sank deep inside me.

And then, when we shattered together and he gathered me close again in his arms, I let the tears fall freely, too overwhelmed to stop them.

"Oh, baby," he said, stroking my hair and kissing my temple. "No, no, it's okay. You did beautifully. That was exceptional. It's okay," he added, then repeated it again and again as I tried to get the tears to stop long enough for me to speak.

"No, no," I finally said. "I'm not upset. Truly. For someone who sees me so well, how can you not know that?" I drew in a ragged breath. "I'm the opposite of upset. I'm—I'm in awe. I'm overwhelmed. I'm still reeling from how close I feel to you right now."

"Catalina." That was all he said before he kissed me, hard and possessive, drawing me in and holding me close. When he pulled away, there was a sharp intensity in his face that I didn't think I'd ever seen before and hoped that I would never forget.

It warmed me and lifted me up—but it was his words that knocked the world out from under me.

"I love you."

I clung to him, my heart fluttering. "Cole." It was the only word I could manage.

He stroked my hair and searched my face, then pressed kisses to my forehead. "Oh, baby," he murmured. "I'm sorry. I'm so, so sorry."

"Sorry?" I heard the squeak of a question in my voice. "For saying you love me?"

"For not saying it before. I thought you knew."

"I did. I do." I closed my eyes and felt warm tears spill down my cheeks. "I just wasn't sure you'd ever say it."

"I've said it every time I touched you," he said. "Every time I looked at you."

"You did," I agreed. And then, happily, I added, "I love you, too. More than I can say. More even than I can imagine."

He kissed me, slowly and gently. "Do you remember when I told you that sex can mess us up?" he asked, thoughtfully.

I nodded.

"It's true," he said, "but I should have qualified it. Random sex. Wrong sex. Unattached sex. All of that can get in your head and screw with you. But what we have—sex mixed with love—sweetheart, I think that's what makes us whole."

twenty-three

The orange glow of the late afternoon sun gave the space under the McGinley Pavilion in the Chicago Botanic Garden a sensual, magical quality, as if all of us gathered for Angie and Evan's wedding had been transported to a fairyland.

The soft strains of the orchestra had filled the area for the last hour, but now the music had begun in earnest, a traditional march that propelled me and Sloane down the aisle to our designated spots opposite Tyler and Cole.

I'd barely had time to glance sideways at Cole when the music changed yet again, this time into the wedding march. Immediately, guests stood and turned, looking back to where Angie had appeared in her stunning, hand-beaded wedding gown with the eight-foot train.

She seemed to glide down the aisle on her father's arm, and there was no sound except for the processional. Even the insects in the gardens seemed to have hushed in deference to this woman who looked so radiant that she seemed lit from within.

I watched, blinking back tears as her father gave her away to Evan, who looked ridiculously happy. As the minister began to perform the ceremony, I stood next to Sloane, my bouquet tight in my hand, and looked out over the sea of faces. Some were friends, but most were strangers, and I was reminded that even though Angie had fast become a focal point of my life, we both had years behind us that the other knew nothing about. Weirdly, the thought comforted me. There was so much still to learn about my friends. About Cole. Hell, even about myself.

I glanced sideways to where Cole stood next to Tyler and Evan and found that he was looking at me, too. I was already weepy just from the fact that this was a wedding, but I saw so much tenderness in his face that I had to look away, afraid that the open emotion I saw in him would cause my tears to spill in earnest.

I concentrated instead on Evan—on the expression on his face that managed to encompass love and joy and passion and every other uplifting emotion.

I wanted that, too, I realized. I wanted to be in Angie's shoes, walking down the aisle to the man I loved.

I wanted to see Cole looking at me that way.

Weddings. I stifled a sigh and forced my thoughts back to the bride. On keeping my smile in place. On trying to remember what Angie's mom had asked me to do after the ceremony to help the staff set up for the reception.

I filled my head with so many thoughts that the actual wedding went by in a hazy, romantic blur that didn't come into focus until I heard the familiar "you may kiss the bride" and saw Evan pull Angie greedily toward him.

After that, it was a flurry of music, another march down the aisle, then congratulations and pictures and hugging and kissing.

At one point Tyler grabbed a microphone and—after the squeal of feedback—he asked for everyone's attention. He started off congratulating Angie and Evan, talking about how they were always meant to be together, and generally delighting the crowd.

"But enough about them," he said. "I have an announcement to make, and it seems to me that a wedding is the perfect venue." Beside him, Sloane was turning a little bit pink, which I found both baffling and amusing since she very rarely blushes.

"Earlier today, I asked Sloane to be my wife and she did me the honor of saying yes. Thank you," he added in response to the burst of applause. "But I have to add that Evan is no longer the luckiest man here today. He has to share that title with me."

"Why not?" someone called from the crowd. "You guys share everything. For that matter, where's Cole?" At which point all eyes turned to find me—not Cole—and I felt my cheeks turning even more red than Sloane's.

Fortunately that's when the staff called everyone back into the pavilion, which now overflowed with food and wine and wonderful music from a band playing softly in the far corner.

I hung back a bit, trying to find Cole, who'd gotten sucked away into the crowd when we'd all been herded outside. I couldn't find him, so I re-entered the pavilion, hoping to see him there. I didn't—not at first—but I did see Sloane. She was on the dance floor in Tyler's arms, and her face was alight, as if candles warmed her from within. She caught my eye, and her smile grew even broader. She lifted her hand, pointed toward the ring, and mouthed *diamond district,* then laughed like a child as her newly minted fiancé twirled her into his arms and kissed her hard in the middle of the dance floor.

And then the other dancers parted, and there he was. *Cole.* He was watching them as well, his expression both wistful and happy. He must have felt the weight of my gaze, because after a moment, he turned and his eyes immediately found mine. For a moment, there was no one else in the world but us. Then he smiled, and the spell was broken, but that was okay. I could handle the rest of the world just fine, because I had this man.

He ignored the dancers and cut across the dance floor, taking the shortest route to my side. "Someday," he said. He took my hand and gazed at me with such longing it made me tremble. "Someday you will make a beautiful bride."

My heart skipped a beat or two, but before I could think about his words—before I could process them, or even allow myself to wonder if he truly meant what I hoped he meant—he'd swept me onto the dance floor as well, and we were lost in the music and the crowd and the gaiety of the moment.

Happy. Such a simple word, but it packed so much punch. That was how I felt with Cole.

There were so many other emotions as well, of course. Desire, lust, need, discovery, hunger, tenderness. And on and on.

But at the core, he made me happy, and the thought was so huge, so powerful, that it propelled me through the rest of the evening.

I was still grinning foolishly hours later, after the cake had been eaten and the stretch limo had whisked Evan and Angie away to begin their fantasy honeymoon. I was standing there, hugging myself near the champagne fountain when Damien and Nikki came up to say goodbye.

"I wish we could stay longer," Nikki said. "We'd love to spend more time with you and Cole, and I've barely seen any of Chicago. But maybe some other time."

"We'd love it," I said sincerely.

Damien gave me a kiss on the cheek, and I noticed the looks of awe and jealousy from some of the other female guests who'd been surreptitiously taking photos with their phones all evening. "You better be careful," I said wryly, "or that's going to end up on Facebook."

"If there's gossip, it must be Tuesday," Nikki said, then tilted her head to indicate Damien. "He got used to it long ago. I'm finally getting to the point where it doesn't feel like I live in a fishbowl. Or, more accurately, I'm starting to feel like a fish who can ignore everything outside the bowl."

I laughed, but I couldn't help but think that I had it lucky with Cole. Yes, he made the Chicago papers frequently, and yes, I'd undoubtedly be included in those pictures from now on, but his celebrity was limited to Chicago. Nikki and Damien were recognized all over the world, and god forbid they were caught up in any sort of scandal because then there was nowhere to hide.

Frankly, I liked my side of the coin better.

"Have you seen Cole?" Damien asked.

"All evening, and usually right beside me," I said. "He pulled Tyler aside a few minutes ago. I think I saw them go down toward the water."

As they left to finish their goodbyes, I searched out Mrs. Raine to get my post-wedding marching orders. A few minutes later, I caught a glimpse of Cole and Damien talking near the edge of the pavilion. Apparently Damien had more to say than goodbye, because Cole didn't look particularly happy.

I was about to go ask what was going on—and if I needed to be concerned about my dad—when Mrs. Raine pulled me in to deal with the caterers and the florist. I hesitated, but I also knew that Cole wouldn't do anything to put my dad in danger—or to let him stay there if danger had found him.

By the time I finished my post-wedding maid of honor duties, the crowd had thinned considerably, and I was ready to go, too. I still wanted to know what Damien and Cole had been talking about, but I could wait until we were in the car to ask.

The only problem was that I couldn't find Cole.

This wasn't a crisis at first—he's a grown man and there were still enough people lingering at the reception that he could easily have gotten pulled aside to talk with a friend. But after more than a half hour passed I started to get truly fidgety.

"Not for at least an hour," Tyler said when I asked if he'd seen Cole.

"He was talking with Damien, and neither one looked happy. Do you know if something happened?"

"Not that I know of," Tyler said. "I know there was trouble in the gallery in LA a few days ago—some kids in Malibu throwing rocks through windows. Could be that."

I frowned. Could be, but it didn't feel right. "At any rate, I've lost him. If you see him, tell him to track me down."

"You've texted him?"

I nodded. "But he probably forgot to turn his phone off silent."

"Maybe he went to the catering office," Sloane suggested as Tyler left to go talk with someone he recognized. "Someone actually delivered documents to a wedding, so they were probably important."

"What are you talking about?"

"You didn't see the messenger? About twenty minutes ago, I think. Maybe he needed to sign something and fax it back."

I frowned, then went to find the woman on staff who was our assigned coordinator. She called back to the office, but was told that Cole wasn't there, and hadn't been there all day.

"Well, he has to be around somewhere," Sloane said, but I was getting a bad feeling.

"I'm going to go see if the Range Rover is here," I said.

Sloane lifted a brow. "Don't be absurd. He wouldn't leave you without a ride."

"I have a ride. You're here, aren't you?"

She frowned, but didn't argue. She also didn't say anything else until we got to the parking lot and found the space where he'd parked the Range Rover empty.

"Well," Sloane said. "That's fucked up."

twenty-four

The benefit of Sloane being a former cop and now working for the knights' investigative company was that she had access to the tracking system on Cole's Range Rover. Not only that, but the system was accessible through a web-based app, and Sloane kept her laptop, camera, and other tools of the trade in the trunk of her Lexus.

"Force of habit," she said with a shrug as she fired up the computer and logged in. We were sitting in the car, and I was watching the screen, tapping my foot because it wasn't booting up quickly enough to soothe my nerves.

When the program was finally up and running, I was just as frustrated. It was gibberish to me, at least until Sloane made a few adjustments and shifted the specs into map mode. She tapped her finger on a purple dot blinking on the screen. "South

Side." She caught my eye. "Pretty deep in, too. And the vehicle's not moving."

"Deep in," I repeated, looking at the lines that represented streets in neighborhoods I'd never seen, and wasn't sure I wanted to. "You mean gang areas?"

"That's what I mean."

I told myself not to freak, but I can't say that I was doing a very good job listening to myself. "Well, okay, then. That's where I'm going."

"That's where *we're* going," Sloane said, and started the car.

"Tyler?" I asked, and in response she tapped the button on her steering wheel to connect the speakerphone.

His voicemail answered, and she glanced at me with a shrug. "He's mingling," she said. "And, no, he's not going to be happy about us going into gang territory without him. But I have years of homicide under my belt and a Glock in the glove box. Your call, though. If you want to wait, we wait."

I shook my head. "As far as I'm concerned, we've already waited too long." I couldn't shake my growing fear that something had gone horribly wrong. I just couldn't understand what.

"Then I'll deal with Tyler later." She shot me a grin as she floored it out of the parking lot. "If he's pissed, that just means I have great make-up sex to look forward to."

"Since you put it that way," I said, then grabbed for my seat belt, figuring that would up my odds of surviving our quest to find Cole.

Even with Sloane behind the wheel it took more than forty-five minutes to reach the Fuller Park intersection where we found Cole's Range Rover smashed into a newspaper machine that may or may not have already been battered in a crumpled metallic heap.

"Shit." Sloane reached into the glove box for her gun, then

tucked it into her small beaded bag. It didn't fit, and the grip extended from the flap of the bag.

I raised an eyebrow.

She shrugged in reply. "In this neighborhood, I'm not worried about having it concealed. Come on. Let's go take a look at the car. Maybe we'll get lucky and he's sleeping off a bender in the backseat."

I didn't believe it, but it was something to hope for, so I followed her out. Across the street, two heroin-thin guys called out from where they sat on the curb in front of a battered brick building that I think was a bar, though I wouldn't swear to it. Their words were slurred and they seemed less than interested in approaching us. Frankly, I considered that a good thing.

There was a bench a few feet down from where the Rover had plowed into the newspaper machine, and I realized this was a bus stop. A burly guy in a filthy wifebeater with an arm covered in gang tats sat there, taking long sips from something concealed by a brown paper bag. He was turned toward us, but I couldn't see where he was looking because the black shades hid his eyes. Even so, I was certain that we were the object of his attention, and I kept a cautious eye on him while Sloane peered into Cole's vehicle.

His head never moved, his position never shifted. But he smiled slowly, revealing a row of gold-capped teeth that glinted in the fading light of the setting sun.

Honestly, I was glad for the gun.

"Anything?" I asked, hoping Sloane heard my silent plea to hurry it up.

"Not a thing," she said. She tried the door and found it unlocked. She tugged it open, peered in, and looked at me. "Whatever the messenger brought him, he either has it on him or he left it at the wedding."

Our gold-toothed friend got up and sauntered toward us.

"You need help, Goldilocks? What's the matter? One of the three bears stand you up for prom?"

I made a face, scowling down at the formal dress I still wore. "Something like that," I admitted.

"Kat." Sloane's voice held a note of warning, and I knew that she was reminding me that this guy might just as soon kill me as look at me.

I straightened my shoulders and cocked my head, forcing myself to appear confident as I looked at him. "You offering to give us a hand?"

"Depends. I'll tell you this much on the house—if you white bitches be looking for the motherfucker who trashed that nice set of wheels, you be looking in the wrong place."

"You know where he is?" I asked.

"I know where he ain't. He ain't around here no more, that's for damn sure. But the mo-fo did some serious damage to my block here before he kicked it into gear."

"Damage," Sloane repeated. "You mean wrecking his car into the newspaper machine?"

"Fuck no. That car barely tapped it. I mean taking his tire iron out and beating the shit out of that thing," he said, waving at the crumpled hunk of metal that once had dispensed newspapers.

I caught Sloane's eyes. I still didn't know what had worked Cole up, but if he'd gone postal on the machine, I knew that it was worse than I'd thought.

"Did you see where he went? Did he walk away? Call somebody? Catch a cab?"

He laughed, and it wasn't a nice sound. "Shit, bitch. You think this be fucking New York City? Folks just step into the street and wave down a cab? You need to go back to the fairy tale you came from."

"Maybe I do," I said. "So you tell me. What happened? Where'd he go?"

"Why should I tell some blond bitch comes asking around about a brother?"

"I'm his girlfriend."

"The hell you say. Your tiny princess ass couldn't handle that motherfucker."

"My tiny princess ass has mad skills," I said. "Now where the fuck did he go?"

"Lady got balls," he said with a nod that might have indicated respect. "No idea where he blew off to, but he tossed three grand at my boy Kray and bought himself a nice new bike right out from under my boy. Sweet set of wheels. Could be anywhere by now."

"He's right," Sloane said. "Without the GPS, we're flying blind."

"So where would he go?" I ran my fingers through my hair.

"I don't know," Sloane said. "Why did he come here? Because it was home?"

"Maybe. Let me think."

We took a moment to thank our informant, who actually pulled the gentleman card and told us to get our lily-white asses out of there because it was getting dark, and the next mo-fo we met might want more than to talk about my crazy-ass boyfriend.

Since that seemed like a good idea, we got back in Sloane's Lexus and headed back toward the highway.

"Wait," I said, and Sloane slowed to a reasonable speed as I dialed Bree in Los Angeles.

I'd hoped that she'd heard from him, but when she said that she hadn't, I asked her to tell me the address of the house he grew up in.

"Is everything okay?"

"I hope so," I said honestly, then promised to call her with an update as soon as I knew anything.

Sloane eased the car by Cole's childhood home—one room on the second floor of a filthy brick building that looked ready to collapse at any moment. There was an old woman on the stoop, and when we asked, she told us that nobody was inside. I considered going in to see for myself, but when Sloane pointed out that the motorcycle Cole had bought wasn't parked anywhere in sight, I agreed that it was better to just get out of there.

"Just go to my place," I said, my whole body feeling heavy and battered. I wasn't sure if it was because I was worried about Cole or simply overwhelmed by the poverty and misery of the neighborhood he grew up in. All I knew was that I wanted nothing more than to curl up and cry.

Well, almost nothing more.

What I wanted more than anything was Cole.

"We're not that far from his house," Sloane said, as she maneuvered her car toward Cole's Hyde Park address. "Maybe he was heading home all along and just decided to take a detour. Let's check there first, then if you still want, I'll take you home."

I nodded, but I wasn't hopeful, and when we got to the house, we found it empty.

"Please," I said, after I tried his phone once more to no success. "Just take me home."

She nodded, and we headed to my little house in silence. Once there, I curled up on my sofa.

Sloane made me hot chocolate, then crouched down in front of me. "Want me to stay?" she ask.

"Yes. No." I sat up. "No," I said firmly. "Go back to Tyler. Maybe he's got some ideas. Call me if you find him. I'm—" I shrugged, feeling useless. "I'm not sure," I admitted. "But I'd like to be alone."

She pressed one hand on the couch for balance, then put her other on my shoulder and looked me straight in the eye. "Whatever it is, he'll be okay."

I nodded, even though I wasn't nearly as sure. We'd come so far, Cole and I. And yet when something terrible had happened, he hadn't come to me. He'd exploded—lost it completely if the newspaper dispenser was any indication—but I'd been completely off his radar.

I knew Sloane was right—somehow, someway, Cole would be okay. He'd work through it. He'd fix whatever problem had arisen. He'd kick his own ass and calm himself down. He would be fine. He would be okay.

And, yes, I was glad of that.

But the bottom line was that when the shit had hit the fan, he'd run from me instead of to me. And that one simple fact felt like a fist around my heart.

Sloane hovered a little bit longer, then finally left on a wave of promises to get Tyler on it and to call the moment they heard anything. As soon as I heard her car pull out of the driveway, I stood up. I wasn't sure what I intended to do, but I knew I needed to move.

What I wanted was to go toe-to-toe with Cole. To tell him he was an idiot. To poke him in the chest and ask him what the hell he was thinking. Didn't he know he could tell me anything? That he didn't have to hide his temper from me? That if he had to explode he could let it all go in front of me?

Didn't he know that I loved him? Didn't he understand what that meant?

Frustrated, I pulled out my phone and again dialed his number. Once again, I got his voicemail. "Dammit, Cole," I said. "Where are you? Call me. You're scaring me, you know that, right? Not because I'm afraid you're hurt, but because I'm afraid—" My breath hitched, and I blinked furiously, forcing back the tears. "I'm just afraid," I finished lamely. And then, because I didn't want to just blather on, I ended the call.

As soon as it disconnected, I called my father on the burner. I wasn't even conscious of making the decision to call, but soon the phone was ringing and I knew that other than seeing Cole, the only thing I wanted right then in the world was to hear my dad telling me that it was all going to be okay.

"Kitty Cat," he said softly.

"Daddy." It was the only word I could manage though the tears that filled my throat.

"Is this a good-news call? I thought you weren't going to call your old man until this whole mess blew over."

"I know. I'm sorry. I didn't mean to get your hopes up."

For a moment, there was silence, then his voice came back on the line, soft and gentle. "Sweetheart, what's wrong?"

That did it. The tears flowed freely. "Nothing," I said. "Nothing to do with you, I mean. It's just—it's just—" I sucked in air. "I guess I just want to see you. But I can't. Not yet. But I had to at least hear your voice, you know?"

"You're scaring me, kiddo. You going to tell your old man what's wrong? You in trouble?"

"No," I said quickly. "No, it's just Cole."

"You have a fight?" he asked, his voice full of protective paternalism.

"No," I said. "But when I find him I think we will." I told him briefly what had happened. How something had upset Cole, and how he'd gone off wild into the night to fight his demons.

"Well, they're his demons, aren't they?" Daddy asked.

"I—well, yes. But—"

"Give him a chance, sweetheart."

"A chance?"

He sighed. "Love doesn't change who a person is, kiddo. Just the opposite. Love lets you strip away all the armor you've put on to protect you from the riffraff of the world. You love Cole?"

"Yes."

"So if he needs time alone, does that make you love him less?"

"No, of course not, but—" I felt my fear and temper deflate just a little. "I want to help him," I finished lamely. "I want him to need me."

"I'm sure he does. But does that mean he has to follow the

script in your head? Give him space. Talk to him. Don't manufacture a problem until there is a problem. I've seen the way that boy looks at you," my dad added. "And trust me when I say that he loves you."

I was smiling when I ended the call, which was a miracle in and of itself since I was no closer to finding Cole. But everything my dad said had soothed me, and it saddened me a bit that Cole had gone his entire life without a parent watching his back.

Except he hadn't.

I cocked my head, turning the thought over as I examined it. Maybe he hadn't had a mother and father. Maybe he hadn't lived the stereotypical life with two parents, a picket fence, and a dog. But he'd had brothers, hadn't he? Tyler and Evan.

And he'd had a father. He'd had Jahn.

I'd wanted to go see my dad, but I couldn't, and so I'd done the next best thing—I'd called him.

Cole couldn't visit or talk to Jahn—but if he wanted to feel close to his friend and mentor, he could go to where he used to live.

He could go to Jahn's old condo.

Nobody answered when I buzzed the intercom, but I told myself it didn't matter. He was in there, because he had to be in there. Because if he wasn't, then I was out of ideas, and that simply wasn't acceptable.

Angie had given me a key and the security code months ago so that I could come in and use the condo's fitness center and pool whenever I wanted. I'd never before entered the actual condo without her advance permission, though.

Tonight, I did.

"Hello?" I called softly as I stepped into the foyer. "Cole?"

There was no answer, and I repeated the call as I moved through the living room and then into the kitchen and bedrooms.

Nobody.

I returned to the living room and stood there frowning. The room looked pristine. Certainly no one had gone and smashed through this area in the mindless throes of a tantrum. Did that mean he hadn't been here? Or did it just mean that he was calming down?

Howard Jahn used to tell anyone who would listen that one of the reasons that he bought this condo as opposed to any other was because the living room was dominated by a magnificent spiral staircase that led to an even more magnificent rooftop patio. Now I turned my attention to that staircase and slowly let my gaze drift upward.

Please, I thought, then walked in that direction.

I climbed slowly, both wanting to find him and wanting to postpone the disappointment if it turned out that he wasn't up there.

He wasn't.

There were no lights on the patio when I stepped through the sliding glass door onto the smooth slate surface. I looked around, peering through the inky night first toward the railing and glass barrier that overlooked the lake, and then toward the fully stocked kitchen and sitting area.

No Cole.

I drew in a breath, letting my shoulders rise and fall as this unwelcome reality settled over me. I started to turn to go back inside when something on a small metal bench in front of the glass barrier caught my eye. A manila envelope. And on top of it, the small green stone that I'd often seen Cole rub when he was worried or frustrated or upset.

I'd changed into jeans before I'd come to the condo, and now I slipped the stone into my pocket. The envelope was a little trickier to deal with. I wanted to open it. And yet I didn't.

I had no idea what was inside that envelope, but I was certain that it had the power to destroy.

Still, I couldn't fight what I couldn't understand. And so I sucked in a breath, pulled open the already loose flap, and let the contents fall into my lap.

Oh god oh god oh god.

Photographs. Dozens of them.

The kind of photos you'd find in magazines that only existed so that men could jack off. And each and every one of them was of me.

Me, spread-eagled on the St. Andrew's cross.

Me, bent over, legs wide, and Cole's cock thrusting hard inside me. Not that he was in the picture—no, only I was identifiable.

Me, bound tight with hemp, a crotch knot at my clit.

I recognized each location, too. How could I not? My house. Our playroom. The photographer had found gaps in the blinds. Had trespassed into my backyard and watched as Cole had taken me—as I'd given myself to him in so many different ways.

Looking at them, my stomach churned and bile rose in my throat. Not because of what they portrayed, but how they portrayed it. Twisting my most personal moments into something cold and harsh and ugly.

Intimacy butchered to become porn.

Who? Right then, I swear I could have killed the bastard who had breached our privacy so violently. But who the hell had done it? And for god's sake, what did they intend to do with these horrible pictures?

I was just about to call Sloane to get her thoughts when my phone rang. I practically turned a backflip to tug it out of my pocket, then deflated when I saw that the caller was Tyler, not Cole.

"Anything?" I demanded.

"He's at BAS," Tyler said, referring to Black, August, Sharp Security. "Just unkeyed the door with his code. I'm going."

"No," I said. "I am. I'm at Evan's condo. I can be there in less than ten minutes."

"Do you know what's going on?" Tyler asked. "What's he doing at the office? Why the hell did he schedule the jet for tonight?"

The jet.

I thought of the weapons room at BAS. And then I thought of the fact that a private plane didn't have to deal with airport security.

"Where is he going?" I asked, feeling a little sick to my stomach as the pieces started coming together.

"Flight plan logged for Atlantic City," Tyler said, and I cursed.

"I know what he's doing," I said. "He's going to kill Ilya Muratti."

twenty-five

I found him in the weapons vault tossing boxes of ammo into a duffel that already held two pistols and a revolver.

"Are you planning to take out his entire staff?" I asked softly. "Or just the man himself?"

He didn't turn, but I saw his shoulders stiffen.

"Dammit, Cole, you can't do this."

"The hell I can't." He ground the words out, raw and rough and so filled with pain they seemed to drip like blood. "It's the only goddamn thing I can do."

"No." I took a step toward him, then another. When I was standing right behind him, I pressed my hand gently to his back.

I'd expected him to flinch away from my touch, and when he didn't, I closed my eyes, the motion like the physical manifestation of a sigh of relief. *Maybe I haven't lost him yet.*

"Please," I said. "Turn around and look at me."

At first I thought he would ignore me, but then he turned slowly, his eyes finding mine. They were cold and determined, dangerous and wild.

I shook my head. "You can't."

"You saw the photos?" His words were clipped, harsh. They were full of anger, but it seemed directed more at himself than at Muratti. "Saw the fucking hell I shoved you into?"

"You? You think this is somehow your fault? Dammit, Cole, this isn't your fault any more than what happened to Bree was on your shoulders. It's nobody's fault except Muratti's and the prick photographer who trespassed on my property.

"And," I added, because I was on a roll, "if you think I did anything with you that I didn't consent to one hundred and twenty percent—that I didn't enjoy at least twice that much— then you are a fucking idiot."

Some of the tension left his body then, and he sagged back to lean against the table on which the duffel bag lay.

"Why are you here?" he asked.

"Don't go to Atlantic City," I said, then tossed the envelope onto the table before handing him the stone. He took it, and as he did our fingers brushed. As always, I felt that shock of connection. More important, I saw in his eyes that he felt it, too. "Don't kill him, Cole. Not even for me."

He ran his hands over his head, then drew in a long breath. He had changed out of the tux he'd worn to the wedding and now wore jeans and a simple gray T-shirt that accentuated the muscles in his arms and chest. Even without a gun, he was deadly. With one, he was unstoppable.

I intended to stop him anyway.

"Talk to me, dammit," I said. I wanted to shake him. To slap him. I wanted to kick some sense into him. But the moment was charged—hell, *he* was charged—and every ounce of reason in me told me that I needed to talk him down. That raging against a man who could so easily give in to rage would be like pouring gasoline on a flame.

After a moment, he held out the small green stone, his thumb rubbing it in slow, even strokes. "Jahn gave me this," he said, without preamble and without looking at me. "Did I ever tell you that?"

"No."

"He left each of us a letter and a gift. More of a token, really. Something personal. Something that held some meaning for him."

"Why was the stone important to him?" I asked.

Now Cole turned his head and looked at me directly. "He bought it on his honeymoon," Cole said. "His first honeymoon," he added wryly. "His wife said he fretted too much. That he needed something to absorb the stress."

"But that's not the whole story." I'd known Howard Jahn. The man had about a million layers. And if he was giving a worry stone as a legacy, there had to be a deeper purpose.

"He knew me better than anyone," Cole said. "Anyone except you," he added, and something that had been cold and shriveled inside me began to bloom and grow. "He knew about my temper. About the crack my mother smoked. About the way I could snap. He knew about the gangs, and he knew what I'd done. More, he knew what I was capable of doing. And he believed that I could hold it all in. That I could control my temper rather than have my temper control me."

"Smart man, Howard Jahn," I said. "I knew there was a reason I always liked him."

I saw the flicker of amusement in his eyes. Just a hint of an instant, but it gave me another thread of hope to grasp.

"He told me that one day I would find a woman who fit me. Who soothed me. Who'd help me cling to control. I'd find her one day, Jahn said," Cole continued. "But he gave me the worry stone to use until then."

He'd turned away as he spoke, looking vaguely at the wall of weapons—pistols and shotguns, Tasers, and who knows what else. But even though he wasn't touching me or looking at me, I knew that he was talking about me—that *I* was the woman Jahn had promised. And that simple knowledge filled me with a bittersweet joy.

That, however, wasn't the end.

"Go on," I whispered. "Tell me the rest."

He turned to me, and his face was no longer closed off. I saw love. I saw adoration. And—god help me—I saw pain.

"You do that for me, Kat. I love you—god, how I love you. But it's more than that. You've done more than slip into my life. Hell, you've clicked into place. You fit me perfectly."

I clutched his hand, tears spilling out of my eyes because there was no way that I could hold so much emotion inside.

"You make me feel whole," he said, his voice cracking with an emotion I couldn't identify. "And all I've done is fuck it up for you."

Something dark and cold wrapped around me, then squeezed tight, making me work for each breath. "No," I whispered. I knew he was thinking of those awful photos. "God no. You didn't fuck anything up. And even if you had, killing Ilya Muratti isn't going to change a thing."

"Yeah," he said. "It will."

"Bullshit. The only thing that will change is that your juvie record will be unsealed."

"Goddammit, Kat. You don't have a clue."

"Because you're not telling me." I had to hold myself back to keep from shouting, I was so damned frustrated. "What do you know that I don't? How the hell did Muratti even get those pictures?"

"Because I fucked up. Because my brilliant plan to keep you and your father safe took a fucking nosedive."

I shook my head, not understanding.

"Muratti cut through the layers of paper and corporations," Cole said. He pressed a finger to his temple and rubbed, as if fighting a massive headache. "I was right that he wouldn't push back against Stark—I was even right that when he found out about me it would deflect attention from your dad. But he pushed harder. Went further. And somehow in checking on me he found out about you. And along the way, the son of a bitch realized that you're Maury Rhodes's daughter."

The words knocked me back like a blow to the chest. "No," I said lamely. "How?"

"On paper, it looks like you came out of nowhere, Kat. That's hard to trace, sure. But it's also suspicious. And a man like Muratti has both curiosity and resources. He can find what needs to be found."

I shook my head, reaching out for the table to steady myself.

"He had someone follow you. Follow us. And don't you know he had a goddamn party when his gopher reported back on the kinds of pictures he'd managed to snag? St. Andrew's cross. Spreader bars. Flogger. Blindfolds. What do you think, Kat?" he asked, his voice harsh with anger and frustration. "You think your dad wants to see a picture of his little girl with a butt plug?"

I winced and looked away.

"*Shit*. Shit, I'm sorry." The harshness was gone from his voice, replaced by a soft gentleness that made me want to cry. "But you have to understand." He drew in a breath. "It's my fault. I know that. I should have seen it coming. I should have done a better job keeping you safe."

"No," I whispered. "It's not your fault."

"Hell, yes," he said, then met my eyes. "I fucked up. But that's a mistake I intend to remedy right now."

"Cole, you can't."

"The hell I can't. Muratti's going to release those pictures, Kat. If I don't tell him where your dad is, he's going to spread them far and wide."

"Oh." It was the only word I could manage. I swallowed. Sucked in air. "We're not telling him where my dad is. I'm not painting a target on my father's back."

"Well, you know, Muratti's not entirely unreasonable." A horrible irony laced his voice. "He said if I release them myself— if I let the whole world see those pictures of you—he'll let your dad walk. No retribution, no nothing."

I met his eyes, then hugged myself. Those pictures, out there in the world. My dad would see them. My friends would see them. My private moments—*our* private moments—tossed out for the gossip hounds.

And there was no telling myself they'd go away. They wouldn't.

I might not be as much in the public eye as Nikki Fairchild, but I'd go through the same hell. At least her portrait had been art. Taken out of context, these were vile. They were the kind of pictures that would make the rounds on social media. That would get tossed up on YouTube.

This was the kind of crap that lived forever, and with a man like Cole August attached to the gossip, it would live even longer.

These photos would follow me the rest of my life.

And Cole had seen that from the beginning. He'd seen that the only way to protect my privacy was to throw himself back in the muck.

"Cole," I said, my heart breaking as I slid my arms around him. He stood tense at first, unresponsive. And then he tilted his head so that his forehead pressed against mine and his arms tightened around my waist.

"You weren't supposed to know any of this. I wanted to keep

you out of it. To keep you shielded from it. But I guess I managed to fuck that up, too."

"Cole, stop," I said gently.

"I didn't think you'd end up at Jahn's," he continued, and I wasn't even sure he'd heard me. "I left the envelope there with the stone as a message to Tyler and Evan. So they would understand what happened if I didn't return. Insurance, you know. Just in case."

He leaned back so he could look at me. "But I didn't think it would be a problem. I planned to go there, kill the son of a bitch and any of his flunkies who got in my way, then come back, destroy the folder, and go home to you."

"Christ, Cole." I could barely get a word out past the jumble of thoughts in my head. "How the hell could you even be sure that would end it? He might have left another set with someone for insurance against that very thing."

"Not his style," Cole said, "so I figured it was a calculated risk. If I was right, you'd be safe. And you'd never even need to know any of this happened."

"And if you were wrong?"

"Then at least the bastard who did that to you would be rotting in the morgue."

I raked my fingers through my hair. "You'd keep all of that from me? Lie to me?"

"You have no idea how far I'd go to protect you." He stroked my cheek, his eyes taking me in, as if studying every line, every pore, every atom. "I want his blood, Kat. And I will have it."

I shook my head, overwhelmed by the emotions swirling inside of me. "You think you have no control, but don't you see yourself? You are nothing but control right now. You're practically vibrating your grip is so tight." I held tight to his hand. "Take it further," I said. "Take it further by stepping back."

"Stepping back?"

"You can't do this, don't you get that? Kill him and you're back where you were before. That's not who you are."

"I'll be whatever I have to be to keep you safe." I could feel the intensity rising in him. A primal, earthy quality, as if he was gearing up for a fight. "I promise you. I can do what's necessary with no problem whatsoever."

I ran my fingers through my hair again, searching for an answer. The truth was, I didn't care if he killed Muratti. From what I knew of the son of a bitch, he deserved to die. But the consequences to Cole scared me to death. "What about giving the land back?"

"Ran that option by the old man. He's way past wanting the land. All he wants now is his pound of flesh."

"What about the son?" I asked. "Maybe he can talk to his father and—"

"No," Cole said firmly. "I did talk to him, and you're right about Michael. He's a hell of a lot more reasonable. But it's Daddy's show and it's going to stay Daddy's show until the old man kicks the bucket."

"You can't force that along."

"Dammit, Kat, I can. I can and I will. Don't you get it? Don't you fucking get it? I love you, goddammit," he said, and the passion in his voice nearly knocked me over.

"I love you, and I will take care of you. I will protect you. I will protect your father. I will goddamn make sure that nothing happens to you—that nothing happens to your father—and that these goddamn photos do not ever—*ever*—see the light of day."

He'd pushed away from the table as he spoke and had moved toward me, forcing me backward to the far wall. Now he had me trapped there, a rack of shotguns to my left.

I was caged in his arms, breathing hard, trying to find the magic words to make him stop and back up. To make him think and figure something else out. Because there had to be a way out. Because I couldn't live like this. Couldn't live in the nightmare that was crashing down all around me.

"You're all that matters, Kat. Ilya Muratti sure as hell doesn't. He's nothing to us." He pulled me close and kissed me hard. "Say it, Catalina. Tell me he's nothing."

"He's nothing," I said, then pulled him roughly back to me. I needed his touch, his hands. I needed it rough and hard and wild.

I had no idea how we would get through this. How we could find an out that wouldn't destroy him or me, but I knew that we had to. I knew, because we had to be together. Because I had to be the woman in Cole's arms—and he had to be the man in mine.

"Christ, Kat," he said, ripping my T-shirt up over my head. "Do you have any idea how much you mean to me? Do you have any idea the extent I would go to keep you safe?"

"I do," I said, fumbling to get out of my jeans, kicking them off, tugging at his. We were wild, frenzied. I needed everything from him then. I needed his protection, his touch, his love.

Dammit, we *fit*. Not just in sex, but in life. In the way we approached the world. In the day to day.

Most of all, in love.

"Kat," he murmured, then lowered his head to my breast. I hadn't bothered with a bra, and his mouth closed over me, sucking, teasing, biting. Sending ribbons of sensation coursing through me, shooting from my breast to my clit so that I was squirming under his touch, so aroused right then that I boldly slid my own hand down and stroked my own wet sex.

"God, yes," he said, closing his hand over mine. "Do you know how hot that is? How hard it makes me to know that you're turned on. That you want me?"

"There's never a moment that I don't want you," I said, admitting everything to him, because he already knew it anyway, and there was nothing left to hide from this man. "Please," I said, hooking my arms around his neck and then pulling him to the ground with me. "I need you inside me. Now. Please, Cole, now."

He didn't hesitate, and as I spread myself open for this man I adored, he buried himself inside me, his body pounding against me, as if by the force of the motion he could make the world outside of us go away.

"I love you," I said as I felt the pleasure rising up and curling around me.

"I love you," I repeated, because I needed to know that he'd heard it, too.

"Everything you are," I said as he thrust harder and deeper, as if each pounding attack on my body was meant to punish himself. "Everything you've done. Don't you get it, Cole? You've stripped me raw and put me back together again, and I love you for it. I love you desperately.

"You gave me the world," I said, as I felt his body tighten inside mine, then shudder in the sweet throes of release.

"You gave me everything," I said, as my own orgasm rolled through my body like a shock.

"Don't take it away from me," I murmured, my body sated and my voice exhausted. "Don't rip it all out from under me. You promised me once that you wouldn't ever leave me. I couldn't stand it if you did. You have to know I couldn't stand it."

He pulled me close, breathing hard. "But you could withstand those pictures being in the world?"

"If that's what it takes," I said, realizing for the first time the full extent of what I'd been saying to him. "It would be awful. But if that's what it takes to stay with you—to really and truly stay with you—then I could handle that and more."

He was silent, and I groaned in frustration. "Dammit, Cole,

what do I have to do to prove it to you? Send the photos out as goddamn Christmas cards?"

He pulled me close, his body shaking a little with what I finally realized was laughter. "Probably nothing that extreme," he said. "But, Kat, I need to know that you're sure."

"I am." I stroked his head, his face. I looked into his eyes, because I needed to make sure he understood just how deeply I felt these words. "I can survive anything if I know you're at my side. If you really want to protect me, take me away. Take me to Europe or New Zealand or some tropical island so I'm not near the Internet or television or people I know. But don't do anything that risks them taking you away from me. Because I will tell you right now—if they arrest you or if Muratti's people hunt you down, it will kill me. And that will be on you."

He studied me. "You're really sure?"

I clutched his hands. "I can survive the photos. My dad can survive the photos. My friends, my career, my reputation. It won't be fun, but it will pass." I drew in a deep breath. "But if I lose you, I will shrivel up. That will be the end of me. Believe me, Cole. Believe me, and decide. Are you going to choose what you think I need, or will you listen to what I tell you I need?"

I pressed a gentle kiss to his lips. "Either way, I do love you. And, Cole," I added, "do you realize what happened tonight? You came," I said. "Without kink, without pain. With just you and me and what's between us."

I watched his face as he took in the moment, realizing then that I was right. I grinned a little, then met his eyes, laughing at the expression of exultant pride.

"Don't worry," I said wryly. "I like the status quo just fine. But it is always nice to have options."

"Yes," he said. "It is."

After a moment, he sighed and pulled me close. "Dammit, Kat, that's what I've been trying to get you to understand. I want the option of protecting you, baby, just like I promised your dad. But that's the option you're just not giving me."

"The hell I'm not," I said. "Don't you get it? You're the shield between me and the world, and that's more protection than I could hope for. You want to be the big strong man, then do what I ask. Stand by me. Take me out of the country until the worst blows over. But don't you dare fucking leave me."

He was staring at me, an odd expression on his face.

"What?"

"I adore you," he said. "I'm not sure how I survived a day without you."

"Then you understand why I'm so certain that I can't risk facing a future without you."

Slowly, he nodded.

"So we tell the bastard to release the photos?" I asked.

"If you're really certain."

"I've never been more sure about anything," I said. "Not about anything except you."

"I don't want to be around when you make the call," I said once we were on the jet.

He cocked his head, eyeing me suspiciously.

"I'm still certain," I assured him, hoping he couldn't see the way my insides were twisted up. "But that doesn't mean I like it or that I'm looking forward to the moment the photos go live."

He studied me, as if searching for deception on my face. I guess he liked what he saw, because he finally nodded. "All right," he said. "I'll head up to the galley."

"Bring me back some wine," I said dryly. "I'll need it."

He nodded, then kissed me. "You are the strongest, most amazing woman I've ever met."

"If I was that strong," I said, "I wouldn't be dragging you out of the country."

"Leaving just means that you're smart." He brushed his thumb over my cheek. "There's good pain, and there's bad pain, sweetheart. Staying would be the bad sort of pain."

"It wouldn't," I assured him. "So long as you're with me, it's all good." I took a deep breath. "Everything else is all set? Daddy?"

"Evan and Tyler will get him from The Drake as soon as I've made the call. And they've arranged for him to spend a few months in Fiji. I can't promise you that he won't see the pictures, but I can promise that they won't be in his face."

"All right. Thank you."

His eyes narrowed. "You know damn well there's no reason to thank me."

"You're wrong," I said, "but we don't have to argue about it again." I took a seat in one of the armchairs, casually tracing my finger over the tabletop in front of me. "Will you tell me now where you're taking me?"

"Paris," he said. "You once told me you wanted to live there."

"You remember that?"

"You're like oxygen to me, Kat," he said. "And how could I possibly forget to breathe?"

I watched him move to the front of the plane, this man I loved who made me happier than I could ever imagine being, and, despite everything going on around us, made me feel safer than I could ever imagine.

I thought about the call he was making—about the pictures that were going to be out in the world.

I waited for the nausea to sweep over me, but it didn't. Just a tingle of unpleasantness, like that uncomfortable feeling when you have bad news to share with a friend.

I'd survive this. With Cole at my side, I would survive this just fine.

It took a few moments, but then the accordion-style sliding

door opened and he stepped back into the passenger cabin. I stood immediately, alarmed by the expression on his face. Not anger. Not disgust or sadness or protectiveness or any emotion that I had anticipated.

No, he looked bewildered.

"Cole?" I took his arm and led him to the couch, then sat beside him. "What's wrong?"

"He's dead," Cole said. "I spoke with Michael. Ilya Muratti is dead."

"Dead? But—how?"

He faced me, his dark eyes unreadable. "Someone broke into his house last night. Got all the way to his bedroom, put a bullet through his head, and managed to get out of the house unde-tected."

I sat back, an odd mixture of shock and relief coursing through me. That, though, was pushed aside almost immedi-ately by fear. "You didn't—"

"No," he said, so quickly and with such force that there was no doubting his words. "And I don't know for certain, but I think that Michael did."

"Michael? You think he killed his own father?"

"I do," he said.

"But why?"

"The old man was a liability. This bullshit with you, the whole thing with the vendetta against your father. Ilya was about revenge and about keeping a tight fist around his empire. Michael is about playing it smart."

I considered that for a moment, letting the ramifications of what he was saying flow over me. "The pictures," I began, my words coming slowly. "If Michael is about business, then there's no reason for him to release the pictures."

"No," Cole agreed. "There's not."

"Do you think he's going to just drop it?"

"He told me as much." A slow grin lit his face. "It's over,

baby. He's even mailing me the memory card. It's not perfect—for all we know he has them saved in the cloud somewhere—but I think you're safe."

I sagged against him, overwhelmed by relief. And as his arms wrapped around me to pull me close, I let myself go and cried.

"There's no reason to leave now," Cole said, when my tears finally stopped and I could breathe normally again. "Do you want to stay in Chicago?"

"Do you?"

"No," he said. "I want to show you Paris. Hell, I want to show you the world."

"Good." I sat up and looked around the cabin, then smiled wickedly. "I want to see the world," I told him. "But first I'm looking forward to the flight. I didn't think about it the first time we flew, but the place has potential. It's not as well-equipped as our playroom," I teased, "but I think this cabin will do just fine."

Something devious sparked in his eyes. "I was thinking that when you move in with me, we can completely remodel your place. Forget playroom. We'll have a full-fledged playhouse."

"When I move in?" I asked, the deliciously decadent concept of an entire playhouse skipping right out of my mind like a stone across the water. "Am I moving in?"

"I figure that's a first step." He took my hand. "Then a ring, then children after that," he finished, moving his hand to press it flat on my belly.

"Oh." I felt breathless and a little dizzy and more than a little overwhelmed. His wife. His partner. *His.* "Is this a proposal?" I asked.

"No," he said.

I looked away so that he couldn't see the disappointment in my face.

I told myself I was being foolish. My father and I were safe. Cole and I were together, we were in love, we were happy. The rest would come soon enough. But he'd said the word, and now it was in my head, and damn me, I wanted it, because it was another way to say to the world that he was mine and I was his.

"Catalina?" There was a world of tenderness in his voice, and I turned to him. "Do you remember once you asked me what my time in Italy was like?"

"Sure." I frowned, a bit off balance by the shift in conversation.

"I lived in Florence primarily, but I spent a month in Rome and almost two weeks in Venice. I know you want to see Paris, but would you mind if we went to Italy after? I'd like to show it to you."

"I'd love to see it. I want to share everything you're willing to give me."

"Good," he said, moving to stretch out on the couch, his back against the armrest. I leaned against him, then sighed as his arms closed around me, trapping me in a way that made me feel safe and loved.

"Are you familiar with the Bridge of Sighs?" he asked.

"It sounds familiar," I admitted. "But no, not really."

"It's an enclosed bridge in Venice. Ancient and beautiful. There is a legend that if lovers kiss under the bridge at sunset, they will be granted eternal love and bliss."

"I like that legend."

"Me, too," he said. "So you might be interested to know that I'm going to take you there at sunset. And when we're beneath the bridge, I'm going to kiss you, just like the legend says. And then, Catalina Rhodes, I'm going to ask you to marry me."

"Oh," I said, my heart skipping in a way that made me more than a little breathless. "In that case I should tell you that I'm going to say yes." I smiled up at him, warm and safe and content in the circle of his arms. "But right now, I think we really should practice that kiss. Don't you?"

"I do." And then the man who would one day be my

husband—the man who loved me and challenged me, who teased and adored me—the man who had saved me in so many wonderful ways—pulled me close and kissed me hard.

I clung to him, letting every fear and worry flow out of me, letting the past slide away so that the only things left in my head were that moment and my fantasies of the future.

A future that Cole and I would face together.

Fall in love with the irresistible, emotionally charged
romance of Damien Stark and Nikki Fairchild . . .

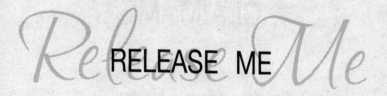

RELEASE ME

He was the one man I couldn't avoid.
And the one man I couldn't resist.

Damien Stark could have his way with any woman.
He was sexy, confident, and commanding: anything
he wanted, he got. And what he wanted was me.

Our attraction was unmistakable, almost beyond control,
but as much as I ached to be his, I feared the pressures
of his demands. Submitting to Damien meant I had to
bare the darkest truth about my past – and risk
breaking us apart.

But Damien was haunted, too. And as our passion
came to obsess us both, his secrets threatened to
destroy him – and us – for ever.

CLAIM ME

For Damien, our obsession is a game.
For me, it is fiercely, blindingly, real.

Damien Stark's need is palpable – his need for pleasure,
his need for control, his need for me. Beautiful and brilliant
yet tortured at his core, he is in every way my match.

I have agreed to be his alone, and now I want him to be fully
mine. I want us to possess each other beyond the sweetest edge
of our ecstasy, into the deepest desires of our souls. To let the
fire that burns between us consume us both.

But there are dark places within Damien that not even
our wildest passion can touch. I yearn to know his secrets,
for him to surrender to me as I have surrendered to him.
But our troubled pasts will either bind us close . . .
or shatter us completely.

COMPLETE ME

Our desire runs deep.
But our secrets cut close.

Beautiful, strong, and commanding, Damien Stark fills a void
in me that no other man can touch. His fierce cravings push
me beyond the brink of bliss – and unleash a wild passion
that utterly consumes us both.

Yet beneath his need for dominance, he carries the wounds of
a painful past. Haunted by a legacy of dark secrets and broken
trust, he seeks release in our shared ecstasy, the heat between
us burning stronger each day.

Our attraction is undeniable, our obsession inevitable.
But not even Damien can run from his ghosts, or shield
us from the dangers yet to come.

TAKE ME

Our wedding approaches.
But our past still threatens.

I've long dreamed of my fairy tale wedding, but it wasn't until I met Damien Stark that I began to believe it was my destiny. Though we both carry secrets and scars, our shared passion heals us, binding us together. Our mutual ecstasy is the brightest light in my life.

But darkness still snakes through the cracks in our armour. Ghosts from our past have moved on, bringing fresh pain that cuts deep and threatens to destroy everything we hold dear.

Damien is my anchor to this world, and I am his. But if we are going to keep each other, we have to fight the shadows of our pasts to move forward into our future.

The seductively irresistible and sizzling hot Most Wanted series began with Angie and Evan's story . . .

Wanted

He is everything I crave, all I desperately want.
And he is everything I can't have.

Evan Black embodies every fantasy I've ever had. He is brilliant, fierce and devastatingly handsome. But he is also headstrong, dangerous and burdened with secrets.

My family warned me to stay away, that I could never handle Evan's dark dealings or scarred past. Maybe I should have listened. Maybe I should have run. But our desire is undeniable, and some temptations you just can't fight.

And from the moment we finally touch, I know that we will never be the same.

Indulge in a scorching, scandalous affair with Sloane and Tyler as the Most Wanted series continues . . .

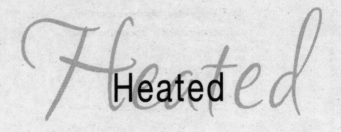

Heated

I knew better than to risk my heart.
But fierce passion comes at a high price.

I grew up believing in right and wrong, good and evil, black and white – that there were some boundaries that could never be crossed. And then I met Tyler Sharp.

Bold, charming, and dangerously sexy, Tyler always gets what he wants. But his smile can be deceiving, his dealings sordid, his ambitions ruthless. I thought I was the one woman strong enough to resist him, but our need for each other is too urgent to deny.

One look and I'm in trouble. One touch and I'm hooked. One night and I'm his. And once I fall, there's no going back.

For updates, bonus content,
and sneak peeks at upcoming titles:

Visit the author's website

http://juliekenner.com/

Find the author on Facebook

 facebook.com/JKennerBooks

Follow the author on Twitter

 @juliekenner

headline

ETERNAL

FIND YOUR HEART'S DESIRE...

VISIT OUR WEBSITE: www.headlineeternal.com

FIND US ON FACEBOOK: facebook.com/eternalromance

FOLLOW US ON TWITTER: @eternal_books

EMAIL US: eternalromance@headline.co.uk